CARAVAN OF THIEVES

DAVID RICH

A Lieutenant Rollie Waters Novel

A SIGNET BOOK

SIGNET
Published by the Penguin Group
Penguin Group (USA), 375 Hudson Street,
New York, New York 10014, USA

USA | Canada | UK | Ireland | Australia | New Zealand | India
South Africa | China

Penguin Books Ltd., Registered Offices: 80 Strand, London WC2R 0RL,
England
For more information about the Penguin Group visit penguin.com.

Published by Signet, an imprint of New American Library, a division of Penguin
Group (USA). Previously published in a Dutton hardcover edition.

First Signet Printing, September 2013
10 9 8 7 6 5 4 3 2 1

 REGISTERED TRADEMARK—MARCA REGISTRADA

ISBN 978-0-451-41925-5

Printed in the United States of America
10 9 8 7 6 5 4 3 2 1

ALWAYS LEARNING   **PEARSON**

For Susan, Bev, and Bits

When you have told anyone you have left him a legacy, the only decent thing to do is die at once.

—Samuel Butler

1.

My father didn't teach me much except how to lie, cheat, and steal, and then lie, lie, lie some more. Mostly it was by example. I was rebellious and stuck to the truth, maybe because I knew I could never live up to the standard he set. I have paid the price for not following his example, but I'm trying to get my head right. I won't say I lie with the smooth skill and frequency he did, but I won't say I don't, either. Somehow the Marines sensed my natural ability in this direction and sent me undercover while in Afghanistan. Mission completed, I went from undercover to under a cloud. And that cloud followed me all the way home.

Not home. Camp Pendleton, where two guys in a black SUV had been shadowing me for a week every time I left the base. At the depot, where I went to requisition a jeep, Staff Sergeant Comeau said, "Why do you keep going out every day if those men are following you?"

"If I don't let them follow me, Sergeant, they'll never figure it out."

"Figure it out, sir?"

"That I'm not going anywhere." The sergeant considered arguing, but returned his attention to filling out the proper form. I said, "Do me a favor, Sergeant."

"Sure. Yes, sir. What?"

"When General Remington asks, tell him I refused to answer your questions."

Impatience persuaded me to take a longer ride that day so I could get a better sense of how serious they were. As far as I knew, I had nothing to hide, at least no more than everyone else. I drove out the main gate, where the traffic was thick. They fell right in behind me and I led them to the coast, then south toward La Jolla. If I weaved, they weaved. When I stopped for gas I did not need, they stopped down the street. It was too blatant to be mere incompetence. They wanted me to see them. Near the UC San Diego campus, I stopped for a burger at Monk's, a spot filled with students, where I knew these guys would be reluctant to enter. They looked like Lifers to me, even if they had already retired, and Lifers are more afraid of civilians than they are of any enemy. If they came into Monk's, it would mean they were eager for a confrontation.

I used to go out with a girl who worked at Monk's. She told her friends that I was a grad student working on my Ph.D. in astrophysics. I enjoyed playing the part for a little while, but I didn't like conning her friends just to con them. Her former boyfriend was drunk and belligerent in a bar one night. "How's the studying these days, Rollie? Find any new stars no one will ever see or care about?"

"The earth has a twin. Did you know that? It's never been seen because it's always exactly on the other side of the sun. We're pretty sure there's life on it. We've caught radio signals because, as you know, they trail behind. And, it seems, stuff happens there before it happens here. It could even mean we all have doubles there." I went on to soothe his doubts by explaining that the government has been keeping it a secret, which is one of the most reliable lies in the world. "I'm going to get in trouble for telling you," I said. He wasn't a bad guy, and I knew he was going to go around telling this story to everyone. I wished I had just fought him. Which is worse: sounding like a fool or getting beaten up by a scientist?

Soon after, the girl told me she could not go out with me anymore because a professor who had been coming into the restaurant for months and staring at her had finally asked her out. She knew I would understand. "He's the real thing," she said. She always lacked confidence, so I told her she was the real thing, too, and I hoped they would be happy.

I lingered in Monk's for forty minutes, and the followers were still outside. This annoyed me, though I couldn't think why it should. Maybe I was just bored and antsy being back in the States, even though it had been only three weeks. I took back roads on the return trip, winding into the desert, through the low hills. It wasn't hard to lose them. I pulled onto a short loop road and came back on the main highway behind their SUV. That was all the provocation it took: the passenger leaned out the window, aiming his rifle at me. I swerved and hit the gas so I'd be too close for him to get an angle for the shot. I rammed the back driver's side of the SUV and tried to push it off the road, but he had too much power. We played that game for a little while. Then the back window came down and I was facing a rifle and I was close enough to recognize it: a Type 88 marksman rifle, made in China, the kind of weapon a sniper might use if he also thought he might get the opportunity for a closer, quicker shot at the target. Like now. He missed his first shot, cracking the jeep's windshield. I slammed on the brakes and spun the wheel, and the jeep swung around the other way. Too far. The jeep careened off the road and down the slope. I didn't care. All I thought about was the copse of cottonwoods about a hundred yards ahead. At eighty miles per hour, I had about three seconds to make it there before the guy in the back of the SUV could set up again. My chances were good because he would get jostled when the SUV came to a sharp stop and I was bouncing around enough to make the shot extremely difficult. I didn't slow down or look back to check if he got any shots off.

The condition of the jeep brought me before Captain Winston, who had a vague sense he wasn't supposed to like me.

"Two guys have been following me. They shot out the windshield. I tried to knock them off the road. That's how the fender got dented."

"You were drunk," he said.

And in the Marines, that meant I was drunk even though I'd been drunk only twice in my life. The first time was to try it out. I hated it. The second time was to make sure I got it right the first time. The captain confined me to the base, which did not suit me at all. If I wanted to deal with the two shooters, and I did want to, I'd have to go off base to do it. I was sure the shooters were sent by General Remington, but I couldn't do anything about him directly. Not yet. Though I spent a lot of time thinking about the day I would.

A day later, I snuck out to a bar not far from the main gate. I chose it because it was populated mostly by civilians who worked on the base or for companies that serviced the base. The idea was to get these shooters in front of civilian cops. I sat down at a table in the corner, under a moose head and next to a photo supposedly signed by Alex Rodriguez. The waitress popped right over, and I ordered a beer and took a menu. I scanned the patrons. The place was only about half full: a long table of men in their forties and fifties who looked like they had taken the day off to play golf. Three mixed groups of men and women, young and old, just off work and settling in for the extended happy hour. Six lonely guys drank at the bar. None was having his first beer of the day. At the far end of the bar, a dark-haired woman was staring at me. I made the mistake of smiling. She picked up her drink and walked over to join me. She was a pretty woman, late thirties, about ten years older than me, with dark hair and blue eyes. Well, blue and a little red. She was drunk.

"Are you a sholdier . . . soldier?"

"No, ma'am."

"May I sh . . . sit down?"

I got up and pulled out a chair for her. The way she looked at me, I thought she might pull me down to sit on her lap. "Well, what do you do?" she said.

"I'm a lumberjack."

"I thought so." She paused and took a long drink. "What does a lumberjack do, exactly?"

The waitress delivered my beer. "And another for the lady, please," I said. I handed over a twenty. When the waitress walked away, I took a sip, then started to get up. "I have to leave now. Excuse me, please. It was nice to meet you," I said. The woman grabbed my sleeve and pulled. Her eyes got sharp and focused.

"No, no. Please. Please. We just met and I . . . I'm really looking forward to . . . later."

She stared at me and let herself go soft again. But now I knew that the slurring drunkenness was an act. I sat down. She emptied her drink and looked around, as if for the waitress, but she might have been checking to see if anyone came in the door.

"Do you think they come in here themselves? Actually make an appearance?"

"Who?"

"All these guys on the walls. Do you think they come around with an armful of posters and photos and a pen and sign the things for, what, free drinks? I mean, if you don't see them sign it, how do you know a machine didn't do it? Or a friend? Why does it matter if it's signed if you don't meet the person, if there's no connection?"

"I met Mickey Gilley once."

"Who's that?"

"I don't remember. A singer, I think. At least that's what he said."

"Maybe the bar owner did the signatures. I would. Your friends are here."

She turned quickly to see the two shooters, dressed as MPs now, scanning the place from just inside the door. She started to rise, but it was my turn to grab her arm.

"You stay." I held on tight and guided her back into her seat. "Besides, if you don't collect now, you'll never see your money."

The taller one stayed near the door. The shorter one, the one who shot at me, strode over to the table. When he got there, he said to the woman, "You can go now."

"Make him pay you first."

She didn't move. He glared at her, then at me. "Get up."

"Sit down."

"Get up or we'll kill you right here."

"Okay." We both knew he wasn't going to kill me right there. Everybody in the place was watching us. The waitress halted halfway to the table with the woman's drink on her tray. The short man was silent for a moment, probably because he wasn't used to people agreeing with him, so I said, "Who do you think killed that moose up there on the wall?"

The woman at my table chuckled, but the shooter took that as a threat. His hand moved toward his sidearm. I yelled, "These guys are not military police. They're imposters. Call the cops." The only person moving in the place was the tall shooter edging toward us. Then the woman pointed toward the bar, at a man on a stool near the middle.

"He's a cop," she said.

Cops seldom do just what you want them to. I wanted him to arrest these guys. Instead, he shrugged and turned back toward his beer. I slugged the short man and kicked the tall one in the groin just as he arrived at the table. Then I picked up a chair and threw it toward the cop at the bar. It bounced past him and knocked down some bottles. If he wouldn't arrest the bad guys, he'd at least have to arrest me.

2.

shaped the still, thick air with my hands, and the unsteady drip of sweat fell along a diagonal line as I traveled back and forth finishing my tai chi routine. Each cell in the brig contains a thousand cubic feet of air, stirred, slowly, by a fan somewhere deep in an air shaft. Somehow the cooler air wasn't making it to my cell. I made a mental note to complain to the management and ask for an upgraded cell, or to have my bill adjusted.

Time was thicker than the air and that was fine with me. I sat on the floor, crossed my legs, and lifted myself into the scale pose. Once I found my balance, I relaxed. I kept my eyes open and stared at the dirty white wall. The mirage took shape, slowly, piece by piece.

This time the mesquite trees formed first. On the right, a twisted clump of leaning bark. The edge of the house came into view. The porch. Two big chairs. The chains jangling above them from where a swing once hung. I could see the low hills behind the house, speckled brown and green. And then more of the house: the shutters, upstairs windows open and curtains waving. I tried to look inside the windows, but I couldn't see anything. I could not get in there. To the left of the house, a startling swath of yellow that looked like bitterweed jumped out.

When I first learned yoga, I was instructed to imagine a peaceful scene and this one came to mind immediately. I enjoyed forming it, filling it out, altering it. I looked forward to lingering there, but the more time I spent there, the less I thought of it as a peaceful place. I had no idea where it came from. I never saw anything like it except in pictures or movies.

This was the first time I had been locked up since my two stints in juvie home, and so far, I didn't mind it. The heat wasn't nearly as bad as in Afghanistan. Confinement was a challenge; I knew I wouldn't be in too long, so I tried to take advantage of the time alone, without distractions. And there was only one door for the people trying to kill me. I didn't know where the shooters ended up after the bar fracas, but in the cell I'd probably be able to hear them coming.

The sound of footsteps could be heard. Three sets. Two in lockstep and another in the lead. I lifted myself into the firefly pose and returned my attention to the mirage. It took a slow moment for the fetid, fragrant air from my cell to envelop Sergeant Matthews after he opened the cell door.

"Dammit, Waters, what the hell . . ." He stepped inside and his boot splashed in a puddle of sweat. "Get up." He pushed me over with his boot. I kipped up quickly and the sudden closeness of the movement made the sergeant flinch. The two MPs at the door moved closer together. "Get him cleaned up. Fresh clothes, too. He stinks like a goddamn mule."

"Nah, if I smelled like a mule, Sergeant, you'd be licking my balls."

Sergeant Matthews slugged me in the gut. Just once. I stayed on my feet. The sergeant started out.

"Where am I going?"

"Why would I tell you that?"

The MPs took my arms and led me out.

The first person I saw outside was General Remington, short, slim, and haughty, watching from across the quad. He was a Marine Corps legend for leading night raids too secret to mention and commanding units too elite to exist. He built the foundation on which my contempt for him lived, but he could not know the depth and strength of the feeling. It was best to assume his hatred was as fundamental as mine. He was too far away for me to be sure his tight, grim mouth was trying to smile. I could have seen it better through a rifle scope.

The sergeant escorted me to the Provost Marshal's Offices. I expected some sort of dressing down from the Assistant Chief of Staff PMO. That would have been overkill, but understandable since he is the one who does all the work running things, like punishing drunk Marines for shooting out their windshields. But the sergeant passed the assistant chief's office and took me to the Commanding Officer PMO: Colonel Gladden. The commanding officer's job is to take credit for the successes and to place the blame for the failures. Colonel Gladden did not like me, but not enough to get involved in a small infraction like this. Either he was forced into it or outmaneuvered or someone fooled him into thinking there was something in it for him.

The colonel sat back in his chair as if intending to leap out when the g-forces abated. His face was a shrine to rage and resentment. Somewhere along the line, he must have noticed it, or noticed how others reacted, and decided to try to hide it with false ease and tinny relaxation. The result was a nasty hiss and eyes that seemed reluctant to focus. His online bio said he was only forty-two, but he looked at least ten years older and probably had since he was a teenager. Maybe it was because his blood was always boiling. After my first deployment to Afghanistan, back at Camp Pendleton for Recon Indoc training, Gladden was the exec and the major recommended me for Officer Candidate School. Gladden disagreed with his assessment. Eventually I got in anyway, and Gladden, not able to take it out on anyone above him, naturally held it against me. I helped him along because I believed, foolishly, that I could make his thermostat evaporate.

The MPs left and closed the door.

A civilian sat across from Colonel Gladden. He nodded at me and looked me over, but Gladden didn't introduce him. Gladden started right in. "You can't stop, can you, Lieutenant?" He paused as if it were a question. "No, you can't. The investigation goes on in Afghanistan and I get reports, I get reports and they're horrifying. Are you a traitor, Waters?"

I stared at him. He was just showing off. What happened there was not his business and he knew it.

"And now you've destroyed Marine property. What's next?"

"Whatever you would like, sir. I'm open to suggestions."

"Do you know a Dan Waters?"

"Yes, sir, I do."

"Who is he?"

I knew that he knew the answer to that one, but I had to play along. "My father, sir."

"It says here he's a scumbag. Why doesn't that surprise me?"

"Because you think everyone is a scumbag, sir."

The other man in the office chuckled. The colonel looked at him like he thought the man was a scumbag. The man did not seem to mind. He was about forty, thin, with curly dark hair and the kind of lines on his face that make people think you're wise. The colonel returned his attention to me. "Your file says you're a hero. But I don't think you are and a lot of other people around here don't, either. You're just another soldier who thinks the rules don't apply to him. Another . . . another . . ." And here he made the mistake of pausing.

"Scumbag? Sir."

Colonel Gladden's hands balled up into fists, his nostrils flared, and he started to get up, but he glanced at the other man first, then sat back down. He didn't call in the MPs to hit me or to take me back to my cell to be worked over. This was a test and Gladden had flunked. For some reason, the other man was in charge here. I turned to him.

"I'm Lieutenant Roland Waters. Everybody calls me Rollie."

The other man reached into his shirt pocket and handed me a card. "Steve Shaw. Treasury Department." Then to Gladden: "May I?" The direct civility nauseated Gladden. He said nothing.

"What does your father do? For a living?"

I could see Dan the first time I asked that question. One hand on the doorknob, he stopped and smiled and said it as if he had been given a special gift: "I'm a middleman, Rollie Boy, best job in the world. The money flows through the middleman."

I said to Shaw, "He's had many jobs. All sorts of things."

"When was the last time you saw your father?"

"About three years ago. Between tours. I was in Arizona, sitting in a bar. He walked in."

"Just like that?" Now the Treasury man sounded just like any cop. "You were there and he walked in, or the other way?"

I could remember the scene exactly as it happened. I sat at the bar. Bought drinks for the two girls next to me. They were giggly, friendly college girls with too little to do, just preparing for the real drinking that would happen later when their friends arrived. I knew they saw me as an exotic specimen, but I didn't mind. I saw them the same way. And I was in just the right mood for company with someone who never took orders without arguing or complaining, someone who thought having bitchy friends was a major problem in life. The dark-haired one was interested and I started to think I had a chance, though I knew she would want to get drunk and I didn't like screwing drunk girls. Then someone poked me in the back. It was my father, Dan.

I remember most clearly the awful feeling of being woken from a pleasant dream. Me wanting to stay there chatting up the girls, Dan offering to join us. I suddenly felt a horrible sense of responsibility; I couldn't do that to them. The pleasant part of my dream was over. I said good-bye without asking for a telephone number and went to a booth with Dan.

I said to Shaw, "I didn't see him when I walked in. He tapped me on the shoulder. We talked a bit. That's all."

"Why were you in Arizona?"

You'll never know that. "What do you want?"

Shaw said, "Just what I asked. Why were you in Arizona?" His voice stayed calm, but he was not going to budge.

"I'd been back from Afghanistan a month and I missed the desert. That's all." I shrugged, hoping Shaw would believe I thought it sounded foolish.

Colonel Gladden never believed anything. He jumped in, "And then last week when you went AWOL, were you on your way to Arizona? You must really like it there."

Had it been a week? "It's very beautiful, sir."

Gladden almost choked. Shaw seemed to be holding back a smile. He said, "In 2003, a few months after we took Baghdad, we began finding stashes of U.S. dollars that Saddam Hussein had squirreled away. Hundreds of millions, in fact. A few soldiers got tempted, grabbed a few bundles as souvenirs. Most got caught. It's safe to assume a few got away with it. I wouldn't know. That's military business." He nodded toward Gladden as if he were in charge of military business.

Gladden hissed, "It's not over."

"Two years ago a man named John Saunders, a former major in the Third Infantry, was arrested in Colorado for beating his girlfriend. He paid his lawyer in crisp new hundred-dollar bills and bragged that there was plenty more where that came from. The lawyer was suspicious and contacted us. It happens. By the time we checked it out, Saunders had been run over and killed. His girlfriend said when he got drunk he talked about shipping home the stolen money in body bags. It's been a long investigation. Day before yesterday, three graves were dug up in a veterans' cemetery in Oklahoma. They didn't find the money. So you know what they did?"

They both watched me carefully. It was easy to act puzzled. I didn't know where the money was, and I didn't know if I was even supposed to answer. A story that included the words "Dan" and "stolen" hardly merited comment in my world.

Shaw went on. "They dropped everything and started searching for your father."

I knew I was expected to say something. "Well, traditionally, Dan has been a lousy place to look for money. Still, I wish them luck. Sincerely."

"He was in Arizona," Gladden said.

"It's very beautiful there, sir."

He pounded on his desk and stood up. "You're going to find your father and you're going to find the money, whether you're in on it or not. And if you don't, if there's any trouble from you . . ." He waited and breathed through his nose a few times, and for a second I thought he was going to start counting with his hoof. "You wrecked a jeep, then went AWOL with a bullshit story about someone trying to kill you. I don't know how long I can lock you up for that, but if you don't cooperate fully, I can guarantee that no matter what happens to the other charges, you'll never see a combat zone again in your life." I realized suddenly that Gladden knew me pretty well. Some people might have considered that a pretty mild threat, but not me. And now I knew Colonel Gladden, too. He was a guy who knew where to insert the needle.

3.

Shaw drove. The SUV was rented because, he said, he thought the bad guys could trace a government vehicle. They had resources. I sat beside him. Pongo and Perdy filled the backseat, two huge chiseled slabs, silent and serious, bumping their heads against the ceiling. Shaw had argued, but Gladden had insisted the two MPs accompany us, or else I was going back to the brig. I'm six foot two, but I felt like a terrier next to them. Their real names were Patterson and Pruitt. We left through the western gate; the ocean sparkling ahead was all we could see.

I said, "Why haven't developers stolen the base by now? Why isn't it all condos and golf courses and ugly mansions with pillars? It wouldn't cost much to bribe the Congress and a few bureaucrats. Certainly less than the cost of a couple of seaside lots. Every time I come out this way, I wonder how long it will be."

Shaw said, "Are you asking me?"

"No."

"You could bribe the congressmen and bureaucrats for a reasonable amount. The problem would be the developers who saw they were being left out. You'd have to buy them off or include them. The pie is big but the pieces would be small," Shaw said, speaking as if he had been thinking about it, too.

"You think that's it? Those zombies look ahead and say, 'I won't eat the body because I'm only going to get a little piece'?"

"What do you think?"

"I think the Marines are too tough, too scary for them to take on. Makes me proud to be a Marine."

"Maybe you're right." He chuckled. He couldn't tell if I was serious.

"Maybe I'll give it a try with the money I find. How much is it?"

"Twenty-five million. We think."

We turned east on I-10, making for Phoenix, where, Shaw said, Dan had lived and worked for the past three years.

"You've got the wrong Dan Waters," I said. "The Dan I know never worked at anything for three years, and he certainly wouldn't do it if he had stolen money to spend."

"Maybe you don't know him as well as you think," Shaw said.

"I hardly know him at all." I know Dan taught me to like this situation: they wanted me for what I knew; they thought they knew more than I did.

Shaw laid out the background, explaining that Dan Waters had been a civilian contractor working with the Third Infantry in Iraq at the same time the money was shipped home. It looked like he either was in on the plot from the start and betrayed the gang, or found out which grave would hold the money, dug it up, and re-planted the casket. I saw no reason to favor either scenario. Each was equally plausible and my stomach tensed and my breathing got short as I contemplated how perfectly this fit into what I knew of Dan. Shaw went through Dan's criminal record, filled with charges I wasn't aware of as well as the many I knew too well.

Shaw had details, but I didn't need the official version. I could see the places to skim, the ways to cheat. I could hear the schemes. Shaw brought up Dan's most recent job, the one he left a few days ago, and my skepticism about that. I didn't reply. I was answering other questions. What did they want with me? Who did they want me to be? A patriot? A child ashamed of his past? An ambitious officer? A greedy chip off the old block? I would give them glimpses, enough to make them praise their own wisdom in demanding my help. I was undercover again, and I liked that.

"Maybe I don't really know him." Lie, lie, lie. "What do you plan to do with him when you catch him?"

"We'll get him to cooperate. Help us catch the others."

The perfect answer because it gave me the opportunity to practice keeping a straight face. Inside I was laughing and trying to remember the last time I thought of Dan as someone who might help or cooperate. "The guys who are after him, who are they?"

"A retired colonel named Frank McColl. He runs a small company providing security to companies doing business overseas. Mainly in the Middle East."

"Frank McColl?"

"Know him?"

"I knew a guy in basic training named Shane Ayala. He had the prettiest girlfriend, stunning, and sweet, too, but he never went to bed with her. No sex. He would screw around with plenty of other girls, but no more than a deep kiss with Lucy. This went on for six months, longer than that. She asked me about it and I wasn't the only one. One night Shane was drinking and decided the time had come to claim his prize and he showed up unannounced at Lucy's place and found another guy there. They were on the couch. Shane went nuts on the guy, but the guy was tough and he clubbed Shane with a baseball bat. I went to visit him in the hospital. He was a mess. But I asked him why he kept Lucy waiting so long."

"What did he say?"

"He told me to go to hell. But I'm thinking if we can get hold of Frank McColl, we might ask him. He left that money in the ground a long time. Years. At least he intended to."

Shaw changed the subject, asked me to make a list of towns Dan had lived in, addresses if I could remember them, friends, bosses, girlfriends. I told him a few short half-true stories about moving from place to place with Dan, between stints in foster homes or temporary parking with friends or business associates. I mentioned Lita, along with her address, because I knew she wasn't there anymore and I knew she didn't leave any forwarding information. I did not mention the smell of beer and cigarettes when she came home late and found me in her bed and how she let me stay there for the night. Or how, in the morning, I would wake up snuggled close to her and I would lie there, still as could be so I wouldn't wake her. Sometimes she would sleep until noon and I pretended I slept, too, and that's why I missed the school bus. That lasted four months. Then she brought home a man who kicked me out of the bed and I kicked him back. Lita called Dan, who showed up two miserable weeks later. There was a big fight. Dan took me with him to Nevada and pretty soon after that I was in another foster home.

Shaw decided we would start with Dan's most recent employer, even though he assumed McColl and his bunch would have beaten us there. "Maybe something we find there will connect to your list or spark some memory."

"Yeah, maybe. Good idea." I closed my eyes and I pretended to sleep. Pongo and Perdy stayed silent as statues in the back. Maybe they pretended to sleep, too. I did not check. I wondered for a little while about ways to escape, but I, too, wanted to see what Dan left behind. The best choice was to go along until I was certain where to find Dan. I relaxed and the mirage slowly formed behind my eyes. A porch swing, shutters, those twisting mesquite trees. Movement in the house? I could not be certain. Maybe a fluttering curtain.

4.

The office was on the first floor in a brick two-story building near Glendale. The sign on the door said "Western Construction." Dan's boss, Alvarez, was caught off guard by our visit. He was a short, trim man, with his belt pulled tight. He looked like the type who watched his diet because of the cost of food. Someone had already been there, he said. He thought they were FBI. Shaw showed his ID. "They had something just like that," the boss said.

"Did they take his computer?"

"No, but they spent enough time in there."

Shaw went into Dan's office. Pongo and Perdy started to follow but stopped when they saw me lingering. I settled my gaze on Alvarez. He met my eyes with a kind of defiance, as if challenging me to accuse him of something. I said, "What did Dan do here?"

"Well, lately it's been collections, which is about all we're doing. At first he sold jobs. We do paving. Did a lot of new developments. That was then."

"Good at it?"

"He could sell."

"I'm his son. Dan's son. Rollie."

Instead of Alvarez being surprised, he surprised me. "Oh, yeah, he mentioned you a few times. But he didn't say anything about you being with the government. He said you were a financial guy in New York."

I was consoled that there was at least one lie involved. I went into Dan's office, followed by the MPs. The computer had nothing personal on it. The drawers were barren, too. There was no appointment book. No checkbooks. Nothing with easily obtainable account numbers or passwords.

There were no photos on the desk or the walls. Shaw looked at me, expecting me to draw a conclusion from this. Dan would have knickknacks around his office, but only things that meant nothing to him. He'd have stuff scattered around to show he was like everyone else. Dan valued the appearance of normalcy very highly.

"Well, we won't find twenty-five million here," I said.

"I can send you back with the MPs on the next flight, Lieutenant. McColl has a big head start and who knows what he took out of here. Where would you go next?"

I turned and walked out of the office. Pongo and Perdy flanked me. Alvarez's door was closed. I knocked and walked in. Alvarez had a phone in his hand and pretended to be interrupted. "All done?"

"They take a lot out of here?" I tried to sound friendly.

"Few things. A book, a photo, but I thought that was something he just bought somewhere." Alvarez was a lousy liar.

"A woman?"

"Nah, some mountains, desert, something like that."

Shaw and the MPs stood behind me now, in the doorway. Alvarez squirmed a bit as if he felt the walls closing in on him. I asked, "How much did he owe you?"

Alvarez shook his head and tried to look disappointed. "Eight thousand bucks, plus."

"Eight thousand? Eight thousand U.S. dollars? You consider yourself a stupid man, Mr. Alvarez? You let all your employees get into you for so much?"

"Looks like I made a mistake."

"And now you want the Treasury Department to believe that you stole the knickknacks and photo frames from his office to recover the money? Plan on getting about fifty bucks altogether on eBay? He owed you about, what, five hundred? Tell the truth, I might pay you off."

Alvarez was living in a world of take what you can get. I could see him making the calculation. "I fronted him about one thousand. But I don't know yet how much he stole," Alvarez answered.

I wasn't insulted. "He stole, but not from you. You don't have enough to make it worth his while."

Shaw and I went through Dan's stuff that Alvarez had stashed away. All junk. A piece of the Petrified Forest. A small cactus, which I suggested Pongo and Perdy should pull from its soil to search for clues. A life preserver with white letters: SS *Useless*. If that was Dan's way of leaving me a clue, I didn't need it. I seized on the photo of a pretty woman sitting in a comfy chair, her hair down and a bottle of beer in her hand. Shaw watched as I studied it. "Know her?"

"It's at least ten years since I saw her. If this is her. Janie. I don't think I ever knew her last name."

"Think."

"I don't think I can help put Dan in jail."

"If he cooperates, I'm sure he can stay out of prison."

I paused as long as I dared. Long enough for Shaw to think he saw me struggling over whether to betray Dan. Shaw was the kind of guy who wanted to believe no man could flat-out hate his own father. And he was the kind of guy who had to believe he was herding me every second. Dan always preached "Give them what they want—or what they think they want." He was a performer at heart, though he didn't leave 'em laughing. No, deep down Dan was a tragedian, dashing hopes everywhere he went and falling, always falling, due to his own well-honed flaws. I hated Dan, but I would never willingly put him in the control of the police. I hated him, but I wouldn't be part of ending his descent because I wasn't done with my hatred; it was just on hold. I needed Dan to be free and horrible as ever so this hatred could run wherever it needed to go. When they pulled me out of that cell, they startled that hatred back to life and I realized how much I had missed it. I said, "She lived outside Flagstaff. Janie . . . Janie Boots he used to call her."

"Boots?"

"Wellington." In fact, Janie Wellington was a foster mother who couldn't have looked more different from the woman in the photo. She was a horrible hag even then, fifteen or so years ago. But the search for her would take me in the right direction and give me the chance to escape. I didn't mind the thought of Shaw and the boys tearing her place apart.

We drove north toward Flagstaff. Pongo drove, or Perdy: I could never decide which was which. I sat in the back with the other one. In the distance, the colors shifted gradually toward red. At first the dull speckle and the striations seemed like spillage, a mistake, and though I'd made this drive a thousand times, the red kept drawing my eyes. Soon, though, the spillage became part of a pattern, the complex, indecipherable, essential pattern of the surroundings, and my eyes began searching for new anomalies.

Suddenly Pongo spoke up. "Sir . . . we don't know what happened in Afghanistan, but we have friends who served with you. They said you're a good Marine. They're behind you."

This was not a welcome compliment. They didn't know what I had done in Afghanistan and they had no idea what I was about to do to them in Arizona. Becoming friendly with them wouldn't make it any harder to do what I had to do, but it would make them angrier afterward and make them work that much harder to find me.

Shaw turned around. "The file I saw was pretty vague."

"I don't think civilians are allowed to know."

Pongo spoke up. "We heard you went behind enemy lines. Alone."

Perdy said, "Undercover. Is that right?"

"You should be a hero," Shaw said. It made me sick to think how pissed off they were going to be and how quickly they were going to change their minds about me. "Why'd they choose you for the job?"

"I guess someone thought it'd be easy to believe I was crooked."

"And then they couldn't stop believing it?"

"Something like that." I wasn't going to tell it on cue. What happened in Afghanistan started out as a misguided adventure, but I thrived. It ended in a way I would never tell the MPs or Shaw. My desire for revenge on General Remington would stay private, too. No investigation, even if it turned on him, could ever satisfy me. I was convinced that what happened there led directly to this mission to find Dan and the money, that the great General Remington was involved. I know I have to tell it and I will, for my own sake, as I need to, so I can see how it helped me and how it led me into the mistakes I made.

"I have a question for you, Agent Shaw."

"Go ahead."

"Why don't you believe I'm crooked?"

"Because you don't want to be anything like your father."

I spent the rest of the ride wondering if he was really that simple.

5.

Janie still lived in the same cramped one-story brick house north of the university. A fenced-in front yard and a small patch of grass in the back. The neighborhood still smelled the same: highway exhaust and weeds. But I was glad everything was the same. I had escaped from that house dozens of times. I was certain I could do it again.

Pongo parked out front. Two small kids were playing in the front yard. They watched us hopefully as we opened the gate and walked up the two steps to the front door. As serious and imposing as we must have looked, I knew they wanted to leave with us. I knew they wanted out of this place. Shaw rang the bell. The door opened and there was Janie, almost as thick as she was tall. A monolith in beige. Beige skin, beige clothes, beige hair. And red lips painted on like graffiti. I once drew an arrow on the back of her pants and wrote her phone number. I figured it would smudge out before she noticed. I was wrong, but it did take three days for her to catch on. It still pleases me to think of all the people who saw it and said nothing to her. Maybe they thought she drew it herself.

Now her eyes narrowed in fake defiance to hide the fear at this unexpected show of authority at her door. I knew her brain was scrambling for excuses to match her vast list of violations and petty crimes.

If Shaw knew I had lied when I said she was the woman in the photo, he hid it pretty well. Janie flinched as he withdrew his credential, but Shaw smiled and said this had nothing to do with current foster children. She still did not want us to come in and she still had not recognized me. She was too busy deciding that Shaw's smile meant he was weak. He turned to me.

I said, "If you don't let us in, Janie, I'll tell everything I know. Everything."

She narrowed her eyes even more and looked me over. It dawned on her who I was, and she wasn't impressed. Janie was a bully first and always. "Rollie? Yeah, I'd expect you to be in trouble with the government."

"I'll tell what really happened to Edgar Ramirez."

"Can't we please come in, ma'am? It's just some questions about Rollie's father, Dan," Shaw said.

First Janie sneered at me, the red slash of her mouth widening as if being stretched by invisible bands. Now that Shaw had given her an excuse to relent, she could relax. She knew nothing about Dan. With nothing to hide on that subject, she could make up any lies she wanted without fear of revealing too much. I knew she would talk a lot, if only to keep me from bringing up that bad subject again.

Edgar Ramirez was a six-year-old foster child who came into the house just a few weeks after I did. He was scared and confused, like we all were. He was also a bed wetter. Of course, he didn't tell Janie what was going on, and she didn't get close enough to the bed to touch it. The smell got bad. She changed the sheets and beat him a little. He kept peeing the bed and forgetting to mention it. The mattress had to go outside. Edgar slept on the floor; I cleaned up the puddles in the morning. But I knew Janie was worried because once in a while inspectors would show up and they would want to see where everyone was sleeping. No way was she going to buy a new mattress for Edgar to ruin. One night I heard movement and opened my eyes in time to see the beige nightmare bend over and lift Edgar into her arms. I don't know if he was awake or not, but if he was, fear kept him quiet.

I didn't see her actually accept the money, but I saw her hand him off to two men and later that night I saw her counting and recounting a stack of bills in the kitchen. In the morning, she pretended to be alarmed that Edgar was missing, called the police and made a big stink, saying he had run away. It wasn't hard to guess that she hid the money in her lingerie drawer: who would want to go in there? I stole a twenty-dollar bill while she was dealing with the police.

Now Janie's natural nastiness was going to be put to good use. We all stood in the middle of the living room. Shaw asked, "Is Mr. Wellington at home?"

"He has to work for a living," she said.

She had not asked us to sit down and that was a good thing. It allowed me to pace while Shaw brought up the questions about Dan. Pongo and Perdy stayed near the front door. I looked at them for the okay to wander into the kitchen. Perdy nodded. I stepped into the hallway and then the kitchen for a brief look around. I was back in the living room in less than fifteen seconds.

Janie was telling whatever she thought she knew about Dan, impressions from long ago. "I always got the impression he just came back from Mexico, but he didn't really confide in me. You might look for him down there."

Shaw asked if Dan brought presents for me. Janie's eyes narrowed again and I knew what that meant: her memory was vague, but she assumed she had stolen the gifts. I nodded toward Perdy again to indicate I wanted to check the bedrooms. He nodded okay. I slipped down the hallway and into Janie's bedroom, which was at the rear of the house. Nothing had changed except that I had grown and the tawdriness now seemed smaller, more comical than when I lived here. I went into the lingerie drawer and took all her money. Then I removed the wooden pole that blocked the slider, unlocked the door, and off I went.

I knew the route by heart. The walls between yards were easy to vault. I expected a dog, a shepherd mix, in the third yard, but he wasn't there. It was like being a kid again, that exhilarating feeling of cutting out, breaking free, ditching. Sneaking out of school early was always more satisfying than just not going. I hated every minute that I lived with Janie, hated most of my childhood, but I was thrilled at that moment to be back in that childhood. The moment I broke free, I felt superior, in charge of the game, as if I had fooled somebody.

I cut out in front, crossed the street, and went through two yards to the next street over. From there it was a short sprint to the mall. I was in the parking lot, searching for an open car, when I turned and saw Pongo and Perdy across the boulevard, coming toward me. I ran toward the mall and knew I would make it easily, but Shaw pulled out in the SUV and blocked my way. The window was down.

"Get in." I hesitated. Shaw said, "If you jump right in, we can lose them and go on our way. If you wait . . ."

I didn't wait. And I didn't look back to see the looks on Pongo's and Perdy's faces.

"Janie told us you usually headed for the mall," Shaw said. Then he tossed the photo from Dan's office in my lap. "Pretty good photographer to make her look like that. Where are we going?"

6.

I was sixteen and back sharing an apartment with Dan in Albuquerque. One night I came home around eleven and I noticed two rough-looking guys sitting in a car across the street. The apartment was dark when I walked in. Dan grabbed me immediately and whispered, "Don't turn on any lights." He counted out two hundred dollars. "I'll be back in a few weeks. If anyone asks for me, just tell them you haven't seen me."

"Where are you going?"

There was no light, but my eyes had adjusted enough to be able to see his charming smile reshape his face, the smile he gave to someone who asked a completely stupid question. It was a mix of condescension and benevolence, which is pretty tough to stand from a scumbag. "I'll be back in a few weeks." And he counted out another hundred dollars.

I went into my room and pocketed my utility tool. I

learned a couple of years before not to carry any kind of knife, not even a Swiss Army knife, even if you're using it to butter your bread. Dan did not ask me where I was going when I left the apartment. The rough guys were still in the car across the street. Could have been cops, could have been bad guys. Didn't matter much. I walked a few blocks to Lomas Boulevard and strolled along until I saw a dark-blue Chevy up on Fifth Street. I broke in and stole the car. First thing I did was fill it up because I figured the trip was probably long and the biggest problem would be pit stops. Then I drove to the back of the apartment building, around the corner from Dan's car. Around three A.M., Dan snuck out the back.

He drove west through Gallup and then turned north. I pulled off the highway a few times, then got back on at the same interchange. It was worth the risk of losing him to avoid having him make me. Truckers dominated the road in long packs that shifted positions according to mysterious rules. I hid behind them, just peeking out occasionally to keep Dan in range. He went all the way into Utah, toward Moab. Before dawn he turned west and pretty soon we were the only two cars on the road. I pulled off, found a gas station and a map. It looked like Dan was heading for Lake Powell, which I tried to turn into a logical deduction by remembering that he once mentioned having been in the Navy.

It took me almost a week to find him, running my

rented speedboat up and down the coves and inlets of the lake and the Escalante River and, finally, the San Juan River. Not far up the San Juan I had to stop. There were rapids ahead. I pulled off as close as I could get and climbed a bit on the rocks to where I could see beyond the rapids. The river curved and smoothed out and widened for a while. There were no boaters and no rafters. These rapids weren't featured on the map I had, so I guessed that meant the tours didn't bother with them. I climbed all the way up to the plateau. Far up the river, I could see a small houseboat moored near a beach. I knew it was Dan.

I walked to a spot where I could spy on him. He had a blond woman with him. Naked, too, which was fine until Dan decided to join her. For most of two days I watched them from above; then I took off. I never went back to Albuquerque and didn't see Dan again until after I had enlisted in the Marines.

As soon as I could lose Shaw, I was going back to Lake Powell.

I had directed him toward the Grand Canyon. He kept asking me where we were making for and I avoided answering, so he said, "You just tell me where to turn." Most people would have gotten irritated or tense, but Shaw stayed as relaxed as a guy with an expense account picking up a dinner check. I assumed he just wanted to show me he could be trusted. After a while, he said, "Why'd you join the Marines?"

It wasn't really a question. He wanted to pretend to

be friendly. "Same reason you joined the Treasury Department. They said they'd take me."

"My father was a cop. And his father."

"So you went into the family business."

"I tried not to. Joined the Army right out of college. Stayed four years. Intelligence. Listening posts in Germany and Turkey. When I came home, I studied for the CPA exam, passed, got a job, hated the job. Everybody in the family said join the force, but I didn't want to give them the satisfaction. So I went looking for a job out of town and found the Treasury."

It was a believable story. I had never hired an accountant, but I think I would want one who was a little more uptight. Shaw was more like the accountant's partner who played golf with the clients.

"Where did all this happen? The family part?"

"Lexington, Kentucky. So . . . I ended up the same, only different."

"Are you saying I'm the same as Dan?"

"I asked why you joined the Marines. You could have easily joined a gang."

"But the Marines gave me food, clothing, and free guns. And, until now, no cops bothering me."

Shaw smiled. He seemed to think I was joking. That was fine. As soon as he turned his eyes back to the road, I slugged him hard with my left. His head slammed against the window and he was out. The SUV shimmied left, then right onto the shoulder. I grabbed the wheel before we went off the road and straightened it out. I pulled his right leg back so his foot came off the accelerator. The car slowed down and I eased onto the shoulder. At ten miles per hour, I yanked the parking brake.

Shaw was still unconscious. I took his gun and cell phone and pocketed them. I grabbed him under the arms and dragged him out the passenger side. While I was catching my breath, he started to come to. "You're only twenty miles from Tusayan. You look respectable enough. Someone will pick you up," I said.

His eyes focused and he rubbed his jaw. "Just stop and think about what you're doing. The Marines are already chasing you. Now you'll have the feds, too. It means jail for sure. You're ruining your life for him. For him."

This wasn't the moment to stop and explain to Shaw that I was not doing this for Dan. I was doing it because Dan had boxed me into this position just the way he always did, and this time I was going to change that forever. "If I find the money, I'll call you. And by the way, Dan would never have slugged you. He'd have talked you into giving him the car."

The SUV had GPS installed so I had to ditch it. Shaw would be in touch with the rental company within a couple of hours. Pongo and Perdy were probably already on it. And then there was McColl, who was chasing Dan. Shaw had not wanted a government car because he thought McColl could trace that. So Shaw believed McColl had friends in the Treasury

Department. McColl probably had active military friends, too. Why not? What did friends cost? A few drinks and an hour with a whore? Maybe a thousand in cash? They could buy a lot of friends with twenty-five million dollars.

7.

I drove to Las Vegas and pulled into the first large hotel I saw, the Mandalay Bay, with about an hour of sun left in the day. The valet service was backed up and it seemed the pressure wasn't going to relent. I waited patiently for my ticket and watched how they worked. Inside I washed up, bought some coffee, and walked around enough to show up on the security cameras if anybody bothered to check. By the time I strolled outside, two lines of cars were backed up. I hung around and counted: three valets driving cars into the garage and two harried valets hustling from driver to driver with tickets. The hotel guests took their tickets and either went in to gamble or unloaded the luggage from their trunks. I strolled past the front car and turned back to watch and time the valets. Each return trip took just over two minutes. I didn't have to wait long for all three valets to take cars up within a minute of each other. I turned swiftly and got into the next waiting car. I was gone before anyone noticed.

Was I going there to save him? I knew better. Did I want to save him? Save him from the people whose stolen money he stole, or save him from jail? I kept struggling to figure out what the mission was, and I didn't like getting closer to my destination without the slightest idea what to do when I arrived. He was hiding out, which meant he did not need a warning. Help him get away? To where?

I should have learned my lesson in Afghanistan: know the goal before you begin the mission. The desert on either side of the highway stayed quiet, patient, and blank for hours, as if waiting for me to supply an answer. But the patience was a trap. I just kept traveling deeper into the darkness, which felt more like a gaping maw than a tunnel that might have an end, all the while yammering to myself to help avoid facing the truth. Flashes of Afghanistan came to mind, mixing with flashes of Dan.

For some reason, I'm good at picking up languages, a skill I was unaware I possessed until I got to Afghanistan. Speaking Spanish was just a survival skill where I grew up. Maybe Dari and Pashto fall into the same category now. I learned a little Dari in my first weeks, but the best lessons came when I went along to the shura, the meetings with tribal leaders. They and our captain spoke and the translators went to work. Before long, I didn't need the translator, though, of course, I didn't let anyone know that. My job was to listen anyway. It was pleasant to sit there drinking tea and sussing out the distrust and wariness and fake sincerity on both sides. Sometimes I would imagine Dan sitting there, telling stories like the pro he was, pausing as if to allow his hosts to beg him to continue but really just to figure what came next, and all the while working on partnerships, alliances, new ventures. The Afghans distrusted pointless conversations with strangers but relished anyone who could convey his points by what he didn't say, by the pauses and change of direction. To visit them without a plan and a goal was more than disrespect; it was a form of betrayal, as if the point of the meeting was to waste their time. And that meant their allegiances would find other attachments. They wanted every word to hold a clue, a hint, an evasion. They would have loved Dan—even though all the while that he spun his web, he would be working out how he could sell off his end of those same deals before he had to deliver. Because when Dan was telling a story, he was delivering all he ever could.

It started with a tap on the back while I was in Helmand Province in the southern part of Afghanistan. I turned to find an Afghan staring into my eyes and looking entirely pleased with himself. There was a problem with that. If an Afghan sneaks up on you and you live, then your nose is defective and you should have it checked because those people smell. They smell bad until you get used to it, then they just smell distinctive. No running water for most of them so showers are scarce. Outside the cities, washing machines are as rare as mink coats. I'm sure Afghans can sneak up on each other and we smell bad to them, or at least distinctive, but it's not something I've ever discussed with one of them. This guy didn't smell.

After three days of trading fire, we had finally shoved the Taliban from Deshu and a jittery exhaustion settled over us. I was in the market, inviting a sandal maker to tea so he could tell us where the caches of rifles and ammunition were buried, when we were interrupted. I turned quickly to face the Afghan, who had his hands out to show he wasn't armed. He spoke Dari with a strange accent, asking to speak to me privately. I checked with the sandal man for his reaction; he backed away. Something was wrong. I answered in Dari and we moved away from the market to a residential part of town where there had been heavy fighting. No one lived there at that moment. The residents and the fighters were gone: fled or dead. The bodies had been cleared out, but the damage wouldn't be repaired for a long time. I stayed a step behind him and kept my weapon ready. Nobody showed any signs of knowing him, so he wasn't local, which might explain the strange accent. I kept speaking to him in Dari, trying to get a fix. He turned down a small lane. No one else was in sight. I hesitated, and he looked back and told me, in Dari, to stay close. I answered in English: "Where the hell are we going?"

He answered in Dari, saying I should come along and he didn't understand English.

"Yes, you do," I said. "You speak Dari with a Texas accent."

"Arkansas," he said. He walked over to a house

where the door was still intact and I followed him inside. I recognized the place because just two days before I had helped clear it. The residents opened the door, bags in hand. They didn't want a fight and they didn't want the place wrecked.

He made tea by boiling the leaves rather than steeping them. That was fine in some parts of Afghanistan, but he didn't have any sugar or hard candies to go with it so it was going to be really bitter. He was showing off his native skills for me; I just wanted to see his face when he tasted the stuff. We sat on the cushions in the main room. "I'm Captain Derek Ballard, Second Marines, First Brigade. I've been seconded to the Counterintelligence and Humint Center at the Defense Intelligence Agency. We were told you speak Dari and Pashto."

"I'm learning."

"Tough languages, but you're going to have to learn fast."

Captain Ballard was an earnest, serious little guy who got right to the point. I found it difficult to trust him. The Afghans never acted that way and never trusted anyone who did. He acted as if he were telling you everything, which probably was not true, and if it were, he was in a lot of trouble anyway. Captain Ballard laid out the mission: our weapons were ending up in the hands of the Taliban; intelligence had determined that they were disappearing after entering the country via the overland caravans from Karachi; everything was checked through customs properly.

Something was going wrong after that.

The captain would go to Torkham, the entry point on the Afghan side of the Khyber Pass, posing as a broker wanting to purchase weapons; I was to go to Karachi and get hired to ride along in a truck as a security man and attempt to find suspects among the drivers and other security people.

"Aren't they all suspects?" I said.

"We have a name. Nawaz Mazari."

"Who are we after, Captain?"

Captain Ballard frowned and his neck moved forward to emphasize his seriousness. He wasn't an Afghan trader or anything like one anymore. He was an angry officer. It didn't take much to strip him down. "You will travel with the caravan and ingratiate yourself with people you think might be involved in stealing arms from our supplies. When you cross the border at Torkham, you will find me and introduce me to these people. You'll attempt to broker a deal. My cover is Abdullah from Kandahar. Understood?"

I understood this was a plan that was not going to work. I wanted to ask him if he thought this plan up himself or if the real geniuses at headquarters pissed on it, too. First, if I could make Abdullah as a Marine then everyone in Torkham would be whistling the Marine Corps hymn whenever he appeared. Second, it would take months and many runs on the caravan to establish trust. The best way would be to wave a lot of cash around and get some entrepreneurial fellow to steal a few weapons on his own and hope that caught the attention of the organization that ran the pilfering.

"I understand," I said. "It will take me a few weeks to grow my beard enough. I can use that time to improve my language skills."

"You start in two days."

"No beard, no me, Captain. I'm not going on a suicide run. Court-martial me if you want." Not every Afghan wears a beard, but every American doesn't. If having one gained me five minutes of doubt in someone's mind, I wanted one.

He squinted his eyes at me and stood up and paced around with his chest puffed out. "You will pay for that outburst, Lieutenant. This operation has been in the planning for months."

"Use the time to dirty yourself up, Captain, maybe have a couple of teeth pulled. I'll go along, starting in three weeks." He was not happy to be challenged, but he agreed.

I traveled to headquarters in Kabul to get the details about Karachi and the caravan. Major Carl Jenkins looked like a schoolteacher: glasses, a mustache, the first hint of a comb-over. He met Ballard and me outside NATO headquarters and ushered us past the gates and the guards. Ballard was wearing his shalwar kameez and swept through as if he thought he were Lawrence of Arabia returning to Cairo. I thought he looked like a foolish adult dressing up for a Halloween party at the country club.

Major Jenkins gave me seed money: one hundred crisp new one-hundred-dollar bills. I told him I needed twenty more. Ballard was always ready: "Why?"

"Because a villager from the south would not have American money in this condition. I'm going to have to go into the market-place and change it and I'm going to have to lose a little bit on each transaction."

"Not a problem," Jenkins said. He seemed to have some experience at this. We talked about communication. There was not going to be any. The meeting seemed about to end. We all stood up. Jenkins came around his desk, and Ballard moved toward the door. I stood still.

"Once the caravan crosses the border into Afghanistan, Americans are in charge. Are we looking for American soldiers?" Ballard stared at me for an answer. This was the moment to run away, go AWOL, disappear. I knew just the right cave for it, but it was in Arizona, and I doubted I could make it there before being caught. Too late it occurred to me that if my Afghan act was good, I had a better chance of getting there in that disguise. "Then it could be anyone. It could be Major Jenkins."

"It's not me."

"Or his commanding officer."

"That's enough, Lieutenant."

"Stop it. Both of you." That stunned us. Neither of us had thought Jenkins had enough starch to give orders. "It's not my commanding officer. He never leaves the office. At least no one has ever seen him outside it. As the captain says, this is the mission. These are your orders."

"You will meet me when you cross the border and vouch for me to the right people."

Hi, Nawaz, I'd like you to meet my old friend Abdullah of Arkansas. He's the one over there wearing the American flag.

"We're going to find these guys and bust them. I promise," said Ballard, now that it was his turn to talk to himself. Major Jenkins studied his shoes. Maybe he wanted to see if they were laced right.

8.

The marina at Hite's Landing on Lake Powell opened just after dawn. The sun splashed against the cliffs across the lake and bounced onto the water. "Ain't got no tackle," said the old man running the boat rentals.

"Going to meet friends. They've already been out two days."

He seemed to believe it. Maybe he just cared about the question. I counted out the cash for the boat rental and the deposit and the gas. I drove aimlessly around the lake a few times to see if I had any watchers, then cruised out north.

Dan was where I expected to find him. He was alone this time and had his clothes on, thankfully. I was the biggest thing on the plateau overlooking the houseboat, and I couldn't crawl under my own shadow to cool off. The heat was bothering me, but it shouldn't have, so maybe it was more than the heat. Dan spent some time fixing an awning. Then the shadows from the plateau fell over the boat and I started down.

He must have seen me coming and hidden. The boat was about forty feet, white, with a roof deck. It rested on two aluminum pontoons. A rubber raft with a small outboard was tethered to the stern and pulled up onto the beach. The boat was called *Not Home*. First I stepped into the water and walked all around the boat. I decided that calling out for Dan would only make him suspicious. He might think it was a warning or that I was being forced to call.

Inside, the boat was clean and well kept. The wood cabinetry was still in good shape. The galley had a small refrigerator and a gas stove and a table where four people could sit if they crammed in close to each other. Two heads. A large bed where Dan slept, and another bedroom with two beds, and a bunk in the passageway, all made up. Aft was a lounge with blue cushions around the sides. There was a box of cigars, Fuentes, on the counter. I took one and grabbed a bottle of beer from the fridge and went outside to enjoy the shade.

I heard him before I saw him. "Rollie Boy, there's no one on this glorious earth I'd rather see sitting in my chair, drinking my beer and smoking my cigars." He came into view, walking along the beach carrying a Winchester Model 70 hunting rifle, low at his side. His hair was thick and white, like a politician's, which should have been a hint to anyone who paid attention, and it accentuated the deep brown tan he had. He climbed aboard the aft ladder, set the rifle against the rail, and held out his arms. "Damn coyote's been checking me out, thought I'd turn the tables on him," he said. "I didn't know if you were dead or alive. It was torture for me." We hugged. "You have to tell me all about it. You look great. Great."

We settled down and agreed that we both looked great and the sky was blue, the sun was probably going to go down, and the stars were going to twinkle in the sky. Nobody asked anyone but himself what are you doing here? How did you get here? How do you plan to get out? At last Dan showed me where I could sleep. I checked out the ridgeline before bedding down and was astounded to see a coyote watching us.

We fished and caught smallmouth bass all morning, enough to make me wonder how long I'd be there eating them, and that made me give in first. "Whose boat is this?"

"Well, I could claim it for my own, but what for, since I get to use it as much as I like without the burdens of ownership." Taxes and licenses and permits. "I knew this guy, big guy, maybe six four, sprout of curly dark hair, beanpole of a guy, had a little wife, tiny, barely five feet, very attractive woman she was, but she ran him ragged. It was funny to watch, painful but funny. She'd want him to check with her for permission to swallow his food. And 'Buy me this, buy me that, take me to Hawaii, take me to France, send the kids to this special school.' There weren't enough hours in the day for this guy to make money at the rate she spent it. His name was Simon, by the way. Simon needed to get away sometimes but could never figure out a good plan until he took the family on a houseboat vacation on the lake here. He went off fishing one morning and came along to the rapids near the river mouth, and it started bothering him what was on the other side and how if he were on the other side, his wife couldn't get to him. So he explored on foot and he thought and he planned and he scouted. He realized that if he could float a boat down here from upriver, it would make the perfect get-away. The problem was that his wife kept a close watch on every penny he made. Every time I talked to him he turned the subject back to the boat. He just couldn't get that vision out of his head, like we all get about a woman sometimes. And it happened at the time I was planning a business venture that could use his accounting skills and he could earn the side money he needed to fulfill his dream and buy a little peace. . . . Now I've been talking and those fish stopped being hungry."

He stopped. It was to check on me, I think. To see if I was going to play my part properly. If not, that meant I was too distracted. I said, "But how did you end up with it?"

"He owed me a little money at the end of things and said I could use the boat whenever I wanted to until he paid me back. I was the only other person in the world who knew he owned it or where it was. His wife never knew this boat existed. When he came up here, he told her he was visiting clients or going to a convention or whatever excuse he could sell her at the time. Over the years, I found it a pretty good place to relax. And he came up less and less until he stopped coming at all. I had moved on and lost touch with Simon. I asked around and found out he got sent to prison at Lompoc, so the next time I was nearby I went over to visit him. Terrible sight he was, too. Skinnier than ever and hair cut short. He shook his head and I could see that he just hated himself. It seems buying the boat wasn't the only way he tried to find peace. His other try was with another woman, and he married her, but he couldn't quite bring himself to divorce the first one first, and it wasn't long before both wives found out and it turned out he had married the same type twice. They got together on his finances and found that he had been working quite a few side ventures, some of which were profitable but on which he could not pay taxes because then his wives would have known about the money. Both wives had divorced him, of course, so he was really looking forward to the day he got out, and he made me swear to take good care of the boat until he could use it again."

"So you have it until he gets out?"

"Poor Simon won't be getting out. He had a heart attack a few months later and died. I didn't think there was any need to go pointing out the boat to the ex-wives; they had pretty much bled him dry. And the government, hell . . . no offense."

People who just met Dan, people who didn't know him, were really lucky because they could think they loved him when they heard him tell that story. For me, the part that stuck the most was the part he left out, the part of the conversation at Lompoc where Dan was checking to see if Simon had implicated him in any crimes.

I knew it was my turn next. Dan would want to know the whole story, and I must have been brooding about how to go about it. We were silent. Then he said, "Do you think that means I stole this boat?" His tone was startling; he was sincere. I looked at him. His face had grown dark and his eyes were sharp and hard, as if he were staring but seeing things that weren't there. The contrast with his face made his eyes seem like they were emitting light. "Do you?" I looked up at the sky to see if there were clouds making the light change, but, no, the sky was still blue.

"No," I said. "You didn't steal it."

"I'll tell you something I've never told anyone else and never will. I never had anything in this life that I didn't steal. Never, nothing."

I laid out for him why I was there and how I got there: Shaw, Gladden, the whole thing, including the shooters who were after me. Dan brightened up considerably when I told him about being undercover in Afghanistan.

"You posed as an Afghan? That's marvelous. And these American soldiers bought it. I always knew you had potential."

"We should get out of here. I stole that car in Vegas and it'll be found at the landing. These guys have the means to put it all together," I said.

"And you think the general put the shooters onto you?"

"He's after me. There was an incident, a bad one."

"Don't be so sure the general is behind it. Doesn't sound right to me."

"Okay." I didn't care about that right now. Those shooters weren't likely to be the first to show up on that river. "Where can we go?"

"Wait," he said. "I want to know . . . You set these guys up in Afghanistan, you got them to trust you."

Was this the moment to say "I learned it all from you. You deserve all the credit"? His flickering eyes and pleased smile seemed to offer warmth and refuge. Inclusion. But I knew the trap: warm yourself at that fire and you'll freeze to death. For a moment, I thought he could not help it: those were his eyes and his smile, all he had. Dan was looking at me with something resembling pride. I felt vaguely ashamed.

"So you had to fool Afghans, too. Who was tougher to fool, us or them?"

"Dan, I'll tell you all about it when we're on the road."

"Three days ago, I had driven out to New River City to try to collect on a job we did at a new development. The boss wasn't in. The secretary looked kinda cute and pretty soon we were on the boss's couch together.

It was easy. Real easy. I'm not bragging, I'm telling you this for a reason. She got up to go into the bathroom to freshen up. Took her purse and took her time. I wandered over to the desk where she had *USA Today*. They have a page with news from every state. I always check Oklahoma. It said the graves of three veterans of Iraq had been dug up. Two of the bodies were left alone, but the third was missing. The secretary had to be pretty fresh by then, but she was getting fresher still. I stood by the door and heard a few words and then she hung up her phone. They'd gotten to her. They had contacted her before I got there and were paying her to keep me there. These guys have resources. I don't think there's a better place than where we are now."

Father and son with fish, beer, cigars, sunshine, and water. A borrowed boat and borrowed time, unless McColl conveniently had a heart attack. And Shaw, too. I spent the time listening unless he asked and prodded for war stories. My reluctance must have come off as youthful sullenness, but I was struggling to isolate each of my resentments and squash them. I wanted to make sure I had Dan right. Filling in that picture had been a lifetime quest, with all the gathered evidence and clues snatched from fleeting moments together or observations of Dan with his women, his cronies, his victims. Now it was uninterrupted access and I couldn't stop staring into the fire, even though I knew I should run.

I even watched him sleep. He was still a handsome man, rugged and strong. I tried to guess how old he was, but it was just a guess and the thought of asking made me laugh out loud. Questions weren't paths to the truth or even to facts; they were cues to start the entertainment, or to change the channel and be captivated for a few more moments. No story ever came off as a rerun. Every moment was fresh; his smile would form and his eyes twinkle a bit and he'd ease in: "I was fishing on the Salmon River up in Oregon when a bear . . ." "Once, at a party in New York, a woman I'd never met before, very beautiful, came up and asked me to walk her home . . ." "They deputized me once in Santa Fe to help them catch a bank robber . . ."

I was on deck, Dan was inside finishing his lunch on the second day, when a raft came around the upstream bend. The rifle was leaning against the rail about three feet from my left hand. The sun was directly overhead. A young man about my age was guiding the raft and a young woman sat in front of him. I yelled out to them as a warning to Dan to stay inside. They waved back. When they came close, the man yelled, "Hey, man, you been down those rapids?"

"Not bad. Between a two and a three. Fun."

"Thanks. See ya."

And the woman waved her thanks, too.

I pretended to fiddle with our motor until they were out of sight. I called to Dan. He came out. "It happens," he said.

"There's the rifle. Where did you hide when I came down the cliff?"

"There's a cave just 'round the bend upriver."

"Wait there. Take the rifle."

I took off immediately up the path toward the top of the cliff. For the first couple of hundred yards or so, it was a smooth, steep wash, mostly in the shade of the cliff. But I couldn't squeeze through the spout where the runoff had created the wash. It had been easy to drop onto the ledge on the way down, but lifting my way up took time. The limestone was gritty and flaky, and I kept falling back onto the wash. I felt like if I didn't see them go over the rapids, I had to assume they were coming back toward us, maybe from on top. At last I wedged myself through and made it smoothly to the plateau. I cut across the bulge where the cliff juts out and the river bends and reached a spot above the rapids. A moment later, they came into view. The man guided the raft out of the current near to the rocks across the river from where I watched. They stayed there talking for a couple of minutes.

I watched them and tried to force myself to consider just walking away. What was the mission? Dan left me often enough, usually in much this way: I'll be back soon. He had come here believing it was safe, never thinking I'd show up. He wasn't asking for my help. Yet by the Rules of Dan, he wanted me to stay: that is, he never asked me to stay or went on about how glad he was that I was going to help him; no blather about us sticking together forever; and, especially, no rosy future scenarios, which were always a reliable precursor to his disappearance. He hadn't offered me any of the money. If he had, I'd have run, accelerating with each additional percentage point. By the Rules of Dan, we were still in the early stages of the enterprise. Betrayal would come in its own good time.

The man pushed off and the current caught the raft and they hit the rapids. I walked back toward the path down the cliff. As I knew I would. The boat was empty. The cave was upriver around a slight bend. Before I got there, I called out to Dan. No answer. "They're gone. Over the rapids." No answer. I moved faster toward the cave opening. It wasn't deep and Dan wasn't there. I hit the cliff face with my fist and cursed myself for a fool.

"Hey . . . up here." I had to step back into the water to try to see him at the top of the cliff. The sun was behind him from that angle. I could see his shape but not his face. "I'll head down. Take me a little while."

On the boat he said, "Ever think about your mother?"

I did not think about her and certainly not there on that river. "I don't remember her."

"I'm trying to figure out who you take after."

"How's that?"

"Not everybody would have come back today."

"She would have?"

"No chance." He did not laugh, though.

Dan reflective was worse than Dan naked. I stared shamefully. But Dan had the charm and the ability to carry the moment as if nothing were odd. "Also, she was nasty and thought the worst of people. Beer. Want one? There's a landing a few miles up the river where we can get more tomorrow or the next day." He returned with two beers.

"We should leave here," I said.

He sat down and scrutinized the cliffs for a while. He started to laugh. Just kept on. Then, "If we die from this, it's due to cigarettes."

"I don't smoke."

"Neither do I. But plenty of Iraqis do. I was over there working as a paving supervisor at the airport. Repairing the runways. Made a lot of friends, soldiers and civilians. One day, I'm talking things over with a young Iraqi, Tarik, about your age, very enterprising guy. He tells me he can make 'tausands, tausands' selling electronics. Cell phones, iPods, that kind of stuff. I wasn't sure I could help him out with any of that, but then he mentioned cigarettes. The main fighting had stopped and the insurgency wasn't in full force yet, but there were casualties all the time. Caskets flown in empty, flown out occupied. Ugly. But I suppose you've seen worse than I did."

"It's ugly."

"One night I took a truckload of cigarettes to the central morgue where Tarik worked. Rough part of town it was, but Tarik told us how to get through. I left my partners watching the truck and went inside. Place was overwhelmed. No vacancies. Standing room only. And the stench as thick as fog on a swamp. I'm waiting for Tarik and I can't help looking at the bodies. There's so many that they're stacked. Horrible and captivating at the same time. And it takes me a couple of minutes to realize that I recognize the second body from the top of the first stack in front of me. And he's an American soldier. He had been anyway. He was in his thirties, dark-complected guy from Oklahoma. Santoro was his name. He'd died the day before from an IED on his way back to the airport. And I'm positive it's Santoro because he thought I owed him money from a little deal we'd done. I'd been avoiding him for a couple of weeks. Tarik came out and we concluded our business. Unloaded those cigarettes in a garage just across from the morgue.

"He paid up, no problems. Twenty thousand in very crisp green dollars. All good, best of friends, looking forward to doing more business, you know how it goes. And before I leave, I tell him he's got an American body there in the Iraqi morgue. Suddenly, we're not friends anymore. Tells me to take my money and forget about dead bodies."

"He's selling bodies, too? Or buying them?"

"Can't be much money in that—too much supply. Where is he getting the crisp bills? And why doesn't he like me recognizing Santoro? I knew there was a lot of money floating around, money that Saddam had stashed away, some of which had been found by soldiers. And there was money the military was throwing around. But I didn't like this money so I gave it all to my partners. Told them it was down payment on the next deal and I let them think I was a sucker."

He smiled at me and held up his empty beer bottle. I came back with two more. The sun had slipped low enough for the shade to envelop the boat, but the light still hit the opposite rock wall, accentuating the striations and swirls of sandy colors. Dan was silent so long I thought he might be done with the story even though I could never remember him stopping midway through a story ever before. I knew better than to prompt him.

At last he said, "If you want people to think you're a sucker, you have to be aggressive, show them you think you're brilliant. You can't act naive. Remember that when you're undercover."

"You told me that a long time ago."

"Did I?" He looked at me like he would have to be careful what he said to me because I might remember. For a moment, I wanted to think it was pride. But most likely, it just meant I fell into a certain category of people who had to be dealt with more carefully. He went on: "I had a job once selling cemetery plots. It was an easy job because if you run into the right type of people, they won't let you leave without selling them. I quit because it wasn't any fun. There was no challenge. For me it was like dealing with aliens. I never once in my life thought of buying a cemetery plot. One time a guy hesitated and I told him if he committed right then, I'd throw in a special tie to be buried in. He wrote the check. I quit. I never spent a minute thinking about death, but Santoro's body stacked there bothered me all night. Why him? I knew he was listed as killed in action, which meant a body was going to be shipped home. Wouldn't matter in any meaningful way whose body would be in the coffin in the ground in Oklahoma, but the why of it stuck in my mind. Next morning at work, a Captain Callahan calls me aside. 'Saw you at the morgue last night,' he says. 'Stay away from there, or that's where you'll end up.' He's a tough guy, Third Infantry, means business. I made a comment and he slugged me and the next thing I know I'm in trouble for messing with a member of the military and they tell me I'm being transferred to Basra the next day."

"That was their mistake. They drew attention."

"Exactly. I left the supervisor's hut and went straight to the back door of the building where the caskets were kept while waiting to be shipped home. There were only eleven that day, all marked. I opened Santoro's. There's a body bag and there's somebody in it. I had to know who. I unzipped that bag."

"And here we are."

"Wrapped in plastic, clean and neat and new stacks of hundred-dollar bills. I knew what I was going to do even before I put the lid back on. Luckily, I got sick in Basra, a little nothing but it got me fired and sent home. Before I left, I managed to get two hundred cell phones for Tarik. Stayed up all night damaging the innards of as many of them as I could."

"That isn't like you."

"Surprised me, too. You're never too old to learn about yourself, I guess. Within a month, I had a job at the cemetery where Santoro's body was not buried."

He stopped for a few minutes again. Night was coming and the breeze swirled up the canyon, fighting the water and making it work. I was hungry, but I did not want to move, not even to reach for my beer.

"I made a mistake," he said. "Same mistake twice. Want to guess?"

I knew what the mistake was and I was surprised he made it, but I couldn't imagine that he wanted to hear me guess right.

"Twice isn't bad."

"Gets you killed in the war. I opened that coffin twice, once in Baghdad and once when I dug it up, and either time I could have taken a share and gone away happy and no one would have ever bothered me about it. But looking at all that money, I just stopped thinking. I didn't even know how much. Hell, I still don't know how much there is."

"Twenty-five million is the number they mentioned."

"I never counted it and I never questioned that I would take it all."

"Does that mean you're going to try to give it back to them?"

"Why lie? I'd do the same thing a hundred times. No way I can look at that money and not try to figure a way to have it all. Let's eat."

I started a fire with driftwood, which was plentiful.

Dan was always eager to cook. I watched him fillet the bass. He liked to show off and offered no instruction. He used olive oil, pepper and salt, oregano, and just a little bit of curry powder. He opened a can of black beans and seasoned those a bit, too. We ate on the top deck under the slight sliver of moon and enough stars to make me feel like nothing and no one in the universe would take notice of Dan or me. Dan smoothed the blanket with reminiscences from days before I could remember. I had run away and hidden in the root cellar. Dan found me, but I was too stubborn or proud or angry to come out, so he brought dinner down there and a sleeping bag. A few nights later, he had guests for dinner, business, of course. He forgot to bring food to the cellar and I walked in looking like I was being raised by wolves and just as angry and indignant. Dan couldn't resist: he tossed a couple of rolls and ordered me out.

Before he went to sleep, he told me that his brother Hal was an all right guy and would help me if I ever got into a jam, even though his wife was a horrible witch.

As he was going down the stairs, I had to ask him, "Why didn't you spend the money?"

He said, "I couldn't."

"Why?"

"You'll figure that out."

I sat up for a long time, listening to the sloshing river and the breeze, watching for shooting stars, and trying to shake it all off so I could figure out what I was doing there and how I was going to stop doing it. The coyote took the night off. A light caught my eye. A bright star rising in the west. It got bigger and brighter and then disappeared. Within seconds, the whoosh of helicopter blades could be heard. Dan heard them, too.

9.

I t seemed the helicopter was hovering downstream for a while, but it was low and I couldn't see it. Dan said, "Let's get the raft."

"Look."

Two rafts could be seen coming around the bend from upriver. We started out for our raft. One shot rang out. We hit the deck. But they weren't shooting at us. They hit the raft.

"Start the engine," I said. Dan went to the helm. I threw off the tie lines. I picked up the rifle and fired a few times toward the oncoming rafts. They didn't return fire, not wanting to kill Dan, but I knelt down anyway. The boat started to move, but the rafts were coming on fast. I could hear the motors now. I fired more and must have hit one guy; he fell into the river. We were out in midstream, picking up speed, and the rafts paced us. We rounded the first bend, still about a mile from the rapids. I went forward to Dan at the helm. "I don't think they'll catch us before the rapids," I said.

"Have any advice on how to take this thing over?"

"Don't think it matters."

The darkness seemed as deep as an ocean. The wind was proof we were moving, but the rock walls were so obscure they seemed uniform. The river was an elevator and we knew the cable was going to break soon. All at once, the walls seemed closer. The wind blew stronger against us. And the churning sound of the rapids drowned out the engine. Behind us, the rafts had pulled closer, hovering nearby like scavengers. The screech of a pontoon scraping a boulder froze us before we were rocked to the left then spun so we were bumping sideways. Dan fell away from the helm into the wall and I hopped over him, then righted myself.

"I'm okay," he said. "Where are they?"

I looked behind: the rafts had stopped before the rapids. But they weren't receding. "We've stopped," I said. "They're hovering behind us." I looked forward, straining against the sheath of black. I could see tufts of white where the water rose and slapped. Dan grabbed the helm and gunned the engine. We swayed a little, but we didn't straighten out. Toward the left shore, I saw an outline, a low strip stretching from the rock wall. Three flares arced from the helicopter for three seconds before they ignited the river and cliffs with the cold light that always signals hell opening up. Flares mean death and destruction to me, either the before or the aftermath. The usual strobe whooshing of the copter blades made it seem as if the light flickered. But it didn't. The light was, as always, mean and hard.

Two men wearing hoods and masks stood on the narrow shore. They held rifles. Two more stood on the other shore. The rafts behind us edged closer. Dan was trying to get us going, but it wasn't going to work because a net was stretched from shore to shore blocking us, keeping us in place. Dan saw it at the same moment I did.

"Can we cut it?"

The flares still burned. We were still boxed in. The steepest, roughest part of the rapids was still ahead of us. I was sure their rafts could outrun our boat. "Let's get in the water," I said. "Where's the fish knife?"

"I'll get it." He came back in a few seconds. "You have a plan?"

"I have an idea."

"I'll follow you. Just let me know when I'm supposed to do something," he said.

We waited until the flares died, then we climbed over the aft rail. The water was cool and ran strong. I pushed off first and grabbed the netting. We made our way along the netting toward the shore until we were just a few yards away. The two men waited nearby and I suppose they saw us even through the darkness, though I didn't have time to check. The net was nylon, but the knife was sharp enough.

"Keep a tight grip. We're going to swing out. Try to keep your legs in front. Let them hit the rocks first," I said.

"I'm ready," he said.

I cut the last piece of the net and immediately we were pushed downriver, holding on to the net, which acted like a swinging gate. I was in front and took the brunt of the bumps. The net had just extended fully when I heard Dan yell, short and sharp. I grabbed him.

"My ankle."

"Hold on to me." The net was going to swing us toward the opposite shore. Flares dropped light through the canyon again. I let go of the net and pulled Dan with me into the current. Instantly, I tumbled and lost hold of him. He shot out ahead of me. I let the water take me without fighting it. Dan rolled and flopped through the chute like a rag doll. I went after him wildly. At that moment, for the first time ever, I worried that Dan might die, and suddenly I was frantic at the picture before me. I was not ready for him to die. I struggled forward and managed to grab Dan's collar. We were around the bend and past the worst of the rapids. We paddled to the shore and pulled ourselves onto the rocks.

Dan couldn't stand without support. "I'd be better off in the water," he said.

"They'd be all over us."

"They won't kill me. Not yet. I'm not sure about you, though. You should go."

"Get on my back."

He laughed, but after he limped along for a few yards, I asked again and he gave in.

The helicopter set down on the plateau and the flares had gone out. I didn't see the rafts coming through the rapids yet. The men on the shore weren't visible in the dark, either. I stumbled along to a spot where the shoreline widened. I set Dan down and went along the rock face, hoping to find a path that would lead up the cliff side. It was a useless gesture in the dark. The whooping of the helicopter blades and the rumble of the rapids conspired with the dark to blot out my senses so I felt like I was the subject of an experiment like the one the Marines once put me through to see how I handled stress. I stumbled my way back to Dan. He was propped against the rock wall, legs bent, looking comfortable, like a guy who drifted away from a party for a little quiet time. His head fell to the side. I was too late reacting. Two men grabbed me from behind. I felt the needle go into my neck.

10.

We haven't talked about the money."

"I don't want to know."

"I was never a violent man. Have no instinct for it. There have been times when I just forgot that slugging someone or threatening to was an option, just like some people forget to lie. You gotta know who you are. Remember that. Not just right now, but the past, too. Remember that. Don't expect much from me."

"I stopped expecting anything from you a long time ago."

He tried to chuckle, but it sounded more like a cough. "I guess you did." The effort at conversation exhausted him again and he fell silent. He might have been sleeping; I couldn't tell anymore because his breath was always labored from the beatings. His eyes were swollen shut. The cell had two cots and a concrete floor. No window. The walls were thin. I could hear the interrogations and the beatings and Dan's relentless, futile attempts to charm the jailers or trick them, whoever they were. I never saw anyone's face. Two men wearing masks would open the door, enter, kick me or throw me to the ground or, if I attempted to resist, inject me, then grab Dan and take him out. No one ever said a word to me. Periodically, a man would drag me to a toilet then drag me back. When I tried to piss on him, he stepped away calmly, then kicked me in the nuts when I finished. The only way to sense the passage of time was to keep track of the cold and the heat. The cold times were nights, I assumed, and the transition came suddenly, without the usual pleasant in-between period of feeling thankful for the relief and hopeful that the middle ground would hold. I was groggy from the drugs they injected and uncomfortable lying on the cot, or the floor, leaning against the wall. Too weak to exercise for more than a few minutes at a time, I tried concentrating on my mirage. Shutters, swing, well, trees: I couldn't hold on long enough to bring the vision into focus. The house swayed and bits faded into a vague background. The voices came from the open living room window in the big house.

They shouted at Dan, "You're a scumbag. A degenerate." And much more. They argued among themselves, someone would defend Dan.

"He's a degenerate, but I like him anyway. He's gonna cooperate if we just ask him right."

Efficient soldiers they were, but they had misjudged their customer if they thought that lame stuff would affect Dan. In another circumstance, I would have felt sorry for them. Dan shouted in pain. Sometimes I thought I could hear the punches landing. I crawled forward on the porch of the big house, closer to the window, closer, but stayed below it. The house changed colors, but the window was always right above my head. Open. I could hear.

"Join us. Join us, Dan. Tell us where the money is."

"He can't tell us if he's dead."

"You took the money, Dan. Admit it."

"I took the money. Plenty of money. Never counted it."

"And where is it now, Dan?" That voice was the boss. Calm and threatening. "Join us, Dan. We have a need for a man like you. Tell us where the money is."

"I don't know."

They hit him and he gagged from the pain.

It became a chant: irritation, diversion, even comfort. Verses repeated like a song that gets stuck in your head. I used it to conjure the mirage and I used the mirage to conjure the conversation, and all the while I strained to see inside the house but I never could. What ritual accompanied the chant? A big pot of boiling water on a platform; Dan tied next to it, waiting to be cooked. But, no, Dan would be suggesting the recipe, selling it to them, withholding the secret ingredient.

When Dan was in the cell, the refrain played. "I never had anything I didn't steal. Remember that."

"I will."

"Figure out who you are."

"I will."

"I never had anything I didn't steal."

I had never seen Dan under physical stress. Plenty of soldiers resort to gibberish after they're wounded or when the attack is too intense. At a small station north of Jalalabad, a captain kept muttering "Go no more, go no more," as if he were in a horror movie. I ran into him a year or so later in Kabul, drinking tea in a cool courtyard, and asked him what it meant. He had no idea, barely remembered having said it. Even through the haze of the drugs, it hurt to see Dan like this. He kept trying to smile, but the swelling distorted his expression, making him look like a guy trying not to vomit in front of his girlfriend.

"Nobody knows me as well as you do. That's why I couldn't stay around. Do you understand?"

"No."

"Yes you do." I did. "It was wrecking my confidence," he said. His voice was a whisper but clear. He wanted to make sure I heard him and understood him. "You're going to make a great middleman." I smashed the butt of my hand against the solid wall, which was as close as I could come to telling Dan how I felt about him. Dan chuckled and coughed. Then he said, "You know where the money is."

"I don't."

"You do. You just don't know it."

"They can hear us." We were whispering, but it sounded like a shout to me. I looked around, as I had a thousand times already, for signs of hidden micro-phones. Whether I found them or not, we had to as-sume they were there. The door opened. Two masked men came in. First they assessed whether I was going to be a problem. I sat back. They came forward and lifted Dan to his feet. As soon as they started out, I kicked one behind the knee. He buckled. The other man threw Dan against the wall and turned to me. I punched with my right. Too slow. He dodged, caught my elbow, and rammed me headfirst into the wall. By then, the other man was up. He slugged me in the kidney, but he didn't have to. I was on my way to the floor, woozy and beaten. I looked up at him. His mouth hung open, showing the gap where his front teeth should have been.

From the next room, I could hear the desperate chorus.

"You're out of your league, Dan."

"National security implications. Join us. Join us."

"We know who you are. We know your past."

"Tell us where the money is, Dan."

"I don't know."

"Bring in his son."

They dragged me out of the cell. I didn't resist. Be-fore we went into the next room, I caught a glimpse of a thin man, medium height, wearing a mask, walking out the other way. I had never seen that one before.

The interrogation room had a window, a desk with a couple of bottles of water on it, and two chairs. Dan was passed out in one of them. They hadn't bothered to tie him to it. His face was raw and swollen from the beatings. Fresh blood dripped on the dried blood on his shirt.

For the first time, I saw faces. Two guys, older than me, in their thirties, stood guard over Dan. They wore combat gear. The one on the right wore gloves. He had blond hair and a huge chin. His eyes glinted with delight. It wasn't because he was going to beat Dan; it was because I was going to watch it happen. The one on the left held a baton. His head was shaved, and when he spoke his words were mush. His mouth did not open properly. Then Blondie said, "Maybe he'd like to take a turn hitting the old man."

The other man said something like, "Ah wanna killminetoo." He was mumbling to hide the gap in his mouth. But then he smiled. The combination of baldness and missing teeth made him look more zany than threatening.

The man in charge sat in a chair facing Dan. He wore fatigues and a black beret without insignia. His skin was tight and tanned and his eyes were such a light blue that he looked possessed or alien, though you could tell they were his pride and joy and he thought everyone was transfixed by them. He said, "Stand over here, soldier, so your father can see you."

I looked behind me. The two who brought me in were guarding the door, masks still on, weapons drawn. I moved in front of Dan. One of the guards had to move aside to make room for me. "You're McColl," I said. He gave me the full treatment with the eyes, blank, disinterested. But I could tell I was right and he didn't like me knowing.

"Your father stole money from us and he isn't cooperating. Now you're going to have to help us."

"You want what you've rightfully stolen."

"Do not be insolent, soldier. You have no idea what you're talking about."

"National security, huh? Top secret. Hush-hush. How about if I take a vow of secrecy and we all put on our masks and do the initiation ceremony? In this case, that would be the Order of the Greedy Fucks Who Washed Out of the Third Army."

The baton came down hard on my shoulder. I buckled for just a moment. Toothless held the baton ready, threatening more. McColl gestured for him to back away. "I know your record, soldier. I respect it. I have no gripe with you. I'm only doing what's necessary to accomplish the mission."

He seemed to think his little speech would convince me that torturing Dan was okay. I couldn't see any sense in arguing with McColl and I had the feeling that I shouldn't have shown defiance to start with. Dan wouldn't have.

"Dan, your son is here. We're going to kill him if you don't tell us where the money is."

Dan showed no sign of life. Eyes swollen tight, head slumped to a side. McColl nodded to the two men beside him. Toothless held up Dan's head and tapped his cheek with the baton to bring him around. Blondie unsheathed a buck knife and looked at me to make sure I could see how pleased he was that it was his turn. The two guards at the door came around and held me by each arm.

"Dan, tell us where the money is. Watch. Here's what we're going to do to your son." Another nod. Blondie dragged the knife diagonally across my chest. I growled low, expelling all my breath so that I didn't scream. Dan's eyes flickered so I know he saw the cut, but they were all staring at me and didn't notice him. I stared at McColl and he stared at me and all I was thinking was that every minute he let me live brought him closer to his own death. I never liked killing and I never hated it, either. It was just the way things had to be. It never made me angry or sad. On my first step into the war zone, I accepted that killing was part of living. But this was different. If I lived, I was going to kill McColl as cruelly as I could. And for the first time, I was going to enjoy it. At that instant, I knew this meant a change in me, not for the better, and I did not care, not at all. I was thrilled to find it there. The blood dripped into a puddle at my feet. Toothless slapped Dan again to make him pay attention. He said something like, "Wake up." McColl turned back to Dan.

"Where's the money, Dan? Where's the money?"

"I don't know," said Dan.

"You admitted you stole it."

"I stole it. I never had anything I didn't steal." Dan

raised his arm slowly. The guards tensed, poised to hit or cut the helpless guy in the chair. Dan turned his face from McColl to me. He pointed at me. "He stole the money."

McColl shouted, "You stole the money!"

"I stole the money. And he stole it from me. I don't know where the money is."

I wanted to growl again, but that would have been the only sound in the room other than the slowing drip of my blood hitting the floor. McColl stared at Dan, and Dan's head slumped to the side as if the gaze had knocked him out. I had the sense Dan did it to mock him. McColl looked at me for a moment, then nodded to Toothless, who, again, propped up Dan's head and gave him a slap. McColl wasn't too quick of a thinker. I could tell that receiving information that did not fit in his tiny compartments made him want to pull the blanket over his head. I didn't understand Dan's game, but I knew there was a game being played.

"Let me make sure we understand you, Dan. You're saying you don't know where the money is, but your son does. Is that right?"

"I'm sorry, Rollie Boy. I told you not to expect much from me."

"I'll try to remember."

"Answer me, Dan."

"You have it right."

McColl had been in command long enough to know he had to respond. He got up and paced over to the window. He looked out for a full minute. The guards stood still, waiting for orders. McColl turned back to the room. He said, "That would mean we don't need you anymore, Dan. Do you understand that?"

Dan's head stayed slumped on his shoulder. I gave McColl the blank stare, a taste of his own medicine. Let him try to read me. He ordered the guards to take me back to the cell.

The air refused to enter my lungs. Maybe it was too thick. I sucked hard over and over again but kept needing more. I forced my eyes open and turned to the other cot. Dan lay still. I drifted out again, but the discomfort came from more than the drugs, and I fought back to the surface and rolled off the cot onto the floor. Dan had not moved. I crawled over to him. He wasn't cold and he wasn't warm and he wasn't Dan anymore. I managed to turn away before I vomited. I straightened him up a bit, folded his arms across his chest. I stood up and pounded on the walls for a few minutes and yelled at McColl. I told him Dan was dead and a lot of things about himself that he needed to know. No one answered. No guards rushed through the door to beat me up or inject me. I kicked the door. And it flew open.

I stepped into the hallway and leaned against the wall to steady myself. The drugs were still clouding me and I knew my movements weren't sharp. I slid along to the room next door. A misshapen rectangle of light tumbled across the desk and onto the floor. No move-ment. No sound. I looked in. The room was empty. On a corner of the desk was my wallet, the fish knife I had used to cut the net in the river, matches, and the car check receipt from Las Vegas: all the contents of my pockets. Nothing of Dan's was there. The light hurt my eyes when I checked outside. There was nothing to see but desert.

The rest of the building was empty. There were eight rooms like the one we were kept in. All empty. The place must have been a storage facility. I walked out-side and the sun staggered me with its intensity, made me bow my head and step back inside for a moment. We were in the high desert: scrub brush, gray rocks and sandy dirt, and small patches of Jimson weed and prim-rose and some blue flower I didn't know. A gravel drive led away from the building and out of sight around a small hill. A jeep was parked twenty yards from the building. I approached. The keys were in the ignition. There was a canister of gasoline in the backseat. I caught motion out of the corner of my eye and spun around. A roadrunner dashed along the drive, into a swale, and behind a bush. The wind purred softly. I no-ticed the sound of a bird repeating a call but couldn't locate it.

From the top of the small hill, I could see where the drive met the road about a half mile out. No other structures were in sight. I turned and looked back at the warehouse. The darkness and nausea and pain and death seemed as impossible and far off as the sunlight and caressing breeze had a few minutes ago.

I gathered my stuff from the desk. My wallet was fat with hundred-dollar bills, twenty of them that weren't there before. I lifted Dan's body to a spot on the hill, then fetched the gas can. Before I poured gas on him, I stood awhile and considered the right words for the occasion. I kept including liar and con artist, which made me start over. Father was a tough one to include also. Did he cheat time, or did it catch up to him? As in every deal Dan ever entered, the results could be tabulated later and debated: who won, who lost, did revenge mean dealing with him again? Staring hard at the body kept time from stretching out, flat and endless, colorless: the world without Dan. Finally I said, "I promise I'll find the money, and I promise I'll kill those fuckers." I chuckled, thinking he would answer: *I've got to go somewhere for a few days. Won't be long.* I poured the gas and lit him up.

11.

Watching the flames did not help me focus on Dan or figure out my plans; everything was too vague and formless. My mind drifted back to Kabul and the start of my trip as a Pashtun villager from Lashkar Gah, traveling to Karachi to look for work. The story was that my wife had died and her family was looking after my daughter. I moved along slowly, practicing my story on everyone I met, watching them carefully for signs of suspicion, and listening to their stories carefully for new idioms and for subtleties of the accents. I stayed away from NATO forces completely. The last week, I spent most of my time in a mosque, making sure I was adequately versed on the rituals of praying. It would be hard to sell my act without that. If anyone suspected me, prayer time would be a major test. Praying is bad enough without having people watching you and judging you so you end up praying only that they like the way you pray enough that they don't kill you. It's the advanced version of what I used to pray for as a kid: get me out of here. Two foster families made me go to church on Sundays, one Baptist and one Presbyterian, and Marion the Bitch tried it out a few times. Of course, I wanted to get out of there, but I didn't hate it completely. I enjoyed watching people there. For kids, church was destructive, just a way to control them, and for about half the adults it was just a phony thing they did to hide who they really were, but for the other half it was a good thing. I could see they needed to be there, and the connection and the prayers and the sermon made them feel less like the louses they knew they were and that maybe there was some way to hope the world was not going to end soon.

Muslims pray enough for everybody. Five times a day. So religion has to be all about the afterlife because even they can see they're not getting a big payoff in this world. It was easy to find a mullah to instruct me. I just told him I wanted to get my head right at last, and I had some money to pay him.

They make a big deal of the idea of being clean before you pray, but that's a relative kind of clean. You have to be cleaner than you were before you started. The physical part is precise; the verbal part gives you some options. It starts with facing the Ka'aba in Mecca and stating your intention, as in "I'm going to say the noontime prayer." Then you put up your hands, palms out, thumbs touching ears, and say "Allahu Akbar" which means god is great. Next you hold your left wrist with your right hand and recite the first chapter of the Koran. It's short and easy to learn, but if you can't learn it, they give you something else to say. Then you have to bow and say some more short praises of god before you get down on your knees on some kind of a rug or anything that isn't the dirt road. When you kneel, the drill is palms down, forehead down, bottom of the toes down, heels up, elbows away from the body, abdomen away from the thighs. More praise of god. You sit up, and your left foot gets tucked under, right foot stays out with the sole showing, hands on knees, fingers spread out. Depending on the time of day, you repeat this a number of times. And you finish by looking right, at the angel in charge of your good deeds, then left at you know who, and you tell them both to go with god and then sort of wipe your face with your hands and you're done for a few hours. It reminds me of tai chi mixed with yoga and a chant. Very peaceful.

I crossed the border into Pakistan without problems. My passport passed muster and no one thought to pay too much attention to me. I guess by then I smelled right. Karachi is huge and spread out, biggest city I had ever been in. They say Karachi is the most convenient port for us to land supplies, which must be military talk for Karachi is the only port because it's completely inconvenient and it brings Pakistanis into the stew, which already has too many ingredients. The work is done by Pakistanis and Afghans and supervised by Americans and other NATO troops.

I worked my way down to the port, past some of the magnificent buildings constructed by the Brits when Karachi was in India and the sun never set. For a moment, I almost understood why we are chasing all this so hard. It's all still grand, exactly the way empire is supposed to look. The muscle shows in every slab. And if you are king of the world, it must seem logical to want to show your muscle, too. Kind of like rich people who have their kids tested to see if they're geniuses; the next stage after having lots of money is proving you're special. But in books, the pain is buried beneath glory and nostalgia. We have resurrected the pain, but I do not see us leaving behind the structures, or enjoying the conquest.

My contact was a short, smiling Pakistani man, Jaffar, in a warehouse office filled with men shouting, begging, eating, sleeping, arguing, coughing, praying, everything but fucking. I was posing as an Afghan, and for about ten paces I felt slick until it occurred to me that half of them were Taliban posing as friendlies and the other half were thieves posing as honest. No one would believe my story on its face, but unless I gave provocation no one would question it too closely.

I fought my way to the desk and presented my paperwork to Jaffar. He looked everything over, including me, and said, "You're too late. All positions are filled."

"I was told to report today."

Jaffar repeated his mantra a few times. I got the letter

back from him and the envelope. I left the building and went to a café, and in the bathroom I took out two hundred dollars and put it in the envelope. When I handed it to Jaffar, he just fingered it a little while he looked me over. Finally he glanced inside, just to make sure. He directed me to the staging area where I was to find the driver I would be riding with.

Rashid was a twenty-four-year-old cocky know-it-all lounging near his truck with his friend Mansour, the guy who already had the job I thought I was getting. Mansour probably already paid Rashid for the chance. I had plenty to outbid him, but this was not a high-paying job and suspicion lurked just below the surface. Rashid dismissed me with an arrogant flick of his hand. I hesitated. Mansour got up and came toward me. He wasn't a big guy, but I let him chase me away.

The next day, before the caravan was scheduled to leave, I waited near Rashid's truck, but out of sight. Mansour did not show up. Rashid got nervous, paced around, asked everyone if they had seen him, made a million phone calls. I knew Mansour would not be there on time because he had been caught having sex with a prostitute in a park the night before. That kind of behavior is frowned upon in Karachi, so Mansour was locked up. The prostitute got away, with only the slightest help from me. I suppose Rashid figured his friend got cold feet. We never discussed it. I offered him one hundred dollars to take me on at the last minute and he accepted. I was in.

12.

The jeep had a compass. The wind was blowing Dan's smoke east. I turned south. Phoenix was south of most places and that was where I thought I might try to start puzzling out Dan's clues. The wind bombarding the open jeep felt like progress, though I wished for sunglasses against the glare and the dust. After a few miles, the U.S. Highway 95 sign told me nothing helpful except that I had never been there before. The gas tank was full and it occurred to me that I did not have to worry about that anyway. McColl was having me followed or watched somehow. A GPS in the jeep for sure, and some sort of backup. If I broke down beside the road, I'd be rescued. Far off on the right, mountains formed a wall up to the sky. On the left, the sky fell all the way down to the brown and gray rock. The road was straight as a rolled-out carpet. It was twenty miles before a car appeared traveling north. A few minutes later, a car came up fast behind me doing at least ninety. I caught a glimpse of a woman at the wheel of the blue Honda as it blew past me trailing blue smoke. I slowed down to let the oily smell dissipate. Twenty minutes later, the Honda was pulled onto the shoulder, hood up. The woman stood beside the car.

She wore shorts, tank top, and flip-flops. Her hair was cut in bangs and pulled back, which made her look younger than she was. I guessed thirty-five. Her skin was smooth and the thin glistening of sweat reminded me of how parched I was. If McColl sent her as bait, he made a shrewd choice. She held her cell phone in her hand and held her ground as I backed up.

"Need help?"

"Thanks. Called the tow truck. They're on the way."

"I'll take a look if you like. Maybe save you some money."

"No thanks," she said, and she tensed and moved backward against the dusty door of her car.

"What would you have done if I'd gone north?"

"Look, you can go now. Leave me alone."

I asked, "You know how far it is to the next town?"

"Fallon is about twenty miles that way." She pointed south. I looked up and down the road and imagined a series of women stationed in all directions, a few on each roadway, there to lure me. If I didn't stop for the first one, the next would appear, more needy or more alluring. The picture made me laugh. The woman got into her car and locked the door. It must have been hotter in there than my cell had been. I realized I probably looked pretty frightening, and there was a slight chance that I was wrong about her reason for being there. I drove away.

First stop was Walmart for some clothes that weren't slashed or bloody. They carried that. I bought sunglasses, jeans, two T-shirts that said "49ers" to give anyone I ran into something to remember other than my face, two plain T-shirts, a pack of underwear, socks, antibiotic cream to put on the cut across my chest, and a backpack to carry it all. The first fast food chain I saw was Burger King; I ordered enough to put me to sleep.

Fallon proved the point that Nowhere and Anywhere have merged in a slurry of chain stores, restaurants, and hotels. For a small town, Fallon is very crowded: most of us live there. I chose the Holiday Inn because they had the sense to claim they were number one in all of Fallon and McColl wouldn't have left me so much money if he wanted me to scrimp.

I sank into the bed and worked at understanding who McColl expected me to be. Greedy. He would get stuck on that and I was stuck there for now, too. It was dark when I woke up, nine P.M. The air conditioner buzzed and coughed, but it kept the desert out of the dreary room. I showered and dressed, planning to eat more, then start for Phoenix. The motel had no restaurant. Two replicas of Pongo and Perdy marched through the lobby as if to remind me that the real ones were still lurking somewhere out there. The desk clerk directed me to Dollard's Steakhouse, located in Dollard's Casino, home of the Dollar Deals.

The air-conditioning wasn't working too well, or the management was too cheap, and the air was thick and close. I walked quickly through the sad, smoky casino to the steakhouse, on the lookout for anyone who might be with McColl's gang. The gamblers, dealers, pit bosses, and waitresses all watched me with that hungry drooling-for-fresh-meat look, though none of their fangs were showing. Maybe McColl sent them all. A fat woman, so fat she had two stools pushed together, rubbed a quarter and licked her lips, but I couldn't take that personally; salivating was like breathing to her. Three blackjack tables, one sparse craps game, and a poker table of five players comprised the action, all of it in slow motion. A few players were cowboys. No one, not even Dan, was a deceitful enough salesman to make Fallon a tourist destination. I figured the rest of the patrons worked at the naval air station a few miles down the road.

The hostess must have been on break, so I took a table at the rear of the steakhouse where I could see anyone coming in. The waitress was a thin, energetic woman in her fifties. She hustled over with a menu. I ordered a draft beer. She turned and said, "Anywhere, hon." And when she moved away, I saw the woman from the blue Honda decide to take a booth on the right side of the room. I joined her.

"I'm sorry," I said, "if I was scary this afternoon."

"And are you sorry that you're scary now?"

The waitress delivered my beer. I said, "She liked this table better." The woman ordered a beer, too.

"How's your car?"

"Fine."

"You work at the naval air station?"

"No."

The waitress brought the beer. "Y'know whatchu want?"

"Another table," said the woman.

"Anywhere, hon." The waitress walked away. The woman looked the room over.

"They're all gonna be the same," I said.

She sat back and sipped her beer and looked me over. She did not seem to be afraid of me. "Why me, with all the beautiful women in this town?"

"They've already turned me down."

She smiled and showed a slight gap in her front teeth, and I noticed for the first time freckles on her cheeks near her nose. "You can buy me a hamburger."

"You know what would be a nightmare?" I said. "Getting stuck in Fallon because your car has a cracked block and you don't have enough money to pay to fix it and you end up working here. Forever."

"You sound like you're a traveling auto mechanic."

"How long have you worked for McColl?"

"Who's McColl?"

"The guy you work for."

"How long have I worked for him?"

"Pick up your phone right now and call him and tell him I know he's following me and I'm going to find the money for him so he doesn't have to send women out onto the highway or thugs into hotels to keep me company. Call him. Call him and I'll let you come with me."

"How many beers have you had?"

I got up, paid the waitress, and walked out. I had just started the jeep when she opened the door and slid in. "Are you gonna be a hard-ass about everything?"

"Only as long as it works. Did you call him?"

"If I call him and say that, he'll know you made me, which he did not want. And I will be stuck in Fallon with no car and no money. Please. Take me with you."

I pulled out without answering her, but it suited me just fine. Even if she told McColl that I knew who she was, it still gave me a conduit to feed him the information I wanted to.

"What's your name?"

"Shannon. You still owe me a hamburger," she said. She already knew my name. McDonald's was right next door. While we waited in the car, she said, "Who are you going to see in Phoenix?"

"My mother."

"How sweet."

"I think she might not be as dead as she used to be."

13.

She slept. I thought. The road was straight and flat and empty. A lake appeared on the left. With the mountains in the west and the lake just a few yards on the other side of the road, it felt as if the world were slanted and we would slide into the water unless I held tight against the tilt.

The open road, a wallet full of money, and a woman by my side: I smiled at the picture. The ghost of my father, leaning in and repeating his clues, demanded to be included. I was not ready for the clues yet, so he whispered, *"Not just a woman. A willing woman. Paid for."* Maybe she was, and I didn't hold it against her. I'm not one of those guys who brags that he has never paid for sex. I have paid, though usually, not always, I prefer not to. The Marines shipped me to Germany for a month of training and my first night out a German girl picked me up in a bar. She spoke no English, none. We went to her apartment, had sex. I was on my way to the same bar a few nights later, the well where I drew water, but a prostitute stopped me and I started talking to her and she was funny. She said, "I like Americans because they believe all dicks are equal." We settled on a price and I had a terrific time. Not because of the sex, that was fine, but because I had been lonely. Horny and lonely. I didn't care that I had to pay for the company.

Arranged pairs and dowries, old guys with some-body's daughter, money lubricates. The stigma sinks to the low-end transactions. A captain lectured me that prostitutes were abused as children, are drug addicts, abused by pimps and beaten by johns. I told him I didn't think that was a reason to deprive them of a liv-ing and the feeling that they were bringing some joy to the world, and he said he would pray for me. Everyone, even the whiniest excuse maker, knows deep down how awful he is. It's only that knowledge that keeps kids at home, despite all parents being abusive in one way or another. I learned not to decide why people act the way they do until I know someone pretty well, and even then, it's a foolish gamble.

Nineteen, riding shotgun in a car full of guys, a night of fake IDs and other lies, and we pulled up to a bar in a strip mall in Tucson. The Raven. To the left of the entrance, near the edge of the building, I saw a guy pull back his elbow, make a fist, and slug the girl next to him in the stomach. She doubled over. He held her up, slapped her. One guy in the car said, "That's Cora Burkle." Another said, "Yeah, I've seen her with that guy." I said, "Let's go."

I was halfway to the couple when I noticed I was alone. All my pals had stayed in the car. The hitter and the girl stopped their dance to stare at me. "What are you staring at?" he said.

"Leave her alone."

He was bigger than me and thick, but his middle was soft. He had long hair pulled back in a ponytail, fat cheeks, and the light from the bar showed the pockmarks. The girl, Cora, was thin. She wore a blue halter top, tight jeans, and a red choker. Her face was the opposite of his, smooth skin and thin features. He turned his back on her to face me. She didn't try to run away from him, which should have been a hint, but even if I'd understood the meaning of that, I wouldn't have been able to stop myself. I came forward within inches of the guy.

"Mind your own fucking business," he said.

I slugged him in the gut, then kneed him in the face when he doubled over. I let him stagger for a second and that was all it took for Cora to attack me. She was pounding on me with two fists like I was the locked door to the medicine cabinet.

"Leave him alone. Get the fuck outta here." And more.

I backed up a few steps to get away from her. The guy had recovered. He pushed her aside and came at me. "Leave her alone, you asshole," he said.

He tried to hit me, but I blocked it and slapped him hard across the face, which always hurts more than people think it will. Cora screamed, "No . . ." as if he had been shot. And she flew onto him, holding him back, protecting him. She hissed at me, "Just mind your own fucking business." She pulled his hand off his cheek and kissed it where I had slapped him. I shrugged and went back to the car. It was empty. My pals were in the bar. When I asked why they didn't help, two said they had slept with Cora in the past month and didn't want the guy to know. I don't know why any of us, including me, did what they did.

Signs announced diminishing distances to Las Vegas, and I chose to believe them so I didn't feel like I was on a treadmill. I tried to focus on Dan's clues, which meant conjuring him: relaxed on the boat, fit and tanned, and in the cell, beaten pale, eyes swollen to slits. If Dan suddenly suggested I get to know who I am, then I knew I better take a close look at who everybody was. Dan could always claim he gave his partners fair warning.

We arrived in Phoenix before dawn. I checked into a downtown motel for a few hours' rest before the Office of Vital Records opened at nine. I showered and fell right to sleep, not worrying about how Shannon spent her time.

The Office of Vital Records reminded me of a high school, a four-story brick and stone building stretched out along the whole block, with a wide, well-tended lawn and a flagpole. One woman occupied the information desk just inside the glass doors. "You have to show some relation to the deceased or that you represent the estate to access the death records," she said. I knew my mother's name from my birth certificate: Gloria Marie Waters, formerly Henning, born 1962 in Tucson. After a little go-round with another clerk, we found my birth certificate and with that, along with my service ID, he felt it was safe to look up Gloria's death information. "I'm sorry," he said. "If she died, it didn't happen in Arizona. There are databases that list obituaries from around the country, but they aren't perfect. They charge. . . . You can use those computers." He pointed across the room.

Dan had mentioned a couple of times that my mother was dead and I remember questioning him only once. "Cancer," he said. There was no reason to think she was dead at all. Shannon had a credit card, which meant McColl would be in on the search. No combination of names and ages matched the Gloria Henning Waters I was looking for in the death records. The only living Gloria Henning was just twenty-six. I found four living women named Gloria Waters in Arizona. Three were too old; one was just the right age.

The town house was in a stylish white stucco building in south Scottsdale. I parked down the street and watched it for a minute. Shannon said, "You want me to wait here?"

"Suit yourself."

"I just thought . . ."

"What?"

"It's your mother, maybe anyway and . . ."

"You don't want to intrude. That's fine. Thanks." A phony act, but I couldn't see why I cared. I left her in the car. Gloria Waters had an end unit, Number 8. A sprinkler missed the small bushes spaced along the edge of the building. An old man walked his poodle, leash in one hand, plastic bag in another. The poodle pissed on a bush that wasn't getting watered. The old man wanted me to smile at the cuteness of it, so I did.

The front door to Number 8 was ajar. I pushed it open and called out, "Hello?" No answer. Shards of mirror littered the marble entrance floor. A small table was knocked over. I stepped inside.

Even with walls punctured, furniture overturned, pillows gouged, drawers and cupboards emptied onto the floor, you could tell this place had been nicely put together. I didn't want to step on the debris because it all looked like such good stuff. Every vase was smashed, every picture slashed. In the kitchen, a bag of Peet's Coffee had been emptied onto the floor. Next to it lay the vacuum cleaner with the bag slashed open. They weren't looking for twenty-five million dollars. They must have gotten the idea of clues into their heads, and unsure what that meant, they binged on the notion of thoroughness and the luxury of their power. They were like morons at an all-you-can-eat buffet, piling their plates because no one could stop them.

She was taped to a chair in the master bedroom up-stairs. A slightly plump woman with dyed red hair cut short, she was wearing a skirt and a bra; she must have been getting ready for work when they came in. Her heavy makeup was smeared. Her eyes burned with fear at seeing me. She struggled against the tape to scream.

"Gloria Waters?"

She nodded.

"I'm not with whoever this was. I'm going to come over there and free you. Is that okay? I'm not going to hurt you."

She nodded again. I moved behind her and pulled my knife and slit the tape binding her to the chair. I pulled it away from her arms. That must have hurt a bit, but she just sat there. "I'm going to pull the tape off your mouth, okay?" She nodded. I looked right into her eyes, which had calmed down. I yanked the tape. She started to sob openmouthed with aching gasps. On the back of the tape, the smudged lipstick matched her hair color. I found a short jacket on the floor that might have belonged with her skirt and helped her put it on. She was able to say "Thank you" in a weak voice.

I found a glass that wasn't broken and brought her water. She had picked up the remains of her phone. "What did they want? What did they want? I don't know what they wanted."

"I don't have my phone, but I'll contact the police for you."

"Who are you?"

I probably stared at her too long. Maybe I was trying to summon some feeling, some connection. It would have been fake. I felt sorry for her. That was all. Maybe the rest would come later, though it was hard to imagine this woman with Dan. Her eyes darted around to confirm that escape was impossible.

"My name is Rollie Waters."

Her expression softened, her shoulders slumped, and I admit that for one quick moment I was confused by a feeling I was unfamiliar with. She rose, her jaw jutting out, and her eyes lost their fear. It was rage.

"Get out of here! Get out of here!"

Not what I was hoping for. "Aren't you Gloria Waters? I'm—"

"My son died twenty-three years ago with my husband. How dare you? How dare you come in here? Get out."

So I was the guy who helped make this the second worst day of her life. And I knew who I wasn't.

Shannon wasn't in the car. I found her about five minutes later at a bus stop on McClintock Drive. The bus arrived just after I did. I managed to grab Shannon before she could push her way on board. A mother ushered her two young kids up the steps and past the driver. The driver looked at me, but I shook my head and said, "Don't." He closed the door and drove off.

I backed Shannon against the jeep. "Call them. Call them right now."

"I will."

"Right now."

"I told you. If they find out you know I'm with them . . ."

"That's over. Call."

She pulled her phone from her purse, called McColl, and handed it to me. McColl answered. "You're tracking me. I don't care. You've sent me a companion. I don't care. I'm going to find the money and then we can deal with each other. But don't ever pull another stunt like you did on that woman today. Never."

"Or what?"

Thank you for asking. "I'll quit looking. Just walk away. And you can torture me until your pants are so wet they fall down. As we both know, it won't do any good because I don't know where the money is."

Silence. I handed the phone back to Shannon. "You ran because you knew."

"I ran because I guessed. When I was sitting there, I just had a bad feeling."

I should have ditched her at that moment. They would not trust her anymore, but if she kept feeding them information, it would create doubt. I thought I could turn her to my side. I should have ditched her.

14.

"hy are you sitting at the edge of the booth?"

"There's a spring broken in the middle and it's really uncomfortable."

"It's near the window on this side. We could switch."

"They're all the same."

I was only six years old when Dan first took me to Chui's Diner. Since that time, they had not made one improvement, bought one new dish or utensil, or repaired one fixture. Most of the customers were the same, too. Chui was a big man in his sixties. His belly has always hung over his belt, and he always wore a bolo tie that sometimes swung into your face when he leaned over to inspect your plate and ask how you liked your meal. In a pinch, Dan would leave me there for the day while he attended to business, which meant I attended to business also, standing on a chair at the sink so I could wash dishes and silverware. Those day sessions eventually developed into sessions lasting days.

Chui and his wife, Rosa, lived behind the diner. I would bathe there and watch TV with them in the evening, then sleep in a booth. Along the way, I learned every job in the restaurant, including cook. I don't know if what I cooked was any good, but I could turn it out fast and accurate. Of course, I ate the mistakes before Chui noticed, or before I saw him notice. I've done about a million crummy things so far in my life, but the one I regret, or at least the one I think about most, is stealing a packet of frozen chicken breasts and selling them out the back door. Chui caught me and I had not been back for more than ten years.

Shannon was looking at the menu and I was putting milk in my coffee when I was slapped on the back of the head. Chui said, "Why the hell you sitting at the edge of the booth?"

"Quick getaway. Chui, this is Shannon."

"Hi."

"Hi. Dan was in just a few weeks ago, said you were doing great, own a ranch in Wyoming, something like that. I figured that meant you were never in Wyoming. You looking for him?" The last part he said hopefully. Chui always wanted Dan and me to act like his version of a normal father and son.

"Dan died." I had to think about it for a moment. "Couple of days ago."

Chui turned and walked away. I signaled the waitress. I didn't know her. She took her time and when she arrived, she was careful to make sure to let us know that despite the warm reception from Chui, we were going to receive the same gentle treatment she gave everyone. "Whaddya want today?"

I told Shannon, "You're safe with the omelets." She ordered an omelet, and so did I. As soon as the waitress walked away, Chui returned with Rosa. She was crying. I got up and hugged her.

"I'll miss him so much, so much. He was my favorite," Rosa said. "And I miss you so much."

"You were his favorite. He talked about you just before he died."

That turned up the tear faucet a few notches. She hugged me again and kissed me and ran away. "Excuse me a second," I said to Shannon and I put my arm around Chui and we walked to the end of the counter where we could speak without being overheard.

"It wasn't good." Chui nodded. He understood. "Did you ever know Dan under another name?"

"I never even knew his last name until he gave me a check one time." We both chuckled, knowing what that meant. "What's going on? If you need help, you know . . ." Chui knew a lot of people in Phoenix, a lot of people with guns.

"He owed some people some money. I'm trying to help out."

"You're a good boy."

"Let me start here. How much was his tab?"

"Forget his tab. I'll start a new one for you."

"Chu—"

"If you say you're sorry again, I'll stab you."

"I was gonna say there's a blue Ford parked just down the street. Could you send someone out there to see if anyone is inside and get a description?"

Shannon was halfway through her omelet when I sat down. We ate in silence for a while. I realized I could ditch the jeep here and have Chui's car if I wanted it, but they would probably destroy the place in retribution. Most people would probably count that a blessing, but not Chui. Ditching Shannon was another matter. Her original version was that McColl would not want her anymore if I knew she was working for him. But I was guessing there would be a revised version. Most people like to hang on to a job.

She finished up and said, "You don't ask a lot of questions."

"Where would you like me to drop you?"

"I didn't know about your father." Maybe she didn't, but she sure knew how to make it sound like a lie. "McColl, he doesn't care who dies as long as he gets what he wants, so . . . you should know that."

"You mean I should be impressed."

"He was Third Army. That's where I met him. I'm a medic. I was. He had started as a lieutenant in Desert Storm. Logistics. And he made a name for himself. When the buildup began for the second Gulf War, McColl didn't want to get stuck in Qatar or some backwater. He fought hard to get a forward assignment and he got it and he nailed it. Remember how fast we got to

Baghdad? Getting the supplies there was a massive operation and McColl specialized in getting his soldiers to go the extra mile. Get it done."

"Do you want more coffee?" I signaled the waitress and she brought over the coffeepot.

"How about dessert?" She had warmed up. I guessed Rosa's tears did it.

"I'm good," Shannon said. The waitress poured the coffee and left and Shannon started right back in, like she was determined to get something on the record, the way people do when they want to establish a lie. "McColl never cared how. Just get it done. He practically owned that airport. Of course, that meant he pissed off quite a few people along the way. Once the war felt won, his role wasn't as important and people who were waiting to undercut him could get to work. He found out he was being transferred back home, so he retired."

"Aren't you leaving something out?"

"I don't know how he got the money."

"That wasn't what I wanted to know."

She understood what I wanted. "I finished my tour, worked as a nurse. In Las Vegas. It took me a while, but I finally fucked the wrong doctor. His wife was head of the nursing staff. I was fired. She accused me of stealing drugs, which I didn't do. Hubby did. So I was out of work. Waitressing. I let my friends know I needed something and McColl came up with this."

Before we left, I checked with Chui. "Two white

guys, muscles, short hair, could be cops, could be military," he said. I kissed him and left.

The blue Ford was gone. Shannon walked to the passenger side of the jeep, ready to hop in, but I stopped next to her. If she was going to stay on, we had to have an arrangement. "I think you better go off on your own. As you said, once I know who you are, McColl will be done with you. He's not going to like you hanging around."

"Take me with you. I can help you. I know McColl. I know his people. I know how they operate." She tried to control her panic with a slow cadence, but her voice sounded brittle and breathless.

"And in return?"

"I get a cut. It's only fair."

"How much is fair?"

"Twenty percent." I laughed. She said, "I don't care how much. Whatever you say. I know his people. I can spot them. I know what resources he has access to and what he doesn't. You need me to get away with this."

"I don't mind having a partner. But we would have to start with some honesty. How much is he paying you?"

"One percent."

I went around the jeep and got in. "I hope you're a better medic than you are a liar."

She jumped in. "Wait." She waited and I waited while she figured out a number I would believe. "Ten thousand. If I stayed with you the whole way."

"I'll pay you fifty thousand. If I end up with the money," I said.

"Okay. Deal."

"And if I don't end up with the money, you can still get your ten from McColl."

"That's nasty," she said, but she was trying to sound flirtatious. "You're nasty." She clutched her purse as if grabbing hold of the future she thought she had connived. I still had a few hours to kill.

Shannon was in the shower. I sat next to the bed in padmasana, full lotus position, and brought up my vision. The clouds looked like rejected cotton polka dots, stuck to the blue, as permanent as stripes on a highway. The chimney, red brick on the right side of the house; the porch; the open windows; upstairs a window with no curtain, but I could not see anyone inside; the chirping of crickets; then a bang . . . how many times? I couldn't tell if I had missed the first few. I realized it was Shannon, out of the shower and banging doors and drawers to let me know it.

She made a little noise while adjusting the air-conditioning and I knew the only way I would get any quiet was by opening my eyes. The show she put on was a good one. The lovely soft bulge of her breasts shimmered just above the towel, which was all she wore. She was tall enough, her legs were long enough, that when she bent forward to search through her bag, I was treated to a peek at her butt. She turned and smiled at me. "You back in the world?"

"Yeah."

She sat on the edge of the bed, bringing along the fresh scent of soap and body oil that seemed like an oasis in the musty motel room. Her hair was pulled up, accentuating her neck and faint, downy hairs too short to be included. She said, "I'm going to call him, Mc-Coll, and tell him I'm still working you, tell him you think you've turned me, but I'm still with him. I want to do it in front of you so there's no question . . ."

She twisted around to face me and put one leg up on the bed. She had freckles on her chest. I remembered that there are days when I really like freckles. This was one of them. I said, "He knows where the jeep is. He'll know I'm here. He can locate the call. Maybe it's better not to do it, anyway."

"I'll wait until you go. I just don't want you to not trust me."

"Do you trust me?"

She stared into my eyes, but her gaze fell. She couldn't lie about it. She couldn't give trust anymore but believed she could still earn it.

"You could do me a favor."

She whispered, "Okay."

I sat on the bed next to her, pulled off my T-shirt, and turned my back toward her. "Next to my right shoulder, something's there . . ." She let her fingers drift gently up to the spot where the itch was and circled it.

"Stitches there. A little swelling, just a little. They must have stabbed you there."

"Thanks." I turned toward her and she stayed close. We kissed. She pushed me back onto the bed and snuggled in close to me as the towel came loose. We kissed some more. My skepticism cleared its throat and mentioned her likely insincerity, but confronted with a superior force it withdrew to let the storm pass. I thought about how I was getting a much better deal than McColl: he just got a phone call; I got freckles and downy neck hair and long legs and . . . I opened my eyes to enjoy it all, and there, before me, was a clock. Who put it there? How dare they? I swore I would rent a cheaper room next time. I slid away from her.

"Where are you going?"

"Wait here. I'll be back."

"I'm not . . . lying to you."

The towel had fallen off her. For a moment, fear and uncertainty twisted her posture and I believed her, but that did not do her any good. She looked away as if trying to find where she threw her defenses. I bent down and kissed her.

"I won't be long." I put on my shirt and went out.

15.

Hal's Discount Furniture sprawls along Apache Boulevard south of the Arizona State campus in a mishmash of buildings acquired piecemeal through years of booming prosperity and astute management. New cheap furniture, used cheap furniture, and, most profitable of all, rental cheap furniture. If you want cheap furniture, something you won't feel like taking with you when you move, this is the place. TV? Fridge? Microwave? Computer? Hal has them for you, and the trucks to deliver and retrieve them, and the countless hardworking, reliable legal and illegal Latinos to do the heavy lifting. Hal, who put it all together, built it with hard work and guts and brains, is Dan's older brother.

I lived with Hal and Marion the Bitch, as Dan called her, and their two children, Melissa and Mark, for most of a school year. The first time I ran away was when Marion started screaming at me because she could not find her earrings. I had not taken them at that point.

The screaming went on for a couple of days and I was the main target. I knew Melissa had been trying them on. I searched around in the den and found them in a drawer where Melissa's hash pipe was stashed, too. Rather than rat her out, I took the earrings and sold them at a pawn shop. I didn't come home, and when I was wandering around, I saw a family moving toward the rear of one of the outer buildings of Hal's Discount Furniture. I followed. They disappeared. I waited. Next two Mexican women came timidly to the same rear door and knocked and said "No tengo adonde ir." The door opened and they entered. I tried it.

Rudy, one of Hal's managers, opened the door and he froze at seeing me. I shrugged and said, "No dire nada, se lo juro." And he said, "Hal knows." The large room was filled with illegals, mostly families, camped out on the furniture awaiting repair. I stayed a few nights until Rudy told Hal, who was worried about me.

Hal's locks the front doors at six P.M. sharp so I walked in at 5:55. A salesman approached and I said, "Please tell Hal that Rollie is here to see him." A moment later, Marion the Bitch came lilting across the floor, pretending not to see me.

"Hi, Marion."

She seemed startled and acted like it took a second to recognize me. "Rollie, how nice to see you." I went forward and we almost hugged.

"You, too."

"You look great. A stuntman in the movies? I think that's what Dan told Hal."

"Starting to do a little acting, too. You look great."

Six o'clock had struck, and the employee at the door looked to Marion to see if he had to toss me before locking the door. She waved him off. "What brings you here?"

"Rollie!" It was Hal. He gave me a big hug and pumped my hand a few dozen times. Hal had the same white hair as Dan, but he had gained weight, wore reading glasses low on his nose, and the weariness of responsibility and marriage had worn him down. Still, his eyes showed that crinkly understanding and amusement, the same look Dan would turn on to disarm anyone within range who showed skepticism. "Have a seat. Great to see you. How's Dan?" And he smiled as he pointed to a living room setup near the rear of the store. I sat in the comfy chair covered in brown microfiber that was probably coated in enough stain-resistant chemicals to weather a slaughterhouse. Hal and Marion sat on opposite ends of the couch.

I was thinking I might as well get straight to the bad news, but Hal talked so I would feel welcome. "As you can see, everything here is just the same. Mark is going to come into the business when he graduates and he thinks he's going to make big changes. Well, maybe. We'll see. And Melissa is finishing up at NYU law school. Hard to believe it. I don't know if you'd recognize her. Tell me what you're doing."

"I'm in the Marines." I made sure to glance at Marion so I could catch her expression: daggers. "I've done three tours in Afghanistan and I'm hoping to go back soon."

"They're lucky to have you. What's up with Dan?"

By now you know I am not sentimental about Dan, but something must have shown in my face because Hal sat forward in anticipation and Marion said, "What trouble is he in now? How much does he need?" Hal shot her an angry look.

"Dan is dead. He was murdered. I can't give you a lot of details. I'm sorry."

Now Hal slumped back in the couch and the slouch made him look like a schoolboy in the principal's office. Marion said, "It's not a surprise."

Hal did not look at her. "Get away from me." She thought about it for a few seconds while staring at him. He would not glance her way. She left.

"I wanted to ask you a few things about him." I wasn't sure he heard me. He just stared and nodded a bit and then started talking.

"He was my younger brother, but he got me laid the first time. I was fifteen. So he was just thirteen. He talked a girl, Jillian Koepke, into doing it with me. Can you imagine that? A little brother. He could talk, Dan could talk, talk the fish out of the water. Our father ran away and we had to take care of each other and our mother. I thought Dan would end up president. You know I made him my partner in this place, gave him twenty percent, but he put up the shares as collateral on some deal and I ended up having to buy them back. But I never cared, no matter how many times he needed money. You had to know him as a boy. I've been very lucky, very lucky."

He covered his eyes so he wouldn't cry, then rubbed his hands together as he looked at me. "What did you want to ask?"

"Did he ever change his name?"

"Of course. I'm Hal Reynolds, and he was Dan Reynolds."

"He said you were half brothers. That's why he was Waters."

Hal laughed. "Of course he did."

"Did you know my mother?"

Hal scratched his head, then pulled his ear, keeping his eyes tight to mine, though I sensed he stopped seeing me. He nodded as if convincing himself of something. "I could use a drink."

I followed him to his office. Marion glared at us as we passed by the office where she was brooding. Hal shut the door and went behind his desk and pulled a bottle of scotch from the bottom drawer. He poured each of us a drink. He guzzled his. I pushed mine toward him. The desk was an old, solid pedestal style, complete with chips and stains and nicks.

"The first piece of good furniture I ever bought. My only extravagance. Here, anyway. Doesn't look like much, does it? But it's solid as a battleship." He stared at me for a little while, then took a sip from my drink. He paused and pursed his lips and breathed through his nose a few times and generally looked like he was going to have to plead guilty to some crime or come out of the closet. For a moment, I thought he was working up to telling me Marion was really my mother. "Dan showed up with you one day. You were about five or six years old. Told me your mother was dead. Never gave me a name. I didn't know he'd been married. Still don't know if he was or not. He had been living outside LA in Ventura County. Then, about I don't know how many years ago, you and Dan were living in Albuquerque not long after you had been living with us, a woman showed up here. Said she was Dan's ex-wife and your mother. She spent a little time trying to put together some reason why Dan owed her money. It was bullshit, but I paid her off. Dan never knew she came around. At least he never heard it from me."

"What was her name?"

"Kate McFarlane." Hal took another drink and did the breathing-through-his-nose thing again.

"It can't be that bad," I said. "She have fangs, or track marks, or a prison tattoo?"

Hal smiled. "No, she was an attractive woman. Seemed down on her luck. Seemed . . . hard . . ." He stopped, but his mouth was poised for more.

"Hard and . . . ?"

"She asked about you. Where you were. I said I didn't know. I'm sorry, Rollie. I just wanted her gone. I should have at least let you know."

"Nah, you did the right thing," I said, and I knew I didn't convince either of us. I was already starting to walk my past through a maze of new paths with Kate McFarlane. Unless it was a con. Suddenly it occurred to me that Dan could have sent her.

Hal must have read my face. "I think she was for real." We talked for a few more minutes. I thanked him and left him sitting there with another whiskey.

16.

Outside, with ever-shifting visions of Kate Mc-Farlane in my head and Dan on my shoulder whispering long-forgotten details, I was halfway to the jeep when I felt the sharp poke in my kidney: a gun or a baton.

"Hands up."

I started to put my hands up then spun and chopped down to knock away the weapon. The baton stabbed hard into my ribs; the tall man who held it was too fast for me, and his partner, Pongo, stepped in behind me to slap his baton across my throat so that it felt like my windpipe was wrapped around my spine. Perdy handcuffed me. It happened in three seconds. This went beyond training; these guys were naturals. They marched me back, past Hal's Discount Furniture, while I gasped for breath. Marion the Bitch glowed with vindication when she saw us go by.

Colonel Gladden stared at me through watery eyes bobbing under half-closed eyelids, which made him look like a junkie who thinks he is ready to face the world. But I knew it just meant Gladden was happy to see me. "Why aren't you dead?" he said. We were in a drab motel room not far from the drab motel where I was staying with Shannon. Gladden paced like a guy who had seen footage of what happens when you bring a black light into this kind of motel room: his problem was that you can't beat up microbes and they like jail cells. Pongo and Perdy stood next to the door. I was on the bed. "And where is your scumbag father?"

"He's dead."

"Sir."

"Sir."

Gladden didn't exactly smile; his face tightened and his mouth drew back and his blank, reptilian eyes crinkled around the edges. Not a smile, maybe it was related to some vestigial expression of sympathy. It was ugly and inscrutable, like a lizard after you've fed him: you pretend that he looks satisfied. But Gladden's insults were as meaningless as sympathy would have been. "And now you're buying furniture?" he said.

"His last wish, sir. 'Get yourself a comfy chair,' he said, 'and an ottoman.'"

"You're going to have to decide, Lieutenant, which side you're on."

"Yes, sir."

"I'm not done. . . . You think you're on your own side. But that is not an option. You want to be sarcastic, go ahead. I'll deal with it later. If I don't, someone else will. But you're in the Marines, you're an officer in the United States Marines, and that means you and me are on the same side. That comes first. You find that money and you return it to the United States Marines. That's your job. Your only job. Do you understand that, Lieutenant?"

I understand that I represent the Independent Floating State of Rollie. My only promise is to not take over the world. I understand that I will never be on your side. "Yes, sir," I said.

"And you return the money to the Marines, not to the Treasury or anyone else, to the Marines. Get it?"

"By 'the Marines,' do you mean return the money to you, sir, directly?"

He lived in a world of commands, of direct orders and blunt talk. Insinuation meant nothing to him. "Yes," he said. "Directly to me. I'm not making you any special offers, Lieutenant. You ran away from these MPs and you'll be charged with that when the time comes. First you have a mission to complete. Now account for your time. Where did you get the money in your wallet?"

He wanted me to be a good soldier, so I played that for him, gave the full report, or as much as I thought it would take for him to believe it was a full report. Actually, I left out some parts so when he threatened to have me beaten there was something to tell him. When I finished, he asked, "Where's the Treasury agent?"

"I don't know, sir."

"Do you trust him?" I had not given that enough thought to make a decision. He jumped in: "They don't." He meant Pongo and Perdy. They stared straight ahead, showing nothing. Gladden took a phone from the desktop and tossed it to me. "Satellite phone. It'll be tougher for McColl to intercept any calls or locate them."

"But easier for you."

"You're in the Marines, Lieutenant. Even when you're in the brig, you're still in the Marines until the Marines say you aren't." He stopped to take pleasure in that last statement. His eyes searched the room for the horizon. I don't know what he saw. "You're dismissed, Lieutenant. Patterson and Pruitt will conduct you back to your jeep."

I stood up and put the phone in my pocket. I started for the door but stopped and turned back to Gladden. "Sir, McColl's men might be watching my jeep by now. Could I be dropped off a few blocks away?"

"Okay."

"And one more thing . . . I could use a weapon."

He leaned so far forward without moving his feet that the room seemed to tilt. His leathery face bulged and the creases grew deeper. Then he laughed, a sputtering cough of the final remnants of something long dry inside him.

17.

thanked Pongo and Perdy for the ride and started walking back toward Hal's Discount Furniture, where I had left the jeep. No pedestrians around there at night, even the bus stop was vacant. The streetlights, headlights, store lights blotted out the stars. The air smelled like what it was: the desert made dirty. It all reminded me of times when I snuck out and just roamed, sometimes walking, sometimes hitching, sometimes riding the buses, just reaching for that feeling that the city was mine, that I was the free loner, anonymous and mysterious. The secret prince of the shadows. But this was different. I was being tracked. As a kid, I took imaginary evasive measures. Now I did nothing to disappear. I didn't want to lose my trackers. Not yet.

Two Latino kids, maybe sixteen, leaned against the front of the Circle K and watched a Ford Mustang parked on the side street. They wanted to steal it and looked like they would talk about it for a long, long time before making their move. Maybe I was wrong, maybe they just liked Mustangs. Gladden stayed on my mind. It was one thing for him to mistrust Shaw: he mistrusted everyone. It was another for him to mention it to me.

A car pulled in fast and parked right in front of the Mexican boys, stopping with a jerk. They glared defiantly into the headlights without flinching. The lights went off, and a tall, broad-shouldered black guy with muscles got out of the driver's side, and his date, in shorts and sandals and a low-cut tank top, got out of the passenger side. The black guy passed close to the Latino boys, ignoring them, then opened the door to the store for his date. The Latino boys never stopped staring at them. After a pause, one of them spit on the car and they moved to the shadows around the side of the store where they could keep an eye on the Mustang.

I drove back to the motel. The small lot was mostly empty. Halfway up the steps to the second floor, I looked back and noticed a black pickup in the far end of the lot, idling. It was not near the streetlights, and I could not see the driver. The curtain was pulled across the window of my room, so I could not tell if the lights were on or not. Before putting my key in the door, I slid back along the walkway to get another look at the idling truck. It was still there.

The room was dark. I was reaching for the switch when the odor reached me. Blood smells. You would think because it's slimy and slippery it would have a thick or oily smell, but it's metallic; the smell of blood reminds me of an armory. This room smelled of blood. I flicked on the light.

Shannon's tongue lay beside her head on the pillow. She was on her back. Eyes wide open. Someone had opened them and left them that way. Her throat was slit. A lot of blood had escaped that way, spread out below her shoulders like a cape. Another long cut ran from between her breasts down to her navel. She wore nothing but blood and that openmouthed, open-eyed expression as if she was just trying to remember what she meant to say.

"Stop right there. Police. Hands up." The voice came from the bathroom. The light came on, and two men in coats stepped out holding guns. I was only a few feet from the door. I put my hands up. The door opened behind me and another cop stepped in. I turned to look at him. "Don't move," the first voice said. But the new cop held his gun forward and made things easy for me. My left hand moved inside his right and grabbed his wrist. I yanked him forward by the arm at the same time my right grabbed his throat. He fired his gun in the direction of the other cops. I swung him around so he was between them and me, acting as a shield, but they ducked back into the safety of the bathroom. I pushed him toward the bed and lunged through the door and slammed it behind me.

They came through the door when I was halfway down the steps. I jumped the rail and landed easily on the smooth pavement next to the parking lot. Staying underneath the balcony, I sprinted away from the bottom of the stairs where they would come down. They were going to blame me for that shot and act as if I were armed. I had to make the end of the building before they could line me up. I was twenty yards from the end when the black pickup that had been idling pulled across my path. The tinted window came down, revealing the driver: Blondie. Smiling. Chewing gum. "Need a ride?"

"Back up," I said. So he would be out of their sight. He squealed back, and I raced around to get in the other side. He peeled out of the parking lot. Two shots hit near us. A few seconds later, the sirens came on. He sped east on Jefferson, then north on Fifth. The sirens were not gaining on us. Blondie said, "When I saw those cops, I thought I better hang around. Thought I might have to come up there and get you out, man. Colonel McColl don't want you wasting time with the police." His voice sounded as easy and friendly as if we were old pals.

Tongue extracted. Throat sliced. Body slit. If he raped her, that would be the only part of the assault that wouldn't be coming back at him. "Thanks," I said. All the while he was careening down streets and cutting through parking lots at full speed, one hand on the wheel, one hand by his side so he could react if I tried anything. The sirens faded. "I should get back and pick up the jeep."

"The colonel will have it brought to you."

"Let me out."

He looked at me for ten seconds that seemed like two hundred. I forced myself to hold his eyes, though I was sure it meant we were going to ram into a wall. His expression was skeptical, the way the eyes of a normal person, someone who isn't a homicidal maniac, get when a woman or man suggests sex out of the blue: Is this too good to be true?

I said, "You think I'm just like you, don't you?"

"We're all soldiers, right. I got nothing against you yet."

"That's two insults. You thought I wouldn't mind that you cut her up."

He turned the other way and spit out his gum, and he turned the truck into a parking lot behind the ASU hospital and stopped.

"What the fuck, man, dead is dead. You want me to put on music while she chokes on my cock? What's it to you?"

I got out of the truck and walked slowly around the back. He got out, and as he came close to me, I kicked him hard in the gut, slamming him back into the tailgate. I pounded a thick, heavy left to his temple. Nothing. Dan chuckled somewhere nearby with one of his earliest sayings: Who hits a numbskull in the head? Blondie hit me twice in the jaw and I staggered back. I kicked him in the gut again. I spun and kicked again, but this time he caught my foot and cranked it. That hurt. I twisted with his force and landed on my face.

He kicked me in the head. I kicked him in the nuts; that was the right place for this foe. He screamed and pulled his gun as I hopped up. The sirens were getting close again. We could be spotted easily.

"Get back in the truck. I'll kill you if you want, man, but after you find the money. Any way you want, man. I'll even cut you up like your girlfriend if that'll make you happy."

My anger was making me stupid, but I could not stop it. I didn't want to. Blondie was not going to be outpunched or outwrestled. I didn't care. "Let's finish it now," I said. And I kicked the gun out of his hand and jumped on him. I pushed my thumbs hard against his throat. His hands gripped my wrists and pulled, but I leveraged my weight and kept pushing. Flashing lights reflected off the building. I looked up and caught a glimpse of a man, a spectator, gaping at us. Blondie used the moment to wrench one of my hands loose. He hit me hard enough to loosen my grip. Headlights swept across us. Blondie scurried for his gun. He leapt into the pickup. "Get in."

I ran the other way, making it to a pathway between two buildings before the cop cars lurched into the lot. I slowed down as I approached the front of the buildings, where I could see two idling ambulances. The pain in my head came from the left and started just above the ear. Later I decided it was a blackjack.

18.

etective Aviles kept telling me I was facing Death. Lieutenant Clarkson said it could be Life, if I cooperated. Death, could be Life, I think Death, with remorse could be Life and on it went: Life or Death. I was facing one or the other. Detective Death and Lieutenant Life. Clarkson asked if I suffered from post-traumatic stress disorder, "Because if you do, you could get Life."

"You mean if I cop to a sickness, you'll let me live, but if I'm healthy, you'll have to kill me?"

"Pretty much."

"I'd rather be healthy and facing Death than sick and facing Life."

Aviles marked that down. He could have been a CPA or an IBM office manager. Fit and trim and buttoned-down, he never laughed at any joke, never smiled, never frowned, never raised his voice. He was conducting an audit. The information would be entered into the proper columns, and if the columns reconciled, he would have the truth, and Death. Clarkson was older, sloppier, heavier, wearier. He did the moaning and made the faces and a few sarcastic remarks and showed impatience. The room was clean, as bright and spartan as an operating room. A table, three chairs. A large one-way mirror for the students or supervisors to observe. I was the patient. The surgery was exploratory and they could not explore beyond the end of their noses.

"This morning you paid a visit to a Gloria Waters. Why did you go there?"

"I was looking for my mother."

"He wants his mommy."

"She says she is not your mother."

"You can imagine how that feels."

"Is that why you killed Shannon?"

I kept expecting McColl's men or Gladden's men to burst in and set me on my way, but the only visitor was a female cop who handed over sheets of paper. Aviles read quickly through the info, returned to the table, and put the papers facedown. Clarkson was irritated by that. Aviles made some marks in his columns, then turned the sheets over and ran through my juvenile rap sheet. One conviction for possession of a concealed weapon, a knife. I explained that it was a Swiss Army knife. Clarkson said, "Those are sharp." But as Aviles read through the list, something happened to Clarkson. He brightened up, looked at Aviles, waiting for him to pause and couldn't wait long enough. He interrupted, "Are you Dan Waters's son?"

How could I have missed this? "I am."

"How is he? He's been lying low these past few years. Haven't seen him forever."

"He's good. Saw him recently."

Clarkson turned to Aviles. "You know his old man. Helped out with that fraud case where the victim killed the sales guy."

Aviles did not remember Dan with the same level of affection. "Yeah" was all he said. Clarkson regarded me with new interest. Suddenly, I was actually alive.

Aviles got back on track. For the twentieth time he asked, "Why did you shoot at us?"

"I had no gun. I didn't shoot at anybody."

"Why did you run?"

"I didn't want to be killed."

"We identified ourselves as police."

"I didn't want those to be the last words I ever heard."

"You're facing death now, but you're not running, or telling the truth."

The truth was flimsier than their preconceptions. I did not know Shannon's last name or Blondie's real name. I had met her alongside a road, though I told them it was in Las Vegas because I thought the idea of Fallon would occupy them for days. I was not going to mention McColl or tell them Dan was dead. Clarkson said, "We just want to verify parts of your story. Your aunt Marion says you left the store at seven. You claim you were with a Colonel Gladden, and we're trying to confirm that, but right now you have no alibi for your time until you walked into the hotel room and we saw you. Give us something we can verify. Where did you stay in Las Vegas?"

"With a friend."

"You know his name? First and last."

"Steve Shaw. He's a Treasury agent."

Aviles leaned forward and scowled for the first time. "Don't think you can bullshit me by bringing in the feds. This is murder. This is not a federal offense. The feds mean nothing here."

"What's the matter, Detective, they turn you down for a job?"

Clarkson laughed. Aviles glared at him, then stood up and left without a word. Clarkson said, "How do you spell Shaw?"

My third cell in a week, alone this time, sink and toilet, rest and peace. Too spent for tai chi or yoga or even summoning my vision, I stretched out on the bunk and tried to put order to my tumbling thoughts. McColl didn't have Shannon carved as punishment for a failed mission. That piece of work was a message to me that he was in control, payback for my threat on the phone. The message I got was that if I found my mother, whether she could lead me to the money or not, McColl would kill her. I decided I would rather get to know her first and then wish she were dead in my own good time. McColl was in a big rush now and I could understand that, but I still could not understand why he took so long to get there. The urge to get out of jail and find the money shot through me and opened my eyes. I was not getting out, though, and my eyes closed again and I drifted away. I had been asleep two hours when the guard woke me up.

He marched me through the short cell block, quiet and still and seemingly empty in the early morning. The air was thick and the smell reminded me of a zoo. The large office was broken into a maze of cubicles by short white partitions. Most of the cubicles were empty. In the far right corner, Detective Aviles stood with Shaw. By the way Aviles was in charge of the nodding, I guessed Shaw must have been in charge of the talking. His back was to me. Shaw patted him on the shoulder and shook his hand, and Aviles, though exhausted, looked like he was satisfied. Most likely Shaw offered him some support at the Treasury if Aviles tried to apply again. Shaw turned to me and waved and shook hands with Detective Death again. Lieutenant Life must have gone home to sleep.

Outside, into the rising sun, back among the living. No longer facing Life or Death, just like everyone else again, facing the search for money. The early-morning traffic moved smoothly and peacefully. A bus loaded across the street and a woman in her forties had to pick up her pace to make it. The bus started to pull out, but she kept moving and the bus stopped again for her.

I told Shaw most of what happened since I hit him, leaving out Kate McFarlane and the comment from Gladden about not trusting him. Shaw asked a few questions in his casual, just-wondering sort of manner, things about McColl and the woman who wasn't my mother and what Hal added to the picture. He barely seemed interested in the answers until he asked about what I would do when I found my mother. "Do you think you'll recognize her?"

"Maybe she'll recognize me," I said.

"What do you want from her? What can she provide? If she knows where the money is, she has probably taken it. If she doesn't know, then how can she help?"

"Could be a dead end. Do you have a better idea?"

"It's just going to be really difficult. I mean, it's the first time you've met since you were a little brat, and now you're in a big hurry for some mysterious clue she probably doesn't know she has. *Hi, Mom, it's me, Rollie, great to meet you—and by the way, where did Dad used to hide things? Things like large amounts of money.*"

"Feelings. I'll try to remember that."

We got into his car, another SUV, and when he turned, the sun splashed through the windshield, showing the tired lines around his eyes. He put down the visor and grabbed his sunglasses from the dashboard. "Where to?"

"McColl has me tracked. The jeep has GPS. He seems on top of my every move, in the jeep or out."

"I can lose him."

"I doubt it. If you come with me, there's a good chance you'll wake up dead."

"Don't you want to lose him?" he said.

"Not yet." I let him digest that. "Why bother? I don't know what I'm looking for, so why waste time losing him?"

"Okay."

"What I don't get is why you don't want to catch him. Where's the big team of federal agents with their windbreakers and walkie-talkies and all that gear?"

He gave me one of his crinkly "Gee, I'm impressed with how sharp you are" smiles. "There's a lot you don't know about this operation, Rollie."

"Like what?"

He licked his lips as if deciding whether to put me in the picture or not. He drove for a little while then pulled to the curb across from a Starbucks. "Will you be here when I come back?"

"Depends how long you take," I said. "I take my coffee black."

When he returned, he handed me the coffee and a muffin and he inhaled a pastry in about three seconds. "I missed dinner last night," he said. That seemed to be enough preparation or dramatic buildup for him. "We want more than just McColl. He's part of a large network. We don't know how many of these money stashes there are around the country, but we believe there are at least five. But this is about more than just recovering money, Rollie. It's about what they plan to do with it.

We have to identify everyone involved and we have to catch them with enough evidence to make a strong case. Right now, we have nothing solid on McColl and your story about the man you call Blondie, his name is Peter Stenson by the way, won't bring a murder conviction. We need more. We need you."

"What do they plan to do with the money?"

"Did you hear any other names when they had you? Any familiar names? Active-duty personnel? Senior officers?"

"Nothing." But I wanted to know more about that. I asked again: "What do they plan to do with it?"

He smiled again. "Maybe you're right. Maybe it's better if I follow you, too."

Without another word, he drove to the motel where I had left the jeep. As I got out, he said, "By the way, Rollie, you shouldn't assume I'm the only one on this case."

19.

led the invisible caravan across the desert: a murderous, martial version of a reality show, *Dead Man's Treasure*, or *Where's My Body Bag?* I was the star and the sacrifice. I couldn't be killed until the end, and then I must be killed. Anyone else was expendable along the way. "Mom, I've brought along some of my new friends to meet you. I guess I've fallen in with a rough crowd. They're going to want to tear apart your life before they end it. And oh, yes, I must not forget, Dan planned it this way." But Dan never intended for anyone to be collateral damage; he would just forget that people got hurt along the path to fulfillment of his schemes. I did not have his gift for ignoring consequences.

The last caravan I was in started in Karachi, Pakistan, and traveled north to the Khyber Pass and into Afghanistan. Rashid drove and I rode shotgun. Progress was slow, just over a hundred miles a day. Food, electronics, cooking utensils, bedding, and clothing fell off the trucks at every stop. The rest was fuel and arms, both guarded more closely. Our rig was loaded with MREs. We prayed in the mornings before hitting the road, stopped three times a day for more prayers and to relieve ourselves. Then one more prayer in the evenings. All that peace and calm kept us from rushing toward our destination. At stops, it was my job to guard the truck with my rifle and a sidearm, a Beretta M9 pistol. When I prayed, MREs disappeared, though that wasn't what I was praying for.

Every junction, every turn, every curve in the road held the threat of violence. At least that was the talk and the way everyone acted. Rashid spoke only of the danger.

"The danger is good for prices," I said. "You rent out the truck for more."

He shrugged. Rashid grew up in Karachi. His father drove a truck for a cousin and saved enough to buy one for his son. Rashid was young and arrogant, and he let me know that he looked down on Pashtun and anyone from a small town.

"We'll see what happens," he said, as if he had a good idea of what might happen.

Private security men escorted us in jeeps and Humvees, fore and aft and interspersed between the trucks. I assumed they were in charge of the looting. Nawaz Mazari, the name played like a mutilated lyric in my head. The danger in saying it out loud would be that someone would understand it. The best I could do was to identify a few thugs more thuggish than the rest, strutting around with the glazed cockiness of gang members on rolling turf. Asking to join the gang would only stimulate them to act out the viciousness of what they regarded as loyalty. A storm slowed us to a crawl, potholes and security stops checked the pace. I suspected everyone, everyone suspected me, everyone suspected everyone so no one had any doubts about who to suspect and the mood was relaxed. In cliques, they joked around about their trucks and how this one drove and that one played soccer. It was a good gig as long as there were no attacks.

As we droned along, my excitement leveled off and I contemplated my new identity, spy, and how it differed from soldier. Is spying a choice or is it nature? Both for me: a relief, a cloak, a release. I was glad to be rid of the rules of engagement, but this assignment was too vague. It would have been more reasonable to try to expose someone who did not want to steal arms.

I had no status and no one to vouch for me. Soldiers have the luxury of rank among their own, who obey it religiously; spies, alone, learn that they must invent their rank and impose it on those who have no reason to respect it. No one came along and introduced himself as Nawaz Mazari, and if I asked around, I would either drive him to ground or give him cause to plant me in the ground.

On the second day, after prayers, a Pakistani security man came up to me with an MRE in his hand. He scooped out the dessert bar, unwrapped it, and took a big bite, and smiled the crumbiest smile I had ever seen. I knocked the bar out of his hands and shoved him in the chest. He pulled his sidearm. I grabbed his arm and twisted. The gun fell and I kicked it away. We had a big audience now. I called him a dog. One of his partners picked up the gun and tossed it to him. I put my palms up and smiled as if it were all a joke, as if I were going to back down now. He pointed the gun at me and his eyes ran over the crowd to measure how far he could go. I picked up the MRE and made a show of dusting it off. I moved toward him and held it out. And, as he reached for it, I took his right forearm with my left hand and raised my knee and slammed his forearm on it. The gun went off. The bullet hit the dust and he screamed in pain. I tossed the MRE at him and walked away through the crowd.

I told Rashid: "If you're going to steal, it should be something that can do some good." He was concerned that the guards would be hostile to him because of me. But I had gotten the attention I needed. And I made sure to pay special attention to the arms trucks during the stops.

At Dera Ismail Khan, the convoy was halted because of delays on the road ahead. We camped outside of town on a flat plain of dirt and sand, grouping the trucks together protectively, like a wagon train, and cooking on propane stoves freshly stolen just the day before. Rashid was frying up khatay aloo, something with potatoes, when a man I had never seen before appeared. He was thick all over, with heavy-lidded eyes. The man nodded toward me and politely introduced himself as Nawaz Mazari. Rashid nodded and put one of the plates away. Then Nawaz invited me to join him for dinner.

The spread was elaborate, with rugs laid, thick cushions, and abundant food for six of us. Nawaz did a lot of the talking about patience and cooperation and respect. He never referred to the fight I had or to the trucks carrying arms which I had been watching. He took a while to make sure the hint was firmly planted and then he got to the main purpose of the powwow: checking me out. Three of the men had been completely silent. I figured at least one was an Afghan. Nawaz asked me about my childhood and complimented me on my fighting skills. I told him that an American had trained me.

"They are very kind," he said.

"Yes," I said. "And very naive." That got a laugh.

"Yes, sometimes they fight against themselves and don't even know it." Nawaz got a bigger laugh with that. It was a successful party. I had no idea whether I passed muster but could not see any benefit to letting the party drag on. When Nawaz started asking about my wife, I told him I was tired and thanked him for the meal.

We spent two long rainy days at Dera Ismail Khan. I did not see Nawaz again. Rashid tiptoed around me and my elevated status. We crawled up to Peshawar, and as we headed for the border, I could feel the tension tightening on Rashid and the others. They were eager to be paid but dreaded journey's end and a possible reckoning and scrutiny of the manifests.

Torkham was a bottleneck with trucks, cars, and pedestrians squeezing in both directions: either way you went, you were still in the bottle. Private vehicles had to be emptied of all possessions, so kids with handcarts hustled the stuff back and forth across the border for cash and whatever they could steal. I left Rashid steaming in the truck and strolled through the Torkham gate.

Captain Ballard, Abdullah of the Ozarks, had stationed himself among the milling crowd on the Afghan side. He looked more ragged and worn, and his chronic anger went well with his new mustache. A big improvement. I slipped past him and loitered in the bazaar, watching to see if he was being watched. It looked clear, so I stood beside him until he recognized me.

"Do you like my mustache?" He had rehearsed the line.

"Is it real?"

He told me he had a room at the chaikhana up the road where we could talk. His Dari had not improved. I was still wary of being seen with him, so I followed a few yards behind him. The road was crowded with Americans and Afghans, military and civilian. When Ballard reached the chaikhana, he stood at the gate outside the small tea courtyard and looked back for me. At that moment, a Marine captain coming from the other direction noticed Ballard and stopped. He grabbed the arm of the Afghan National Army lieutenant who was with him. And pointed out Ballard. It was clear that the Marine recognized him, or thought he did. Ballard spotted me, so he went through the gate and up to his room. I lingered just down the road to watch the Marine captain and his ANA friend. They were giving the chaikhana a good once-over and the ANA guy was nodding: he would be checking it out. They walked on. I went inside.

I passed through the courtyard into the small, dark restaurant and lingered there a moment. The ANA man was not coming in right behind me, so I went on toward the rooms, which were in a building attached to the back. I knocked on Number 10 and announced myself in Dari. Ballard opened up.

"Don't you get tired of speaking only Dari?" He looked tired overall. Being someone new was exhausting work even if most of it consisted of waiting.

The answer was yes, but I kept speaking Dari. "Sometimes I speak Pashto, too. Outside, just now, it looked like someone recognized you. A Marine officer. A captain."

"I didn't see him," he said in English.

"Maybe you should back off. At least get away from here."

But Ballard was only interested in whether I had

made contact with potential weapons sellers. I agreed to come back the next day after bringing up the subject with Nawaz.

I could not find Nawaz that night or the next morning until I was halfway to the chaikhana and he was coming back toward the border. His eyes were bright and excited, his breath was shallow. The little ANA lieutenant was with him, and he was equally agitated.

"We must talk," said Nawaz. "Have tea with us this afternoon, please." He did not introduce his companion. They seemed eager to get back to the trucks.

"I look forward to it." The commotion at the chaikhana was apparent from a hundred yards away. By the time I arrived, the body, Ballard's body, covered by a sheet, was being loaded into a van. Two ANA soldiers helped the police hold back the curious. Maybe the ample supply of dead bodies helped people develop a taste for more. No U.S. troops were on the scene. Except me. I asked a boy what happened. "A man was knifed. Slit his throat," he said.

"Pashtun?"

The boy shrugged. If he thought the victim was an American, he would have said so. Ballard would be treated as an Afghan and his death would not be reported to the Army for days. His Arkansas accent would not help him.

The van pulled away and the onlookers drifted toward the bazaar and the border. The ANA soldiers backed off and groups of men slid into the tea courtyard, grabbing the tables of those who were leaving. I watched, deciding whether it was worth trying to catch a peek inside Ballard's room. My eye caught a familiar face: the Marine captain who had recognized Ballard the day before. He was sitting alone at a table at the back, next to the restaurant wall. He took off his hat to wipe the sweat off his shaved head. And then I recognized him. He was known as Junior, not as a term of endearment: it was an epithet earned by his arrogance and disregard for everyone ranked below him. I had seen him strutting around at Camp Pendleton and at the mountain warfare training center as if he were a Congressional Medal of Honor winner and being treated that way, it seemed to those of us lucky enough to keep our distance.

I remember asking a sergeant about him. "Stay away from him if you can," he said. "He expects others to pick up his messes."

"Why does he expect that?"

"His father is General Remington."

I was confident Junior would not recognize me and I was willing to risk the chance that he would.

20.

I was as blind in this caravan as I was in the last, burrowing without knowing the direction. Coffee and gas in Blythe, California, classic oasis and most inauspicious gateway: the unmarked green door that lets you into the biggest, wildest club in the world. I was hoping that as my followers avoided being seen by each other, I might spot one or two, but no luck. On past Indio and the first in the chain of golf courses that take you all the way to the ocean. How excited the first pioneers must have been to come through Death Valley and sight the first flag hanging limp against its stick. Thousand Palms, Palm Springs, and not long after Banning I turned north on 210 for a short stretch before cutting off on State 330 toward Big Bear and Lake Arrowhead. The desert grew grayer, speckled with shrubs, until the road wound around and climbed enough to find the pines. One car kept appearing in my rearview mirror. I assumed it was Shaw. I turned onto Route 18, switchbacking all the way to Big Bear.

I parked before reaching the mall, where all the followers would have an easy time watching my movements. I stopped in a small market and asked the clerk if he knew Gloria Waters, mentioning that she had a butterfly tattoo on the underside of each wrist. I asked for the manager so he could say no, too. I made up a name, Ron Wilson, and asked about him, too, so that when they were quizzed later, they could help McColl waste some time. All that, the butterflies included, was fantasy. Kate McFarlane was never mentioned. Under the arch and into the village mall, I was on my way toward the jewelry store for more meaningless questions when I saw the tattoo parlor and detoured there. Same questions. I returned to the car and drove down the road to the Boathouse Fish Company, same routine. Willy's Tavern.

From there I strolled over to Schmidt's Bakery. A thin woman, about five foot three, sat along the right wall opposite the display case, sipping a coffee with difficulty because her hand shook when she lifted the cup. Her hair was short and gray. She was forty-six years old. Her name was Loretta Sexton. I kept my back to her while I asked my questions, loud enough for her to hear. I knew she would be looking at me when I turned. I met her eyes and shook my head slightly. She understood and turned her attention back to her coffee.

Outside I paused to look around as if considering whether it was worth inquiring at more stores. Mostly I just felt happy to have found Loretta, happy she was still alive. I knew I could rely on her when the time came. And I wanted her to know I would be coming.

It was four P.M. If I rushed down the mountain, I could hit the worst of Los Angeles traffic, which would help percolate everyone's impatience and frustration. I wanted them aware of each other, jockeying for position, distracted. I made a few extra freeway exits and entrances so they had to work a little harder because my route did not make sense. I parked in a lot off Hollywood Boulevard just after six thirty. The street was already crowded: tourists from around the world and around the country there to see the pavement and the facades, tourists from around town there for the clubs, and the locals working the way locals would anywhere they could find a crowd.

Lush Life is a dive bar on Hollywood Boulevard. The last time I was there, maybe five years earlier, it was filled with bikers and only bikers. Only two bikes were parked outside this time. Now punctured punks and goths and hipsters inhabited the same grimy, burgundy Naugahyde stools and booths. Fake color stripes in hair, genuine black clothing, and pale skin comprised the regulation uniform, along with piercings and tattoos designating a secret rank which I could never penetrate. The transformation at the Lush Life suited me just fine. I could still feel hostility and paranoia when I sat down at the bar, but I guessed these patrons would be less nasty than the bikers were when the mood struck them. The ugliness of the goths' appearance is complete and deliberate, aggressively off-putting. I respected them for it. Goths reacted to my respect with suspicion, which made me respect them more.

The bartender was the same guy from years ago, shaved head, thick forearms covered with a dense, colorful pattern, two earrings. A small statue of Popeye with designs drawn on his forearms similar to those on the bartender's forearms stood beside the vodka bottles next to the mirror behind the bar. I ordered a Bud and sipped slowly for a while. A few stools away sat another shaved-headed guy, about thirty, with two young girls, too young to be in a bar, all gotten up in their best black. Outside, in back, was a patio for smoking that looked like it held a few patrons. I did not go back there.

The bartender did not have much to do yet besides chat with the waitress, who looked like her sadness would outduel her frailty in keeping her from making it through the night. When I ordered a second Bud, I asked him, "You get your arms done locally?"

"Down on Highland, about two blocks," he said.

"Who would I see?"

"Titus is the man. Three dollars."

I laid down three dollars, then added a hundred. "Did Titus have a woman working for him, Gloria Waters?" I said. "She'd be late forties, early fifties by now."

"He had a few women there. Only one I remember about that age. I think her name was Jessie," he said.

"Could you describe her?"

"Could you?" He pushed the hundred back toward me. "I don't know what the game is, pal."

"Butterfly tattoos inside each wrist." The bartender just stared at me. "Someone is going to come in here in a while and ask you what I've been asking about. I'd like you to tell him the truth," I said. I pushed the bill back at him. "Please buy them a round. I'm going to ask them the same questions." I pointed to the trio down the bar. The bartender took the bill and served the drinks.

I walked over and introduced myself and asked about tattoos and Gloria Waters. They all knew Titus, and the girls struggled to remember someone else's name there. "I think it was Shelly," said the one with the pink streak in her hair. "Not Shelly, something just like it. Sarah, Samantha, Julie, Jody? Maybe it was Gloria," said the one with blue and pink and blond streaks.

The guy said, "Why don't you just go over there?"

"I'm waiting for someone." I went back to my stool and made my beer last another twenty minutes. Then Blondie walked in with Toothless. I finished my beer and smiled at Blondie and walked out. He followed me, Toothless staying behind to grill the bartender and patrons. He wouldn't appreciate their attitude and I started to doubt he would be able to discern that they were telling the truth. Blondie grabbed my shoulder. "You were in there a long time," he said.

"The beers are cheap and I was thirsty." I kept walking, turned onto Highland. He moved with me and grabbed again, firmer, and turned me toward him.

"We're getting tired of the runaround. This is taking too long."

I started walking again. "First, if you touch me again, we're going to fight again. Right here. And that will bring cops and this will take a lot longer. Second, if you come into any establishment where I'm asking questions, I'm going to walk out and stop asking questions and this will take forever. Now fall back and follow me like a good boy." I made sure to stare into his eyes and smile to infuriate him more.

By the time I reached the tattoo parlor, Blondie had dropped from sight.

The music wasn't loud, but it seemed to come from every corner of the small storefront area, which was plastered with designs from the floorboards up to and including the ceiling. I couldn't see any pattern to the placement, any categories, but I did not spend a lot of time looking. Two reclining chairs flanked the counter, with stools next to them. A thin man in his fifties appeared from a back room. His short hair was gray and so were his eyes. He wore a black T-shirt and black jeans. Flames covered his neck giving the impression of a high, starched collar. He waited patiently for me to stop looking around and to speak first.

"I'm looking for Titus."

He nodded, keeping his eyes on mine. I broke with his gaze and looked outside before I spoke again. I didn't see any of the followers. I met his eyes again and decided Titus would react best to the truth.

"I need minor surgery. You can name your price. It'll take about ten minutes." He still did not speak, so I went on. "There's a transmitter sewn into my right shoulder blade. I'd like to have it removed. If we wait too long, there's a chance they'll come in here to see what's going on. Either way, there's a chance they'll come in after I'm gone. I'd rather you didn't tell them about the procedure."

"What should I tell them?" he asked.

"That I was asking for Gloria Waters, a middle-aged woman with tattoos on both wrists."

"And do I know her?"

"Better if you don't. But that's up to you."

Titus did a lot of thinking, none of it out loud. Finally, he said, "Come in back."

I moved around the counter and through a curtain. Titus held open a door and we entered a small room where he did piercings. "Take off your shirt," he said.

I did that and turned my back to him. He moved his fingers gently across the incision, then pushed a bit harder below it to see if the thing moved. He motioned for me to sit.

"Do you want an anesthetic?"

"I'd rather not," I said.

I sat down with my back to him and he took a little while preparing. He swabbed the spot for a minute. Then he showed me the knife he was going to use. Wordlessly. He slipped on gloves and started to cut and a buzzer sounded: the front door. He looked at me and

I looked toward the front. He handed me the scalpel and went out. I could feel a trickle of blood seeping down my back.

"We just wanted to see how much it was? How much for just a little tattoo on our ankles, y'know, a heart or something?" It was a girl's voice, giggly.

Titus said, "One hundred dollars each. Plus tax." Silence. It was easy to imagine the two girls looking at each other, neither wanting to be the first to declare her preference. Then the buzzer sounded and Titus returned. He picked up a piece of gauze to sop up the blood, then he looked at me with a question in his eyes.

I said, "I don't think so. They know where I am because of the tracker. They'd wait before they got suspicious."

He took the scalpel from me and returned to the task at hand. It took a few seconds for him to complete the cut. He grabbed the transmitter with tweezers and dropped it in a shallow bowl. Round and flat, it was the size of a watch battery.

"I'll need that."

He went about his business sopping up the blood, then tearing open a new needle and sewing me up. When he was done, he swabbed it with disinfectant again. He rinsed off the transmitter and handed it to me.

"How much do I owe you?"

"Nothing. That was fun."

Fun? I should have guessed. I took three hundred

dollars from my wallet and laid it on the table. He held up one finger to ask me to wait. From a closet, he pulled a large sketch pad from an easel. He flipped some pages until he found the one he wanted to show me. "Take a look."

A businessman stood in front of his closet in a dress shirt, collar open, mouth open, getting ready for the day. His mouth was dark and empty inside. Lined up along the right side of the bar were tongues instead of ties. His hand reached out to make his selection for the day.

There was not much to say and no good way to say it, which was the way Titus wanted it. We studied each other's eyes for about a minute. I grabbed him and gave him a hug and walked out.

McColl was sitting in the driver's seat of the jeep. Blondie and Toothless fell in on either side of me as I got near. They escorted me into the passenger seat and melted away. McColl had his own key.

"Which way?"

I told him to drive west on Sunset. He was wearing sunglasses and in the initial silence, the one meant to establish that he would talk when it suited him, I bet myself about how long I would have to wait before he turned to me and took off the sunglasses and gave me the benefit of the full stare. Near Sunset and La Brea, he said: "The money is not for me. I want to make that clear. I have no interest in money. Never have. Wouldn't have joined the Army if I did. I'm interested in service to a cause."

I thought the glasses were coming off, but not yet.

"It must have occurred to you that all attempts to lose us are futile," he said.

"I haven't tried to lose you." I made an elaborate effort to turn in my seat to check if the others were following. They were.

"I think we're taking the wrong approach to this. It's inefficient. We should be working together."

"It will be more efficient if you call off your dogs and let me get on with the search."

He didn't answer until we came to a red light. He turned to me for the big moment. Off came the glasses, leaving only the strange light-blue eyes. "Join us. You were meant to be part of our group. We have a mission that I'm certain you would embrace. And your skills and ability will be big assets to us. I know you were not close to your father, and I hope you can understand that he was impeding the mission. That could not be tolerated. I think you can understand that. He was a casualty. I'm sorry for that, but there was no other way. Join us."

He put his glasses back on and hit the gas. I stared straight ahead. McColl was just an extreme example of a type I ran into throughout my life. Foster parents, teachers, cops would try to get in on my hatred for Dan. They presumed a bond based on disdain for him. Some were trying to ingratiate themselves; others just wanted a place to whine. But my hatred was private and I never met anyone worth sharing it with. McColl seemed to think I'd say "Yes, I didn't get along with him, thanks for killing him for me." I didn't. Instead, I thought about killing McColl right there. Unfortunately, he had no weapon that I could take from him and I would have a hard time fighting Blondie and Toothless without one.

"We've waited seven years for this. We're part of a truly exciting plan. . . ." He was making it sound like a time-share opportunity. "It's enormous. At last the right moment has come. If you commit to us, I can brief you. Until then, I can tell you this: this stash of money is only one of many around the U.S., and the money from all these is only a small portion of the funding we will ultimately have. It's an opportunity you were made for." He did everything but pull out a pen and a contract.

"I'll have to think it over," I said.

"Where are we going?"

"You don't have any problem following me, right?"

He pulled over, took his keys, and got out.

I made enough effort to lose them to give me a chance to call the Mondrian Hotel on Sunset Boulevard and make a reservation for Gloria Waters.

The valet took the jeep, and I rode to the rooftop bar, which was busy with a crowd far different from the one on Hollywood Boulevard. The bouncers at the door gave me a long once-over before letting me join the crowd. My T-shirt wasn't from the right store. This bunch still believed they could please the wide world with their clothes and jewelry. They were aggressive only in their supplication: Notice me. Take me to a place where I can get more of this. And all poses and postures were designed to camouflage that attitude. And they all failed. Of course, the dominant color was white. I ordered a beer and walked around looking for a spot to ditch the transmitter among the couches and huge potted plants. At the door, the manager was talking to the bouncers and looking over at me. There was the answer.

I grabbed the arm of a waitress just a little too roughly and set my beer on her tray. "This beer is flat. At these prices it shouldn't be. I know beer. Get me another one."

The moment she left, the manager stood beside me. "Is something the matter?"

"Depends who you are. You're not her boyfriend, are you?"

"I'm the manager."

"Oh, good," I said and shook his hand. "Gloria Waters, I'm supposed to meet her here. Do you know her? I'm sure you must. Gloria." I let him edge me toward the door.

"Sure, Gloria? Sure. What's your name?"

"Rollie."

"Rollie. Are you a hotel guest this evening?"

"Nah. Not yet. Maybe I'll get lucky," I said, and I moved away from the door so he had to bump me and I could slip the transmitter into his pocket.

"Maybe you'll be more comfortable waiting for Gloria in the lobby." I had to give him credit: he said it as if he had just thought of a great idea.

I shocked him. "Okay. But if she comes up without me seeing her, be sure to tell her I'm down there."

21.

I was certain I had lost them, all of them: McColl, Gladden, Shaw. But I could not shake the feeling of being followed. The itch made me crane around and look out the back window of the bus as it cruised up Pacific Coast Highway. The short Indian woman in the seat next to me who was holding a stuffed pillowcase on her lap said, "Are you being followed, too?"

"Careful," I said. "I think they can hear everything." She gathered her pillowcase and edged past me to a row near the front. I slid over to the window seat. The itch stayed with me, though I refused to scratch it again. The bus moved slowly through the Malibu traffic. Surfers bobbed in a loose, smug pack. Slowly one turned and paddled farther from the beach, another followed, and another, like a flock that mysteriously decides it would prefer to occupy the tree over there. The bus lurched forward before I could watch the rest of them form a wedge when they followed.

Hal had said Dan arrived from Ventura County with

me in tow, so to justify my trip there, I formed pictures of Kate McFarlanes who had stayed behind. Kate McFarlane, local flower, plucked by the dashing scoundrel Dan, replanted in the loving family garden, where she thrived, despite her missing petals. Kate McFarlane, the wild child, tamed and brought down by the infamous Dan; they say she gave birth and now will never leave the hallowed ground where she met her match; she can be found at sundown on the bluff above the beach, staring into the horizon, remembering. Kate McFarlane, harried mother and wife, facing the emptiness at the end of her PTA eligibility, but sometimes, after sneaking a morning shot of vodka, she pulls out a necklace and remembers a time when her heart was full and the world seemed young and easy. It was a sickening bunch of soap opera versions to cover the one I feared most: a vagabond Kate who flitted into town and stuck for a few years before coasting along. She would be tough to find.

"She'll be there, or close by," Dan said.

"When was the last time you checked?"

"If I had to check on that, I might never have left." I stared at the empty seat next to me, reading the smile Dan wore at that whopper. It was his "I can still surprise you" smile.

"No, you can't," I said. And I saw the Indian woman looking at me.

Ricky Severinson was a first lieutenant, Annapolis man, who had the wrong disposition for war. He counted the minutes. Discomfort, impatience, and fear combined to torture him daily. So great was his torment that he assumed all the men in his platoon felt the same way and therefore his job was to do everything he could to alleviate their pain. We fought the heat, the dark, the dirt, but we rarely sought the enemy. To fill the endless, panting hours, Ricky talked about his father, who had invented the shopping cart ad, those photo ads that go in the folding basket of your shopping cart. He was rich and vicious, and Ricky went to the Academy to spite him. But the old man pretended to be terribly proud when he heard everyone talking about how proud he must be. Ricky decided the appropriate next ploy would be to leave the Academy. His father countered by putting his photo, in uniform, on all the shopping carts in their small Connecticut town with the caption: "Proudly Serving Our Country." Ricky graduated and was commissioned and sent to lead me and a few unlucky others. Eventually our battalion leader noticed our indolence and got around to screaming at Ricky, who finally led us out to look for the enemy and into an ambush at sundown. Ricky and four others were killed.

I only tell that story because Kate McFarlane had her photo all over the shopping carts at a Vons on Channel Islands Boulevard in Oxnard. A mortgage broker.

Blond hair, clear, focused blue eyes, thin face and nose, sharp chin, pearl earrings, and a single strand of pearls across the top of a blue dress. She looked efficient, part of a ruling class who could help the peasants make good choices.

I just thought how uncomfortable I would feel putting bacon or Twinkies in the basket if she were watching.

For ten minutes, I was sure it was her; then the doubts crept in, and I welcomed them as guests who would keep me in line and serve as protection against Dan, laughing on my shoulder, whispering warnings and lies. Or truths. *"Try to match that photo with me,"* he said. *"If it works, you've got the wrong woman."*

First I bought a used bicycle because I had arrived on the bus and I did not want to take the risk of stealing a car until I needed to. Kate's office was in a strip mall near the Channel Islands Harbor between a real estate office and a dry cleaner. It was not yet noon when I took a seat in the window at a Starbucks kitty-corner from the office.

I waited, hoping she would come out for lunch so I could follow her somewhere, get a sense of who she was, who I would be dealing with. The Gloria Waters experience hung over me. Her rage still hurt worse than any punch from Blondie. I imagined myself traveling from town to town, accusing women of being my mother: which did I dread more, their rage or their affection? Two women came out, neither could have been Kate McFarlane. A man left. That was it for a while.

By one fifteen, I decided to face her. The door said

"Wakeman Mortgage: A Full-Service Brokerage." Four front desks stood unoccupied. Beyond, dividers formed cubicles. I walked back there. "Hello?" A slovenly man in his fifties held his sandwich an inch from his mouth as he peeked from his cubicle. Crumbs dotted his blue button-down shirt. "I'm looking for Kate McFarlane."

He pointed with the sandwich, and when I turned, Kate was standing there. She wore a tan sleeveless dress cut at the knee and sandals with heels. Her blond hair was pulled back tight, just like in the supermarket photo. Around her neck hung a thin silver chain with a star that had diamonds, or things that looked like them, on each point. She was pretty; the photo was not doctored.

"I'm Kate."

"I'm Robert. Robert Kent. We're moving to town, my wife and I, and the time has come to get a mortgage."

"Great. Did someone refer you?"

"My shopping cart."

She led me to a small conference room and was just warming up the spiel about how the folks at Wakeman gave the best mortgage when her phone rang. She was going to pretend she did not care who it was until she saw who it was. When she came back, she said, "Robert, please forgive me, but something has come up and I'm going to have to leave. A closing. Maybe someone else in the office can help you."

"I can come back later."

"It would have to wait a few days. I'm leaving town tomorrow."

"After the closing." That would have been a good moment for the unveiling, with just us and the guy with the sandwich and crumbs. But I hesitated and told her I would come back next week. She barely seemed to hear me. Whoever had called had all her attention. I took her card and retreated to my lookout post at Starbucks.

I was barely settled when a silver Mercedes sports car pulled up and Kate popped out of the office like a teenager sneaking out on a date.

I hopped on my bike to follow, which was easy with all the traffic. They went over the bridge to the harbor and parked and walked out on the pier to a boat about seventy feet long, sleek and modern and expensive. The guy who drove the Mercedes was about Kate's height, gray hair pulled back in a ponytail, shorts and sandals and a polo shirt and, of course, sunglasses. I guessed sixty-five, but the gray hair might have been fooling me. A thick Asian man greeted them on board and brought out a tray with drinks and snacks. A second man, who could have been the twin of the first Big Boy, appeared and climbed to the top deck.

Kate went below. Ponytail Man conferred with the big servant, who pointed to something on the deck that I could not see. A moment later, two men about my age walked along the dock toward the boat. One carried a black backpack. Ponytail Man welcomed them with a handshake and half hug. The young guys looked all around before sitting down. The backpack came off and the guy checked with Ponytail Man before setting it down. Ponytail Man gave a nod, directing him where to place it. Everybody picked up a glass, a toast was made, and everybody drank. Ponytail Man did a lot of talking and the two young guys looked at each other and a moment later one picked up a backpack and they were off.

One of the Big Boys took a second backpack, identical to the first, off the deck and went below. On cue, Kate came outside, having changed into shorts and a blouse.

I wandered along the dock as if I were just passing the time, coveting the boats. Ponytail Man noticed me before Kate did.

"Nice boat."

"Thank you."

"My wife's father has one similar. Not as big, not as nice."

"Around here?" He said it like he didn't want anyone else around here to have a boat like his. The big servant came out of the cabin to check me out. He looked like he could lift the boat.

"Marina del Rey," I said. Kate had recognized me. Even behind the sunglasses, it was clear she was uncomfortable. "We're moving up here. Her mother lives nearby."

"Hi, Robert, this is embarrassing," Kate said.

"No. Who could blame you?"

"We're having a spur-of-the-moment party."

"You're old friends?" Ponytail Man tried to act relaxed about it.

"This is the young man I was talking to at the office when you called."

Ponytail Man looked me over, then glanced back at his servant. Big Boy up top was watching me, too. All four of them stared at me behind sunglasses. For a moment, I felt like the next dead guy in one of those alien-bugs-posing-as-humans movies. They could have shooed me away, but the suspicion and paranoia at the coincidence would have drowned them on their cruise.

"Join us for a drink. I'm Scott."

"Cool." I hopped on board, making sure not to pay too much attention to Kate despite Dan's voice cooing over and over, *"It's her, you've found her. What do you think? She has the answer."*

She was nervous. Scott was studiously casual. The huge servants swiveled their head to keep an eye on me. Samoan, I thought. They looked more like bodyguards than butlers.

"So you were overseas?"

"Afghanistan. Third Marines. Looking for a job now."

"And a house," Scott said.

"And a house," I said. One of the Big Boys came around to refill Kate's white wine and Scott's scotch. I asked for a beer. Kate started right in, the way she had at the office.

"I just think all you veterans deserve all the help we can give you. I'm just so grateful. We are, aren't we, Scott?" She did not cede the floor to Scott, though, maybe knowing she was unlikely to get it back. "You give so much and what do you get in return? This country has its priorities screwed on wrong. We have to take the country back and it starts with honoring the people who make the sacrifices. If we want to win these wars, we have to commit ourselves fully. If that means casualties, then so be it. Don't tell me those people feel the same way about life that we do because if they did, they wouldn't give their countries over to terrorists and maniacs. They'd stand up for themselves and we wouldn't have to."

"Thank you, ma'am," I said. She was shrill and confused and completely revolting. I wanted to laugh because her coarseness threw a mocking knockout punch to the sentimentality I had been fighting since I had first heard her name.

When people in the military romanticized military service, I thought they were full of crap but I gave them some leeway, figuring it was just something they needed to do to cope with it all. When people out of the military romanticized military service, they were just full of crap.

Scott jumped right in on the downbeat like a soloist in a jazz quartet. "People who don't work are living off the government, while people like you come back and have to struggle to make ends meet on your own. We can't change things the way we'd like to, but we try to do what we can," he said, and he leaned forward with excitement and looked at Kate, who was caught off guard by the pause, still draining her wineglass. A Big Boy arrived with my beer. Scott got up.

"Excuse me a moment." He hustled into the salon, followed by Big Boy. Prostate or cocaine? Dan's rule: assume both.

Kate took up the sword. "It's about respecting the laws. If you come here and the first thing you do is break the law, how're you gonna have any respect for any other laws? I mean, c'mon, that's common sense. You're dodging bullets and they're lining up with their hands out." She paused to pour herself more wine and sip it. That seemed to bring her back to her sales pitch. "This is your lucky day. We can help you find the house you want and hook you up with a mortgage. . . . Are you working yet?"

"Not yet."

"Doesn't matter. The VA has one-hundred-percent mortgages and we can get you one where you come out of it with extra cash to tide you over the first few months. This is what we do. This is how we help."

By committing fraud. "One mortgage at a time," I said, smiling. She looked at me with her mouth open as if she just remembered that she forgot to flush the toilet. "Are you okay?" I said.

"Oh, yes, I just thought of something. You reminded me of someone."

"Kate, I want to talk to you alone."

"We have to take this country back. We have to reward hard work again. We have to protect our liberty." She said it by rote, still lost in the moment. She hadn't heard me. Somewhere along the line, Kate had stopped by the Kool-Aid stand and bought a few pitchers full of the stuff. It practically came gurgling from her mouth. Yet as each moment passed, I became more and more convinced I was sitting next to the right woman, the one Dan sent me searching for. Maybe she was the one lucky person in the world who had completely blocked the Dan experience from her memory, and when the picture was erased, my image went with it.

Dan popped up: *"I never had anything I didn't steal. Even you."*

I was not impressed. *"I'm not impressed. You only stole to win the game, not to get things you wanted."*

"Take a close look. That game was too easy to win. It was not about winning. I had to leave her and I had to take you. Can you blame me?"

Blame would blow back at me, as useless as pity, and Dan was beyond punishment. I concentrated on Kate. Maybe she trained herself to only look forward. Neither she nor Scott wore a wedding ring, so she was a hot young thing for him and he was a catch for her. I did not want to ruin her gig, but she was making things difficult.

"Make up an excuse to get off the boat. I have to speak to you alone," I said. She giggled nervously. "Where can we meet?" I was hoping that open-jawed moment had cast a shadow on her brain, hoping she sensed who I was.

She said, "We're leaving tomorrow for Mexico. Maybe when we come back."

Scott reappeared, with lots of new energy, before we could pursue the subject. "Hey, so have you two been talking about the future? Where to live in Oxnard? Let me give you a tour of the boat before the guests arrive. There are only five in the world like this one. I had to get on a waiting list for three years. Paid in full in advance. C'mon, let me show you." I followed him inside, passing close by one of the Big Boys, who just swiveled his head to watch me pass.

"It's designed and made by a Spaniard named Astendoa. Fifty-eight feet. Three state rooms. Three heads . . ." He droned on: Raymarine electronics, Kohler cooling, two 750-horsepower diesels. I kept thinking about Kate and how to get her alone. I wanted information and I wanted to know a little about who she was and I did not have much time. Close up, Scott looked seventy: tired and hopped up at the same time. He showed me the head, which was air-conditioned. In the elaborate galley, a female servant, also Asian, worked efficiently at putting sushi and other hors d'oeuvres on platters. The Mercedes key hung on a labeled hook next to the stove. The other hook said "Aston."

"You have an Aston Martin, too?"

"Another waiting list, but worth it."

Maybe Kate had been smart enough to put him on a waiting list. We moved on: the lower helm, the fly-bridge, the engine room, with all specs at the tip of his tongue. He had memorized them; Dan would have made them up. I took a deep breath when I made that comparison and he asked if something was wrong.

"Just envious," I said. I knocked Dan off my shoulder so I could concentrate on this moment. "This is truly beautiful. But I don't want to take up too much of your time."

He smiled as if he were waiting for me to say that. "Never say that to anyone. If you are getting what you want from them, then take the time. It's your time, not theirs. If they want to stop, they will. It's something I learned in business, and as you can tell, it's paid off handsomely."

"Thanks. I'll keep it in mind. And when I buy my yacht, I'll send you a bottle of champagne. First, though, I have to buy a house around here."

"How strange that you happened to come by this boat. What a coincidence."

A Big Boy had come in behind us. Behind me.

"Yes."

"It is a coincidence, isn't it, Robert?"

"Isn't it? What's going on?"

"I mean, you're not stalking Kate, are you? Or me?"

"Look, sorry to disappoint you. Kate's an attractive

woman but a little old for me and you're not my type. Neither is he." I nodded toward the looming hulk blocking the door. "I just got out of the Marines. I've been home from Afghanistan for six weeks, so the last thing I'm looking for is a fight. I'll leave. Nice to meet you. Thanks for the tour."

Scott held my arm. His smile made him look like a mad doctor trying to convince me to just try one treatment, but behind his eyes raged the battle between skulking paranoia and his desire to be grandly magnanimous: uptight versus cool. "Don't be angry, Robert. I'm an attorney. I have lots of enemies. I had to ask. Let's go have a drink. Maybe we can help you."

Big Boy was gone when I turned for the door.

22.

Kate greeted the guests as they came aboard, two couples in their fifties. I was introduced. A Big Boy brought around drinks. More couples arrived and I drifted toward the bow, trying to figure out the best way to get Kate away from there. Two women in their fifties came forward and we all said hi and wasn't it a great boat. The harbor was quiet and calm, a scene waiting to happen. A sailboat motored out. One man at the tiller, another working on the sails. A Big Boy appeared and gestured with his finger for me to come along with him. I excused myself to the women and followed him upstairs to the top deck. Scott was holding court with Kate by his side. When he saw me he waved me over to him and when I was facing him he raised his voice and said, "Everyone, everyone . . . I want to introduce you to Robert Kent, a true American hero. Robert is just back from serving two tours in Afghanistan as an Army captain, where he led his battalion on raids into Taliban strongholds, capturing hundreds. Thank you, Captain Kent, from all of us. To Captain Kent."

Kate sure knew how to pick them. Maybe she preferred the really big liars, maybe she couldn't tell. She gave no indication that she knew that he had made it all up. Everyone took a sip and then tried some polite applause, which was made difficult because they were holding their wineglasses. A few of the men stuck their hands out and I shook them. Oxnard is a military town, so they all had to have met lots of vets, but they acted like me being there was a big deal. Maybe I was Scott's first veteran. Maybe they just wanted him happy so he would be in the mood to pull out the free cocaine later.

Someone tapped me on the shoulder and I turned to a short, attractive blond woman wearing a low halter top. "When are you going back? I mean, you must like it by now, right? It's a thrill, right? I'd like to hear about it." And more of that. But the same itch that bothered me on the bus made me raise my eyes past her toward the bridge where I had stood. Two men occupied the same spot.

"I'm down here," the woman said.

I did not know the men, and had no time to understand how they could have tracked me. When they saw me they straightened up and one started to point, and they left immediately. They were coming to the boat.

"Thank you," I said to the woman. "That's very kind."

Scott had begun rambling on to a man next to him. I leaned close and whispered in his ear, "I have to speak to you alone."

"In a minute."

I whispered again: "I'm DEA. In the galley. Now. Bring Kate." I made sure to smile and hold his shoulder so he would stay steady. He looked at me, mouth open. I walked below.

In the galley, I shooed away the servant. Scott and Kate arrived promptly. A Big Boy guarded the entrance. Scott thought he would try a little lawyer talk: "You lied to me, Robert. You—"

I cut him off. "Here's what I want you to do: get everyone off the boat immediately. Tell them anything you want to, there's a tidal wave coming, the wine is poisoned, anything, but make it happen fast. There are two very, very bad guys coming and you don't want them on board and you don't want them hurting your guests, but they will if you give them the chance."

"Why should I do anything you say? I don't care about the DEA and I don't trust you."

"Because I won't come after you for the cocaine import business you're running and the money laundering and the taxes and the funny-money mortgages you help Kate peddle."

His brain was coated in coke and booze, but he could figure his position pretty well. It took five seconds for him to turn to Kate and say, "C'mon."

I held her arm. "She stays with me. I have to talk to her."

He thought she was an informer and it shocked him. "You?"

"No! Fuck this guy."

"Go. Make it happen fast."

He went and Big Boy went with him. I held on to Kate. "When the others are streaming off the boat, you join in. Go to Scott's car and wait there for me."

"No. Leave me alone. Let go of my arm."

I took off her sunglasses. "Look at me, Kate. Look at me. I'm not DEA. My name is Rollie Waters. Does that mean anything to you?" It was clear that the name meant nothing, which was an improvement over the last try. "I'm Dan's son. Your son."

"I have no children." She said it the way people say it's a beautiful day or they're doing fine. So much for the mystical mother-son connection.

"Kate, these men are going to hurt you if they find out who you are. You have to get off the boat and meet me. You can't let them get hold of you." Behind her, I could see the stream of guests leaving the boat and the two thugs looking them over to make sure I wasn't sneaking away. "I'm Dan's son. I'm your son. I'll meet you at the car." She put her hand to her throat and tried to regulate her breathing. I thought she was going to vomit. Her world had revealed itself to be a nightmare, the one she always suspected was waiting for her. I put the sunglasses on her and turned her around and she went out.

I grabbed the keys to Scott's Mercedes from the hook. The two Big Boys stood on guard at the stern as the last of the passengers left. Out the window I could see Kate among them. The two thugs pushed through them on their way to the boat, but they had not identified Kate. I waited in the galley for the fight to start. The Big Boys just told the thugs to go away and that was it. A shot went off. I caught a glimpse of a thug being thrown to the deck. The sounds were reduced to grunting and swearing. I moved forward. The space on the stern was tight, so the two fights kept bumping into each other. A thug and a Big Boy were wrestling and the other Big Boy recoiled from a punch and toppled them overboard into the water. As I came out, I grabbed the railing below the fly deck and, swinging up, kicked the remaining thug in the jaw. He fell backward and I jumped down, landing on his knee. The crunch was awful. I smiled at Big Boy and ran down the pier.

Scott had abandoned ship, too. "I'm taking your car," I said. "Don't tell anyone I have it."

"It's a crime to impersonate a federal agent."

"Do you want to trade threats, Scott?" He didn't. "If they ask about Kate, say she was there but left with the other guests. You don't know where she went. I need your car for a few days. I won't hurt it. Kate, get in."

She looked to him for instructions. "The full wrath of the law, Scott. That's what you're facing," I said, in case he was starting to forget.

"Go with him. If he hurts you, I'll have him killed. I'll do it myself." He was as gallant as he was honest. She could not hide the disgust from her face.

"I'll fill it up," I lied.

23.

She remembered Dan with bitterness and anger. He had promised her the moon, but she ended up waiting tables and bagging groceries and drinking. No fond acknowledgment of his enveloping charm or wistful regret at not being able to reform him. I waited for the watchword of Dan's victims, *I'd do it again; it was fun while it lasted,* but she had never reached that stage. Dan was an evil genie who had tricked her and stolen her golden locks, and she had spent the rest of her life dreaming of getting them back.

I drove north toward Ventura for no reason other than she had started talking and I wanted her to keep going. I was foolish to fear that she would clam up, though. Once the self-pity faucet turns on, you need a power tool to turn it off. She was crying recycled tears while I thanked Dan for sparing me this act. I would have had to run away.

"I was beautiful. That bastard, that bastard told me

to have the baby and he'd take care of everything. I was eighteen. What did I know? I couldn't take care of myself, how could I take care of a little kid and he stuck me out in the middle of nowhere and brought around his business associates and then he disappeared for weeks at a time and what was I supposed to do?"

I was the wrong person to ask. "Where was that house in the middle of nowhere?"

"He told me he owned it," she said. I made an effort not to tense up. "Ha! I found out it belonged to the damn monks and he didn't even pay rent. They let him use it. That did it for me. I was out of there."

"Monks," I said.

"Monks," whispered Dan. *"They're honest."*

At that moment, I knew the money was there. "Where is it? That house . . ."

"What're you writing a book?"

"Yes."

"I don't think I could find it if I wanted to, and believe me, I don't. Near Ojai. Somewhere above Ojai. The monks own a big place and that house."

"Big, sprawling place? Hacienda style? Front porch swing?"

"Yeah."

"I remember it a little. You don't have a photo of those days, all of us together, hanging outside the house?"

It was as if I had reminded her of a task left undone, a burner left on, a debt uncollected. Panic gathered behind her eyes. Her bad dream was accelerating. Dragged away from hope and pleasure, she felt the past squeezing her in a dreaded embrace: she could not remember her locker combination, she had to make a speech that she knew she should have prepared for.

"What else do you want to know? I gotta get back."

At a red light, I asked for her cell phone. She did not want to hand it over.

"You can't go back for a little while," I said. "I have to take the battery out of your phone so no one can find us." The light turned green. I went through and pulled off to the side of the highway and waited until she handed over the phone.

I asked a few more questions to make it seem like I gave a damn about her life after Dan left and up to today and so she wouldn't suspect my only interest was in the location of that house. The parts she told me went like this: community college, dropped out; modeling, burned out; men, still trying. I was pretty sure those were the highlights. As we entered Ventura, she relaxed a bit. She asked about Dan, sheepishly. "What's he doing now?"

"He died," I said.

"I'm sure someone killed him." Her one moment of insight.

"It was in New York. A woman dropped her bag on the subway tracks. Dan jumped down to get it for her. He threw the bag back but slipped climbing up and the train crushed him."

"Are you really writing a book?"

"Yes. About Dan."

"You'll probably be good at it." She said it with a pout and meant it as an insult. She was the same young girl Dan fell for, clueless and skeptical at once. I could understand why he married her; he thought the cluelessness would go away, that he would have a partner who saw through him but still loved him and still craved his charm. Somehow it made me want to lean over and kiss her on the forehead and hug her. "I suppose you look a little bit like him. He was handsome, I'll give him that," she said. I had planned to park her at a motel somewhere up the coast, but she would be back at the boat in a flash no matter what warnings I gave. I realized I would have to take her along.

I used the computer at the public library in Ventura. The only place near Ojai with monks was a Buddhist monastery on the northwest side of Ojai, bordering the Los Padres National Forest.

Kate's lament that Dan did not pay rent might have been true and it might have been a fantasy she had and it might have been a Dan story. My favorite was the no-rent version because it meant Dan had charmed them and a proper coating of Dan charm could last a lifetime. My least-favorite version involved rent. I struggled to concoct a solid lie for the monks, one that would get me access to the house and time to search it alone.

24.

A small shrine near the road marked the entrance to the Veruvana Retreat. "Oh, damn, this is it," Kate said. "This is the place." I turned up a long paved driveway flanked by sycamore trees. After a few hundred yards, a parking lot opened on the left. I stayed on the drive until I came to a large mission-style building. A small sign near the door said "Veruvana." Ahead of us, across the drive and up an unpaved path, stood a two-story building that looked like a chapel. Scattered among the trees were small shrines and prayer spots. On the other side of the drive were two large greenhouses. Everything was well kept and neat, but the silence made it seem as if the place were abandoned. Wind chimes added to the effect.

The terrain was right, the trees and bushes, even the sky; it all meshed with my vision. Beyond the main building, the driveway continued up a hill and around a corner. I looked back toward the entrance and could see the parking lot below me. Two shiny white SUVs, three green vans. But the architecture was wrong, all mission style. I was looking for a wood farmhouse.

"Everyone is in the dining hall. Can I help you find it?"

I spun, startled out of my own meditation. His right shoulder was bare and his head was, too; the rest was covered in a saffron robe. He wore sandals which did not look like they would help him creep up silently.

"I was hoping you had rooms for my mother and me."

"Do you have a reservation?"

"It doesn't seem too crowded. Do I need one?"

"Everyone is in the dining hall. But I'll check."

We followed him into the main building. He disappeared for a little while, and when he came back he told me we could have two singles in the Samoner retreat, which sounded okay to me. Cash confused him and made him disappear again. At last he took the money and an extra hundred as a deposit. I parked my car in the empty lot and hiked back up, and he showed Kate her room first and told us dinner was still on if we were hungry. Kate decided to skip dinner.

The dining hall held four long tables with benches for seats. At the head of the room, near a stage, a buffet was set up. The ceiling was high, with arched beams of dark wood running from the floor all the way up. I looked around for the statues of Jesus, but they had all been taken down. This place used to belong to the Catholic Church.

I never went to summer camp or to prison, but I imagined it would be something like this setup. Instead of gangs with their different colors, you have teams with their different colors, and you all eat the same slop and do what the guards or counselors tell you to. Instead of punishment, you call it fun. Or in this case, instead of drudgery, you call it enlightenment.

Men and women sat in groups, filling most of the spots at the tables in bunches with matching colored T-shirts. Where one color ended and another began, an empty seat marked the territory. Their ages ranged from the mid-twenties to a few who looked in their sixties. A few monks were salted into each group. For conversational purposes? I hoped not. I did not see any interaction between the groups while I ate, silently, at the edge. At last an old monk stood and everyone seemed to understand that meant dinner was over and they filed out in a very orderly fashion. I followed.

We trooped into a meditation hall, where the teams deployed onto mats with admirable fluidity, which I assumed was due to the competitive natures they had come here to shrink. I found a mat in the back. When I looked up, I saw the old monk who had led the procession staring at me. I had to act as if this was what I came for, so I joined right in with the puja. Maybe the old guy watched me the whole time. I didn't open my eyes to find out, but it felt like he was right there. My vision was sharp. I could have counted the leaves on the cottonwood tree in front of the house, drawn the pattern on the lace curtains, kicked stones along the dirt driveway which matched that drive leading above the main lodge. The monk watching me did not matter. At the end of the chanting, a monk rose and walked to the front of the room and began to give a talk, a little dharma lesson.

"When we are not at ease, we are diseased. When we are not possessed, we are dispossessed. When our minds are not able, we are disabled. When we are not at rest, we are distressed. . . ."

This guy had the accent and inflection of a native English speaker but used the language like someone relying on a guidebook for translation. He droned on for thirty minutes at least, or, as I came to think of it, eternity.

As I walked back to my room, a monk joined me. "I'm Mark."

"Rollie."

"I saw you chant. You've done this before."

"So?"

He flustered easily. "I didn't mean anything by it. I—"

"You meant who am I, why did I come here?"

"No."

"I'm a guy who has chanted puja before and wanted to do it again so he came here. Good night." Maybe from the inside he was a devout young man, pure of heart and intent. From the outside he was a snoop who was fooling only himself.

I went to Kate's room. She was already under the covers. I pulled the chair a bit closer to the bed. "I'm sorry about Scott," I said.

"There's a million Scotts. You probably did me a

favor. He's so coked up lately even the Viagra doesn't work."

"Lucky you."

She laughed. "He's lucky to have me anyway." She yawned and closed her eyes for a few seconds. "I'm sorry. I took some pills."

The scent of sandalwood filled the room, though no candles were burning. The windows were closed and shades pulled down. I felt like I was supposed to say something sentimental, something about always looking forward to this day, but she hadn't done anything lousy to me. She didn't deserve that lie.

"Are you really a Marine?"

"Don't you believe me?"

She rolled her eyes with mock impatience, the way a teenager would. "Oh, yes, every word." I laughed and she smiled.

"I am a Marine."

"My father was, too." I waited for the next line: and one, and two, and three . . . "He loved Dan." She yawned a bit and sipped some water from a plastic bottle. "Did you find what you're looking for?"

"I'm just hiding out."

"It's okay with me. There's nothing I want in this place, no matter what it is. I knew that the second we got here. It even smells the same. And I know he didn't leave anything worthwhile because he never had anything." She stopped to yawn. "By the way, I've been meaning to tell you, your real name is Jake."

"Jake." I realized that was only half an answer. She read my thoughts.

"Reynolds. At least it was. Jake Reynolds."

"What's yours?"

"Kate. Kate then, Kate now. I've been married a few times." She yawned again. "I did come looking for you once." She paused. "Not really. I came looking for money, but I did want to see you. Don't blame me, okay. Please. I just . . . I'm not made for it."

"I don't blame you. Not at all. It all worked out."

"Really?"

"Really." Maybe I had an odd look on my face because I couldn't think of anything to blame her for.

"Maybe we can talk more tomorrow. You can take me back. I won't tell them anything." Her eyes were closed.

"Tomorrow."

Back in my room, I sat in full lotus and brought up my vision again, a trial run for later that night. I strained to see more than ever before. Meditation as frustration. Every foray inside felt false. At last I let my mind go blank and stayed like that as long as I could. At one A.M., I went out.

I crossed the lawn toward the rear of the main building, then cut over to the driveway. I walked beside it so not to crunch on the rocks. A quarter moon shed enough light to keep me from falling in a hole. About one hundred yards up the drive, a wooden fence, chained and padlocked, covered in vines, blocked the way. A sign read:

**PLEASE DO NOT ENTER.
PRIVATE PROPERTY.**

The fence was twelve feet tall and looked flimsy, like it was there for show. I pulled at it slightly and saw the chain-link fence behind it. I walked to the right side of the gate to see if I could go around. No go, the fence continued up along the side and widened before disappearing in the night. Same thing on the other side. I followed along the side away from the buildings.

When I was sure I was completely out of sight and sound range, I climbed over the fence.

My cottonwood was waiting for me, a shimmering silhouette against the sky. I stood next to it and turned all the way around. Little bits and pieces felt like they were coming back to me, but that might have been wishful thinking. I did not want that. The swing hung still but on the left side of the door, not where I remembered it. The windows were closed, no fluttering curtains, but most of the rest was the way I had built it. Three steps up to the porch. I sat down in front of the house and looked it over to make the corrections.

I went onto the porch and pushed the old swing. The metal chains creaked in the hooks. The door was locked, but I knew exactly how to get in. The second window started to move when I pushed up, then quickly stuck. I wedged my fingers inside and lifted. The window screeched and the curtain fluttered in salute.

White sheets covered the furniture. I crossed into the large farmhouse kitchen. The appliances were relics, at least forty years old, strangers to me, evoking only some generic past. Anyone could have claimed it. What should I picture to give it meaning? Is this where Kate burst into tears because her cake fell? Out back, the low black humpback hills slumped protectively.

There was a den, furniture covered, including an old TV and a stereo. I tried to remember what music Dan preferred. I could see him listening to anything anyone else wanted because he was not really listening. He was figuring. I tried to let it all flood back in, but not much came up other than vague, muddy shadows which I could not trust. I had no photos to prompt me with false memories, and not many stories from Dan. I lifted the sheet on the dining room table and saw Dan tossing me the bread as if I were there, as if I remembered it. But what I remembered was that it was a Dan story. Nothing more.

Without a flashlight, searching for the money would be useless. I climbed out the window and made my way back to my room. I had spent two hours at the house. It felt like five minutes.

25.

Good morning, Rollie," Mark said, just as I had finished my oatmeal. "The lama would like to see you. Please follow me."

The signal that the meal was over had not come yet. I rose anyway and followed Mark past the smug glances of the campers who had never been summoned by the camp director. When we got outside, I said, "If you see the woman I came here with . . ."

"Oh, I should have said, she came down early and asked for a ride into Ojai. That was around seven. She said to tell you." Maybe she figured there were a million Kates, too.

The lama was the old guy who had been staring at me the night before. He met us near the greenhouses. Mark quickly excused himself. The lama gestured for me to follow him along a path that led into the woods. We walked about fifty shaded yards to a clearing and a pond. A gazebo and deck jutted over the water.

"My name is lama Gyamtso. If you're uncomfortable

calling me lama, you may call me Henry. Henry Holland was my given name. This is our reflection pond. I rarely get to spend any time here when we have guests."

I assumed the cash had caught his attention along with my seeming experience at puja, and he was going to make a pitch that I hand over whatever fortune I had and sign up with his crew. These outfits always needed fresh blood and money. I kept quiet waiting for the pitch. "Mostly we cater to groups. Very few individuals and none without reservations."

"And none with cash," I said.

"And none with cash, and none has ever snuck up to the farmhouse, at night or during the day, ignoring the very clear signs and the very tall fence. You must have had a purpose. Please tell me why you went there."

His voice held no rancor or tension or threat. To break from his gaze, I picked up a stone and tossed it into the pond. "I lived in that house."

It was his turn to be caught off guard. His eyes grew wide and he looked away as if to calculate the meaning of that statement. He said: "I've lived here almost thirty years. No one named Rollie Waters ever lived in the farmhouse in that time."

"I'm Dan's son."

He froze, so still I thought he would have to be rebooted. At last he said, "Tell me about Dan."

"He was a charmer, a con artist, a deadbeat, and a sport, a wise man who wasted his wisdom foolishly. He could be trusted to finish what he started, only it was never what you thought it was." I almost went on, but I wanted to avoid anything that sounded sentimental because it might make him suspicious that I was faking it.

"Would you say he was greedy?"

"Once. And it killed him."

The lama's eyes were distant, like a guy watching scenes in his head. "Tell me how he died."

I told him some of it, leaving out the money. He jumped right on that. "You haven't told me," he said, "why they killed him, or why you were there, or why you survived."

"You first," I said.

"Dan's son was not named Rollie."

"I found out yesterday that I was Jake. Dan never mentioned that."

That seemed to satisfy him. He looked around to make sure no one was nearby. He gestured and I joined him on another path that led farther away from the buildings.

It would be tough to live here and not be contemplative. The trees seemed to be individually designed and engineered to let just the right amount of sun glide through at just the right intervals. Birds and crickets provided just enough background noise to keep the silence from feeling creepy. The lama spoke softly, confidentially, in a tone that matched the surroundings.

"This property was a convent. The Sisters of Mercy. A decision was made by the church authorities to consolidate and the property was put up for sale. Our group was renting an old campsite near Carpinteria. Our founder, who is dead now, envisioned . . . all this. He raised money from many sources, but mainly from one woman who donated a large chunk of the down payment. No bank would lend to us, but we found a private lender. We spent the next two years improving the property and building. We dredged that pond, refurbished the housing and the chapel, constructed the main reception area. It was a great time, building time. Then the lender realized the potential value of the property and convinced the rich donor to join him in taking it back.

"We were on the verge of losing it all. Dan had been renting the farmhouse from the nuns and we had continued the arrangement. We didn't know much about him, but we asked if he could help. Dan went away, off and on, for a few months. One evening he appeared, just after dinner, with the title and the deed. Free and clear. All he asked in return was perpetual use of the farmhouse."

I could tell he was not finished. He was searching for the right way to phrase something.

"How did he do that? He couldn't have bought the land," he said. "All these years I've wondered. Dan is a legend here. Every novice, every monk knows about him. When he visits, it's a highlight. He chants with us, then . . ."

"Tells stories?"

"I sit at the pond replaying that evening he returned, trying to imagine how he accomplished it all. . . . It's unfathomable."

For a moment, I thought this was a clever ploy, some Buddhist trick, a way to check if I was really Dan's son. But this guy, sixty if he was a day, sounded like a troubled kid pleading for the secret behind a magic trick.

I asked, "Did Dan ask for money before he began?"

"We gave him twenty thousand dollars."

Dan did not tell me this story, but I knew enough about the way he operated to parse it out. Print the legend they say. And since he was dead, I could stand doing Dan this service.

"Remind me of their names, the donor and the backer."

"She was Gwen. I don't remember her last name. He was Norman Simpson."

"Right. Yes. . . . Both late forties, early fifties at the time?"

"Yes."

"Here's how it worked," I said, as if I were Dan himself. "First Dan flies down to New Mexico and plunks down some of your money for the right to buy a piece of worthless desert. It costs him about five thousand dollars, and he makes sure to overpay a bit so he can make friends down there. Then he goes to Del Mar down the coast from here where he knows Gwen likes the track. Dan's about twenty years younger than Gwen. He turns on the charm and throws some of your money around, and suddenly Gwen feels young again. The world seems brighter. He tells her he's in the energy business, and he hints, very tenderly, that he is about to make a huge score, the score of a lifetime. A game changer. Simpson is Gwen's boyfriend by then and very protective because Gwen is worth so much money. Gwen makes the introduction and Simpson has to make sure Dan is not a threat to his meal ticket. Now Dan wants Simpson comfortable and certain that Dan has no chance if they go up against each other. And the way Dan reassures him is to act like he thinks he is the smartest guy in the world and is holding all the aces. Dan wants Simpson to think he is a fool, which isn't difficult because guys like Simpson like to think everyone else is a fool. This dance takes weeks: days at the track and on the golf course, dinners overlooking the beach, trips to Las Vegas.

"After a night of drinks, Dan tells his new best friends about a property he has in New Mexico bursting with uranium, the high-grade stuff. As the night goes on, Dan lets slip that he doesn't actually own the property yet; he has an option to buy it, for which he paid two hundred thousand dollars. A big chunk of his inheritance. Simpson suggests a trip to New Mexico to check it out, offering to help Dan with financing the deal. By now, Simpson is completely enthralled by Dan and at the same time convinced Dan is ripe for the taking. Dan rejects the offer a few times until, after suffering heavy losses in a casino, he gets sentimental, wanting to visit his secret treasure chest with his new best pal. They drive down together. Sure enough, the Geiger counter makes all the right noises because Dan had it rigged to detect radon. Dan recites like an Irish poet as he paints pictures of his dreams, big dreams of empire and alliance, monopoly and domination. He's giggly with enthusiasm. They celebrate. Wine, women, and song: women supplied by Dan. Simpson thinks he is getting Dan loaded and into position so he can move in for the kill.

"The next day, they fly back to Los Angeles and Simpson asks Dan up to his office to talk business. Simpson intends to make the kind of deal on Dan's land that he made on this property, one where he could call in the loan and take over the title. Simpson explains that he knows Dan is hard up for cash. Dan hears him out patiently and expresses his delight that Simpson is interested in the New Mexico property. 'You can have it,' Dan says. 'The price is two hundred thousand dollars . . . and the former convent property.' He had never mentioned this place before. Simpson doesn't understand. Dan repeats the offer, keeps the charming smile shining in spite of Simpson's growing tension. Then Dan reaches into his briefcase and extracts an envelope, which he pushes across the desk. Dan keeps his eyes on Simpson as he opens the envelope and pulls out the contents: photos of Simpson naked with the naked prostitutes. 'It's real simple,' Dan tells him. 'Gwen is worth close to two hundred million. You have about a million in the convent property. New Mexico could be worth a billion someday. If you make the deal, the worst you come out with is Gwen. If you don't make the deal, you own some buildings in the woods near Ojai. By the way, I called Gwen earlier. She's meeting us here in about an hour.' Dan keeps quiet for a little while to let Simpson see the One True Way. Then, to close the deal, Dan lowers the amount Simpson would have to pay him to one hundred thousand. How much did he bring back to you?"

"Ten thousand."

"The rest were legitimate expenses. Everyone was happy."

The lama thanked me a few times while he chewed it over, enjoying all the subtle flavors he had been craving for so long.

We had circled back toward the buildings. The lama led me into his office, a small cedarwood room with saffron-colored cushions on the floor in one corner and a desk and chair opposite. Behind the desk, a tall bookcase was filled with hardcover volumes about prayers and holiness. One shelf was devoted to Christianity and another to Judaism. Buddha supervised it all from the middle of a credenza which ran along under the window. The lama invited me to sit on a cushion. He unlocked a desk drawer, pulled out one of those wooden boxes that are a puzzle to open, and he opened it in a couple of easy moves.

He laid ten thousand dollars, crisp ones, in a packet on the desk.

"Is this what you've come for?"

My turn to freeze. He brought it around the desk with him and tossed it on the floor in front of me. He sat down facing me.

"Dan left that and a lot more in the house about seven years ago. He's only been back three times since and he never touched the money."

"You checked."

"It's easy for an alcoholic to give up liquor if there is none for a thousand miles. The challenge is in keeping your temptation close at hand. As I'm sure you have learned, facing one's weakness develops one's strength. It's hidden where you used to hide. I think Dan knew that I had found the money. I think it pleased him to test me in this way."

Dan the Great. Dan the Legend. Dan the Zen Master. I got up and told the lama to keep the packet of bills. "Payback for the money Dan didn't replenish."

"What are you going to do with it? The rest . . ."

"I have to give it back."

"Who does it belong to?"

"It's complicated. I have to figure that out."

"If you have to leave it here in the meantime, it's safe."

He didn't want it for himself, but he didn't want to let it go, either.

The monks and novices lined up to give me their hands-together bow. I checked with the lama and he understood and shook his head: don't mention Dan's death. Two monks carefully opened the gates and I drove up to the farmhouse.

The body bag was in the root cellar behind a cabinet and a wheelbarrow and four old tires. It was heavier than I expected. I paused to imagine myself living down here for days, as Dan claimed I did. I could believe it.

The money had been safe there for seven years. The lama had explained himself honestly. I had to consider leaving it. But two things had changed: he knew Dan was dead, and he knew I would be taking it away soon enough. He might decide those were divine signs that the time had come to make his move. And more likely, he might decide his connection to Dan was so close that Dan would want him to have it, had always intended for him to have it. I loaded the money into the trunk of Scott's car.

26.

was carrying ten thousand dollars to be used for bribes, or to grease the wheels for Captain Ballard when we met up in Torkham. That money felt as heavy as the stuffed body bag I had just found. Ballard's death should have meant the mission had ended since my role was to report to him. But Junior's smug face haunted me. All I could report is that he had tea in the courtyard while Ballard was murdered. I wanted more. Ballard had been intent on playing out his fantasy to the end. I was not finishing this for him.

I spent about eight hours over the next few days with Nawaz. We prayed together and I told him about my village, slowly bringing up our difficulties in defending ourselves.

"You deserve the right to defend yourselves," he said. "But sometimes rights do not matter without money to accompany them."

"I have some money with me. I'm only looking for someone who can be trusted."

"My cousin might know someone who can find weapons."

He was asking what weapons I wanted. I had given this issue a lot of thought. Three trucks in the caravan were carrying M2 .50 caliber machine guns, a fancy weapon. It was heavy, more than forty pounds with the tripod. And it required belted ammunition, which was also heavy. Because I would need help transporting them, I did not want them.

"Those machine guns that we brought from Karachi are very powerful and accurate," I said.

"And reliable," Nawaz said.

"Yes. Solid. Excellent for defense, for defending a fort. Moving them can be difficult if you want to move quickly."

"They are heavy," he said.

"But .50 caliber is good," I said. Nawaz listened patiently while I discussed the relative merits of various weapons and their usefulness for my situation. "The M107 .50 caliber sniper rifle, if your friend could find those . . ."

Nawaz shrugged. "Very expensive. But he might be able to obtain them."

The Marines train you to use the weapons and clean them, but they never mention the black market cost. At DIA, we had not discussed further funds for me. I was caught off guard for a moment and worried that it showed on my face: the long, long list of lousy deeds I had contemplated did not include selling my weapon to the enemy. I was surprised by the omission. But Nawaz must have assumed I was already bargaining. He said he thought he could bargain it down to eight thousand dollars per weapon. When he saw that I was not prepared to enter that territory, he changed the subject to the quality of the food in Kabul and soon got up to excuse himself. I stopped him. "Let's make sure we want to go forward before I bring all the money. I'll buy two of those rifles for eight thousand dollars."

Nawaz flashed anger at the challenge. I wanted that. "I don't have time to waste if people cannot pay."

"I told you what I would pay for two. If your cousin can deliver, I will buy twenty." He hesitated.

"Come," he said. And we went to meet cousin Abed in a house nearby. Abed was the ANA lieutenant I had seen with Junior and the next day with Nawaz after they had murdered Ballard. He was young, early twenties, small and clean-shaven. His eyes were light. He greeted us and dismissed the men he had been meeting with. After an hour, we started talking money. We settled on $9,500 for two, plus $84,000 for the additional eighteen rifles to be delivered. I paid him $4,750 on the spot. Nawaz and Abed walked me out. They said they would contact me soon. As I walked away, Abed spoke loudly, without yelling: "Watch out. Duck!" In English. I winced, but they couldn't see my face and I kept walking.

The next morning, Nawaz and Abed picked me up in an old Ford. Abed was driving and wearing his uniform. It's easy to understand why the Germans covet Paris; it's beautiful. It's difficult to understand why the Brits, the Russians, and the Americans have coveted a country where Jalalabad is one of the nicer-looking cities. The road from Torkham to Jalalabad traces the Kabul River, and as we neared the town, thick splotches of green appeared in the gray-brown desert. We passed cornfields and groves of olive trees. We did not talk much.

Abed parked the car in town. He walked to the line of tuk-tuks and instructed us to get in. Abed sat next to the driver, facing Nawaz and me. Abed told the driver, "The American base."

Abed showed his papers and talked to the guards and his story was good enough to get us thoroughly searched a few times. We only had to wait half an hour to get inside, passing most others who knew they were in for a long day. We sat in a mess for civilian workers, American and Afghan. Abed knew a lot of men from both groups. Hellos and nods. I was sipping soup when the star of the show swept in along with a young lieutenant named Nance. They sat at a table across from me. Junior was in full attaboy mode, slapping backs and bumping fists. I stared right at him. If he was going to make me, I wanted to know and the base was the best place for that to happen. I could surrender and never have to see Nawaz and Abed again. But I could read Junior and he did not see through me. He broke the gaze first, turning away with a sneer of superiority, which is a bad habit when you're staring your enemy in the eye. Soon he and his companion were gone, and Abed with them.

They took with them my last chance for escape, though I spent the next few minutes lying to myself, pretending I would just hand over their names and be done with all this. But I knew the truth: I had fallen through a fissure in the earth into the Land of the Louses; I would not escape without a fight. No one at DIA was going to believe me, and I would not believe any of them.

"Let's go," I said to Nawaz. I got up and didn't wait for him. Maybe it was posturing in front of Americans instead of Afghans that made me antsy. Maybe it was that no one suspected me. Suddenly I just wanted it to be over. The weeks of posing and now being on a base with other Americans sickened me. I walked quickly out of the mess, down a corridor, and out into a courtyard. Nawaz caught up with me. "What is wrong with you? Abed will be coming back to look for us."

"I don't like to be left alone in there with them. I could feel them staring at me."

"We'll be done here soon. Come back."

I shook my head, but before I could start away, Junior and Abed were coming toward us. Abed was not happy to see us outside. I brushed past him. Outside the gates, I turned on him.

"Don't ever leave me alone with them. I don't know you well enough for that." Abed was conciliatory. My sudden change of heart could not alter the course. The scent of money and betrayal was too compelling for them to give up. The deal had been struck. All was well. We were moving forward.

The next night, Abed and Nawaz delivered two of the rifles and I handed over the rest of the payment. I promised to return with the remaining cash within a week.

27.

After I left Dan and the blonde at the houseboat, I wandered toward California, stealing cars, riding the bus, hitchhiking with no intention. The future looked flat and I pulled down my sails because I was not ready to skid off the edge of the world. Officially I was not yet a runaway. Dan wouldn't be looking for me for quite a while and school was out, but I was sleeping in strangers' parked cars and work was intermittent. I drifted up from San Diego to Los Angeles. My Spanish helped, but most employers weren't fooled and didn't have faith that I would do the work as diligently as a native speaker. I was passing a clothing store on Melrose when I thought I saw someone who looked familiar in the window. I stepped back and stared. The guy was a raggedy mess, skinny and dirty and lost. I was staring into a mirror. Some kids along the road had mentioned a refuge for runaways in the mountains. I hustled up bus fare.

I was waiting outside the bakery in Big Bear,

deciding if I could stand being in there with the smells but without the taste. Loretta walked out. She was in her thirties, thin and tough. She shook slightly. Multiple sclerosis had begun to work on her, but it was not much of a factor in her life.

The negotiations were quick. She wouldn't tell anyone anything and I wouldn't, either, and she would feed me until I was ready to leave and I would help her rebuild the place. She could kick me out whenever it pleased her. No trial. Loretta would not inquire about my past but would listen if I wanted. She did not want to know about any crimes or warrants.

Loretta was the anti-Dan. She could lie, cheat, and steal as well as he could, almost as well, but she did it to help others, her stray dogs, as she called us. Her charm was in her lack of charm. She had taken over an abandoned campsite with ten small cabins in Fawnskin, a village on the north side of the lake. Private donors, some were churches, and state money funded the refuge. If anyone tried to interfere, even visit, Loretta would drop everything to deter them. Loretta believed the best way to get people to grow up was to give them freedom. All scrutiny was censorship.

She fed me and I worked. In the months I was there, twelve runaways came through. Eight were girls. Some only stayed a few nights. Loretta threw two out for stealing from stores in the village a second time. When the police inquired, Loretta told them the shopkeeper had tried to get the girls to pose nude. I was older than some of the runaways and became Loretta's assistant. She even let me cook.

Dennis Shelton showed up looking not at all ragged. A big guy, bigger than me, with broad shoulders, handsome and strong, he claimed to be sixteen, but I thought he was older. On his second night, he disappeared with Becky, a girl who had been there for two weeks. Becky was fourteen. She came back in tears but would not say much. The impression she gave was that she did not volunteer for whatever went on between them. The next day she slipped away. Loretta spoke with Dennis. She wasn't reporting any of the details, but he stayed. Ten unpleasant days later came the repeat, this time with Amanda. She told the story in tears. Loretta kicked Dennis out. He threatened her. I was eavesdropping. When he pushed her, I stepped in. That was the worst beating I had taken up to that point. He capped it off by clocking me with a frying pan.

But Dennis did not leave the area. He was camping out on a ridge above the lake and not far from a spot the kids went for Sunday picnics. Loretta warned everyone, but she stuck to her complete freedom policy: do what you want, pay the consequences. Dennis lured Amanda away from the group two Sundays later and raped her. No doubt this time. I took a large carving knife and set out for his campsite.

He had chosen a good spot. The climb was steep and tough. He saw me coming long before I reached the top, even though I came up the back way, the difficult

way. I could hear Dan suggesting something more subtle, but I was in no mood to listen. At the very top, a
promontory jutted out to the right of the path I was
taking. Dennis stood there taunting me, "Hey, it's Mr.
Frying Pan Man," while the sweat leaked into my eyes
and my muscles burned.

And then he went flying past me like Superman, but
with a shocked look on his face like his powers had just
deserted him. The first rock he hit was about thirty feet
below me. After that, he was a sack of meat. I scrambled up the rest of the way and lifted myself onto the
promontory. Through the trees, I caught a glimpse of
Loretta moving steadily down the other side of the
mountain.

The police decided Dennis fell. They came around
the refuge cautiously, reluctant to deal with Loretta.
Was Dennis violent? His past showed tendencies in that
direction. Had anyone come around looking for him?
Loretta told them no one came and they could go. Rel-
atives claimed the body. Loretta and I never spoke
about what happened, though I stayed a long time at
the refuge and even longer in Big Bear.

I knew the body bag of money would be safe with
Loretta, and if I died, she would use it for something
worthwhile.

She wasn't at the bakery this time, so I went over to the
refuge. We hugged and kissed and she said, "They were
following you the other day. Did you bring them here?"

"I've lost them for the time being." She looked at

Scott's car. "Borrowed," I said. "I'm glad to see you. And I'm glad to see the place." The place did not look good. The cabins needed paint and repairs, and weeds had overgrown two of the paths. She had only eight kids there. The MS symptoms were stronger. Loretta used a cane. I had forgotten how little she was, wiry-thin and short. In memory, she was my size. Her nose and chin were sharp and her eyes bright so she always reminded me of a bird, and that seemed exaggerated now. She made a pasta dinner, no meat, for the kids. They cleaned up and drifted out, all but one boy who kept staring at me. "He's okay, Kevin. Not the cops." Kevin shrugged and went out. Loretta and I ate alone.

"The kids are the same. They're great. The only thing wrong with them is they don't know they could own the world."

"You might mention it," I said.

"Just sound like a liar to them. Encouragement starts to sound like a taunt after you've been hit enough." I ached realizing how much I missed her. "The state is cutting us off," she said. "The churches won't contribute if we're not a state-sanctioned entity. I told some of the private donors to come through, but I seem to have lost a step. The Mormon church in Ar-rowhead wants to take over. I don't want to give the kids a place to run away from."

I told her about Afghanistan and she wanted me to speak to her in Dari and Pashto and Arabic, so I did a little showing off.

"I didn't think you'd last."

"Me neither. The orders are tough, the rules, but it satisfies something." Loretta's eyes widened as if she were going to scold me. "Not the killing and not the being shot at," I said, and she sat back. "It's the feeling of exploring. Always something new, even if the newness is only new danger. Even the boredom feels like it's on the way to somewhere."

She did not answer for a while; then she said, "I'm sorry to hear it." The anti-Dan.

She sat next to me on the couch and I put my arm around her and she rested her head on my shoulder. I let her sleep like that a while, then carried her to her cabin. She woke up but I shushed her.

In the morning, I rented a storage locker in Big Bear in the same place Loretta kept one, paying for one year in advance. I hauled the money in there and unzipped the bag. For about two minutes, I stared at it all just to see if I would be moved by it. Maybe if I had more time to give the exercise, it might have had an effect. I removed about a million dollars and put half in each of two backpacks. Loretta was in the bakery, waiting, in case any more kids got off the bus. I ordered coffee and a cranberry muffin for me and a scone for her. Her hand shook and I thought she was going to spill the coffee. She caught me looking and spilled some on purpose and laughed without smiling.

"I might call for this key. It's best if you can leave it

somewhere where I don't have to get it directly from you. If I'm not back in two months, consider it yours."

"It's a refuge, you know. You can stay since no one knows you're here." That was as close as I ever heard her come to asking for anything. She didn't touch the locker key.

"They'd find me eventually."

"Then even the boredom will feel like it's on the way to somewhere." She held her bird eyes on mine when she said it. At first I took it as a taunt, but it dawned on me that she was thinking of herself. Loneliness had festered. Maybe my visit made it worse. Loretta had set up a world in which everyone she cared for and who cared for her left her. Complete freedom. She still did not touch the key. "It will be behind the counter here. What name should I put on the envelope?"

"None. Just describe me."

I drove back to the refuge and put one of the backpacks in Loretta's closet.

28.

Any idea how to get them to believe I'll give them the money? Ideas that don't involve them torturing me for the information?"

"Make demands."

"Negotiate."

"They'll think you believe them. They're vain. They'll think you believe they intend to keep their end of the deal."

The bartender came over and I ordered a beer. I'd been having this conversation with Dan over and over during the ride down to the outskirts of Phoenix. Dan kept telling me I was the one who had the money.

"You're the one who has the money."

"They could say no and just torture me."

"They might. It's a risk. They might use a little torture just to make sure you're sincere. But, it's a risk for them, too. You might die, like I did."

"They can promise anything."

"So can you. And you have the money."

"They're going to kill me as soon as they have the money."

"I don't know about you, but I like to spread the money around. Offer some to everyone. They'll all agree and all plan to screw you. Did you bring any of that along with you?"

"Yes."

"Seed the mine."

"Good idea."

"Try to make sure you know what you want out of it, and you'll get it."

"Like you? Why didn't you spend the money?"

He didn't answer. I asked a different question.

"Why didn't they spend the money?"

"They're going to tell you that as soon as they think you're giving it to them."

"Because they'll think I'm dead."

"Like me."

First I called Shaw. "I think I found the money," I said.

"Where are you?"

"Fine, thanks. How are you?"

He waited before replying, then said, "I'll say it again: Where are you? That's first."

"I'll be near Tucson. Be ready. If you can have help there, that would be good. I'm going to be there with McColl."

"Tell me where you are, Rollie. We have to talk this over. I can be in Tucson in ninety minutes."

"Just trust me. Please."

"Because you've been such a trustworthy guy so far. My jaw still aches. You called me for a reason."

"I wanted to check in with you so you'd know that I'm okay and I'm on the trail. If you're near Tucson when I need you, that would be really . . ."

"Helpful."

I hung up. I called Gladden next. "Reporting in, sir."

The conversation was pretty much the same as the one with Shaw except that I could hear Gladden choking on his bile, and see the veins straining against the skin and the eyes bulging. And Gladden bothered to make threats and remembered to call Dan a scumbag.

"How much reward money am I gonna get?"

He screamed, "You're still a Marine, mister."

"Just checking, sir." I hung up. I spent the rest of the day making preparations.

29.

The good thing about flying in to Blythe must be that you can fly right out. I stood on the dirt between the runway and the access road at the Blythe Airport, watching the air shimmering off the concrete and the dirt and the main building and the four small planes baking near the sheds. I thought about what it would be like growing up here and how strange it might look the first time I went to a place where the air wasn't shimmering. The mountains were miles off to the north. It was a great spot for an airport, wide open and flat, but it seemed like a waste of good desert.

I could see the helicopter long before I heard it. It circled twice. Blondie sat with his legs dangling over the side and a sniper rifle cradled in his lap. Toothless hopped out past him and frisked me, then escorted me inside and we took off.

Blondie smiled at me. "Welcome aboard, pal."

The pilot turned to me. "Buckle up," he said. He

took off his shades and smiled, too. It was one of the shooters who chased me at Camp Pendleton, the short one. I buckled in and when Blondie saw that had been done, he lifted the butt of the rifle and slammed it down on the back of my head.

I woke up on a twin bed in a small bedroom. It was dark. Curtains were drawn across the single window on my left and a fan was blowing across my face. I reached out to turn it off and knocked it over.

"He's up," someone said.

"He's up" echoed down a hallway. The door opened and a light came on, making me wince. Blondie appeared with Toothless. "How's that head, pal?"

"Fine."

"Good." And he slapped me hard across the side of my head. My brain rattled and the pain dug in where it was safe and could stay awhile. "Get up. We'll show you around."

They led me down a hallway lined with framed photos of horses, some being ridden by McColl and some by a woman, but I could not stop to get a good look. We entered a large living room organized around a stone fireplace. Everything was ranch style: leather couches and chairs. One sofa was cowhide, splotched white and brown so it looked like a great place to sit if you were planning on spilling coffee, or cream. There was an elk head mounted on the wall, and a bear's head. As we headed for the front door, it opened. Mc-Coll stood there basking in the outside spotlight.

Blondie and Toothless moved me back so McColl could enter.

"Welcome, Rollie. Hungry?"

The dining room was more of the same: rough-hewn wood and leather, a table that looked like it weighed a thousand pounds. Sitting there, eating a steak, was a woman with short blond hair and huge breasts and a blouse at least one size too small pulling tight against them. She barely looked up when we came in. "Oh, I was so hungry and I didn't know when you guys planned to start, so I just went ahead." She said it like she had to but didn't mean it. She wasn't sorry.

"Rollie, this is Jessica." He was proud, I could hear it, and he wanted me to be impressed.

"Jessica."

She nodded to me and took a bite of her steak. McColl sat at the head of the table, so I sat across from Jessica. McColl started right in about the ranch and how much they loved it there: the wind, the sand, the stars. Luckily, that took only a couple of minutes. Unluckily, he then got to the horses. Jessica chimed in about this horse and that horse, and how the rescued wild one was healthier than the expensive auction-bought one, and this one only ate crunchy peanut butter, and that one was so gentle. There are golf bores, ski bores, even gambling bores. Marion the Bitch once detained me for half an hour about how she won two hundred dollars at the poker machine in just ten minutes. Pet bores top the list for me. I wondered how

McColl would feel about himself if he substituted cats for horses in that conversation.

Steaks were served by a white-haired older man in a cowboy shirt and jeans. He removed Jessica's plate and brought her coffee a moment later. Something happened between McColl and Jessica, some signal. As soon as she sipped her coffee, McColl got down to business.

"Why did you change your mind now, Rollie? Why did you decide to join us?"

"I haven't." I let that sit for a moment and watched what went on between them. Jessica was not surprised. McColl did not like it that she was letting him know it. I went on. "First I would need to know what I was joining. And I'm still a Marine. I'd have to deal with that. And then there's the Treasury agent."

Jessica said, "Is that all?"

"A percentage of the money. A finder's fee."

"How much?" A hard edge took over McColl's voice. He thought this was going to be easy. He must have said as much.

"How much were you paying Shannon?"

"Shannon was to be paid ten thousand dollars if she got you to lead us to the money," McColl said.

"And I suppose you didn't have to pay Blondie any extra to kill her. He'd pay you for the chance. Quite a savings. I'll need five percent, plus Shannon's take."

McColl squinted at me, then slowly widened his eyes, an expression he had practiced. His hands rested on either side of his plate. Maybe he wanted to kill me right there. Or have me killed. I didn't think he was the man for the job.

Jessica said, "I was under the impression you wanted to join us, Rollie. Is that incorrect?"

"As I said, I don't know what I'd be joining."

"You put us in a difficult position. We can hardly be expected to tell you everything about what we represent if you make no clear offer in return."

"Put you in a difficult position? That's a good one. I get thrown into this situation I know nothing about. You kill my father, sew a transmitter in my back, follow me around the southwest while I'm trying to find the money for you, ask me to join up, and then won't tell me what it is I'd be joining. I'll leave right now and there's not a damn thing you can do about it. You can't torture me because you can't risk killing me. And I couldn't describe the place to you anyway. I'll have to take you there—when the time comes. If it comes. I told you what I need and none of it is unreasonable. Now if you want to negotiate the amounts or discuss how to take care of my issues, I'm listening. If not, give me one of those jeeps you can trace. I'll take it now and lose it later, just like last time."

I returned my attention to the steak so they could send their messages to each other via nods and winks. And, suddenly, I was hungry.

Jessica spoke: "Maybe the general . . ." I looked up in time to see McColl give her an odd look that made her change course. "Treasury Agent Shaw and Colonel Gladden and the MPs have traveled to Tucson. We wonder what the reason is for that. Would you know?"

"I told them to."

"I'm having a hard time trusting you, Rollie." Mc-Coll thought he found the crux of the matter. I was relieved that the meal and the presence of his wife had not sped up his mind.

"If you have trust issues, work them out elsewhere. I keep telling you the truth, which is more than I can say for you."

McColl was flummoxed. He knew how to give orders and how to get rid of people who didn't follow them without question. Everything else was beyond him. Jessica stepped in. "The money isn't ours to give. But because of the trouble you've experienced, a small payment could be made. Say fifty thousand dollars. That's part yours and part Shannon's. I think when we've shown you what you have the opportunity to be part of, you'll think less about money. As for dealing with Colonel Gladden and the MPs, I think the role envisioned for you involves staying in the Marines until the end of your current enlistment. Gladden might not believe your story entirely, but he has superior officers whom he must obey. And he will. They are with us. You might have to spend a little time in the brig, but no formal charges will be filed and you'll be released. We're sure of that. As for the Treasury, I wish you hadn't told the agent that you found the money. You'll just have to convince him you were wrong. The Marines will want you back and that will end your involvement as far as the Treasury is concerned."

I know McColl couldn't have worked all that out, so Jessica was the brains. It all fit nicely: easy promises for a dead man. I told her I wanted a hundred thousand dollars, and we settled on seventy-five thousand. Jessica did the agreeing and made it look as if she were asking for McColl's approval. When we finished that part, she reminded him it was time to give me the grand tour of the place and to explain the mission.

Blondie and Toothless leaned back against the corral when we came out of the house: rustlers in fatigues. They tensed up and scrutinized us, wondering if they could kill me now or if they would have to wait. Their disappointment only brought a shrug. They'd still be hungry tomorrow. I looked back and saw Jessica framed in the doorway.

McColl showed me the new stable and introduced me to the three horses they currently owned. "Shame we won't have time. Blue here is a great ride." Beyond the stable was a warehouse with a satellite dish on the roof. On the way there he started his story. "Some forward-looking officers in the Army, Marines, and Air Force got together during the early days of Operation Iraqi Freedom. It was clear that politics would trump good sense. It was clear that our country would gain very little from this massive effort. The Iraqis had problems we could not solve and the cost of trying was going to be prohibitive. Also, it was extremely doubtful that they would ever be reliable allies for us. We could never depend on their oil. And we would never be repaid for liberating them from the tyrant. We saw that it would take years for the worst of the fighting to end. The political bickering would continue far into the future. But eventually, the U.S. would draw down the combat troops, leaving only a support force. At that point, Iraq would be up for grabs. We don't want to let it fall to our enemies, or another tyrant."

"You're planning on taking over Iraq?"

He hit some numbers on a keypad and the door clicked open. I followed him inside. At this point I was expecting tanks and Stinger missiles, but the big main section was almost vacant: two forklifts, four stacks of pallets about eight feet high, and three jeeps. A small living room section was set up against a wall about midway across the space with two couches and a large TV and a refrigerator.

"Iraq is a made-up country. Made up after World War One. We don't see any need to continue that construct. It would take another dictator, a brutal dictator, to keep it going. Iraq is a ninety-year blip on history's radar, a failed experiment. One area in particular is eager to separate from the rest of the country: the northern provinces where the people are Kurdish. They were brutalized into submission under Saddam and have little loyalty to the larger entity. And they have the oil fields to be self-supporting. They can pump two hundred fifty thousand barrels a day easily and we think there's plenty more. We believe that with a little help, this area can achieve independence and become a useful ally to the United States." His stride lengthened and his chest puffed out as he talked about it. He needed this moment. Probably the long wait was getting to him. Killing Dan and chasing me made him itch for more action. He wanted his role acknowledged.

The far end of the warehouse was closed off. McColl tapped in some more numbers and we entered a large room with five computer screens on desks set around the perimeter. A huge map of Iraq hung across the back wall with an outline of the targeted provinces: Dahuk, Ninawa, Arbil, Kirkuk, As Sulaymaniyah, Diyala. On a table in the middle was a relief diorama of the territories McColl and the farseeing men dreamed of conquering.

Two technicians worked at computers. McColl stood behind one of them, a heavy man at least fifty years old. "Where's Gladden tonight?"

The technician brought up a map and zoomed in on a blinking spot. "It's a Best Western motel in Tucson," he said.

"And Agent Shaw?"

The technician went through the same routine. He smiled when he said, "He's at a Best Western just three miles from Colonel Gladden."

"This is just one of my western command centers. We have access to every database, every database in existence. Here . . ." McColl went to the computer terminal in the middle, the one with the largest screen. He stood over the keyboard, typed a little, and my military records came up. My status was listed as "Temporary assignment, liaison Treasury Department."

"If I want to, I can make changes," McColl said.

"Can you make me a colonel?"

He logged out and moved to the diorama. "We knew we would need seed money, and the funds that Saddam had stolen fit our needs perfectly. We arranged a shipment and storage method that would last until our moment came. Our group is ready. The time is fast approaching for action. That's why we started to retrieve the money."

"Twenty-five million won't go very far."

"You're right." His chest was heaving with pride now and his blue eyes were twinkling. I was afraid he was going to burst into song. "We have five more stashes just like it around the country. And we have other resources. And immediately upon taking over we will be repaid out of oil revenues. We've been planning this for years."

"How will you transport the oil?"

"Pipeline. There's one through Turkey—"

"They won't like a Kurdish country on their border."

"—and one through Syria."

I was elated by the insanity of it all. And the stupidity. The marvels Dan would have worked with this setup danced across the screens. They had missed their big chance when they killed him. In the field of divide and conquer, misappropriation of precious resources, and criminal land grabs, Dan was a rare and special natural resource, worth much more than twenty-five million to them. And I doubt he would have needed that much to have gained the entire region and left the rest of the country thanking him, at least for a little while. The Republic of Danistan. Too bad.

I reached into my back pocket and retrieved a scrap of paper and handed it to McColl. He read the numbers on it. "Coordinates?"

"Yes."

McColl read the note to himself, then read it again out loud: *"You thought you could skip out on me. But now I have ditched you for a long time to come."*

"It's my father's way of saying he left me money." I had written it last night.

"Where did you find it?"

"I went back to the river where the houseboat was. I hadn't seen him much the last few years. Figured that was one place I knew he had been. If there was going to be a clue, that would be a good place to look. He had buried the note in the sand against the rock wall. Marked the spot with a circle on the rocks. It was something he showed me when I was a kid. I looked on a map. The coordinates are for a cave he used to take me to. He liked to explore caves."

McColl and I stared at each other for a long

moment. I could see him trying to decide what to say. This was taking too long. All that was important was that he bought the story.

I said, "What role do you see for me?"

"I'm sorry we got off on the wrong foot, Lieutenant. You're just the kind of man we have been looking for. With your gift for languages and ability to go undercover, we see you transferred to Iraq and stationed near Kirkuk. From there, you'll be able to operate in advance of the event. We have allies there but it would be a big help to know which are most trustworthy. We've been aware of you for some time, Lieutenant. The undercover mission in Afghanistan was a test and you passed. You're in the right place now."

McColl didn't come out and claim Captain Ballard was part of his group and I couldn't imagine he was. If that mission was a test, it had to be in the sense that someone in the group became aware of it and kept an eye on it for recruiting purposes.

I did not like the notion of secret tests. I liked having the option to decide to fail. Failure was not an option for this bunch; it was destiny.

30.

Traffic—no, not traffic. Traffic moves. Eight lanes of cars, trucks and tuk-tuks and motor bikes, engines running, drivers sweating, swearing, singing along to the radio, talking on cell phones, shrugging shoulders, shaking heads, edging each other out for a five-foot advantage. Kabul. Not a war zone but an occupied city. It was easier to walk to the NATO headquarters than to ride. But when I got there, I realized I did not want to go inside. I didn't want to change out of my Afghan identity or explain myself to the guards. Distrust swirled in front of me like a wraith. I walked close to the barriers and watched the soldiers watching me suspiciously, and as I prepared my explanations of why I should be admitted, I kept being delayed by the thought that I suspected them, too. My instinct was to stride forward and toy with their paranoia, then vaporize it, but the closer I got, the slower I went. Like forces repel; my paranoia met theirs, and the force field became impenetrable.

I retreated to a shop and bought a phone and called Major Jenkins. He came to the shop and I made him wait while I watched for followers, his or mine. Every place I thought of where we could meet was either too public or too private until I remembered the one place where no one paid any attention to the surrounding crowd.

The Soviet Cultural Center looked like it should: a bombed-out shell that resembled what a '70s-era Phoenix apartment complex would look like if gangs had Stinger missiles. Afghan culture had taken over; the chefs were tasting their own creation: opium. Enough interior walls remained to give the place the feel of a maze, a sort of cherry of confusion on top of the despair sucked up in blue smoke. I stared at Jenkins outside the remnants of the fence long enough for him to finally recognize me, then let him follow me inside. In the land of a zillion rugs, almost everyone sat on the bumpy dirt floor. If they noticed us, we were only a distraction from the thin, ungraspable wisps that always vanished too soon, like satisfaction. We made our way to the eastern section, where the morning light came in through the windows and shell holes, driving the inhabitants away.

Jenkins was not as uncomfortable as I was hoping he would be.

"Captain Ballard is dead," I said. If it bothered him, he hid it well. He listened patiently for the rest. I told him some of what I knew and that I had decided to carry on the mission. I expected a reprimand. Part of me even wanted it.

"Have you met the sellers?"

"No." I liked Jenkins, but everyone's first thought is how to survive. Maybe he knew Junior, too. Maybe he knew the general.

"The deal is set for the day after tomorrow, fifteen hundred hours, outside of Jalalabad. Get me a GPS for my truck. You can station people in the hills with cameras. And you can block the road back. Pick them up."

"I can get you the money in a few hours and the GPS. But to get the support, we'll have to go upstairs. I'll try for choppers after you give the signal that the deal is done."

"Who is upstairs?"

"Army CID."

My heart sank. Army CID might be good at arresting soldiers who get drunk and out of line, or go AWOL, or even those who get trigger-happy, but keeping secrets was not something they knew about. They knew about paperwork and procedure. And I knew there was no way around this. Jenkins had spoken it, so it was going to happen. "I won't meet with them." It was the most I could hope for.

"They won't come here anyway," Jenkins said.

"They wouldn't be allowed in."

The next afternoon, Jenkins drove his jeep past the back side of NATO headquarters and I jumped in. The road was clear and we were on the outskirts of town in twenty minutes. He handed me a thick envelope of money. I counted out ninety thousand dollars.

"We'll collect the difference afterward," he said. "You might have contingencies. When the transaction is complete, you signal the spotters by giving a thumbs-up to the sellers."

"Will there be spotters?"

"We got the okay."

"Good, but no thumbs-up. These guys are not selling to a Marine, they're selling to an Afghan. If the spotters can see my thumb, they can see that the transaction has gone down."

"Calm down."

"Ballard was calm. I didn't see it happen, but I'm pretty sure the people I'm doing business with killed him. They'll be standing behind me. The people standing in front of me are U.S. military traitors. I'm gonna take a wild guess that they might consider just ripping me off and leaving my body in the road. I'm the meat in the sandwich. Now I've got to rely on the timing and the subtlety of CID. Are you going to be there?"

His mouth turned down and he looked all around, everywhere but at me, before he answered. "I'm a desk man. I have other operations I'm running. We didn't start out to . . . This wasn't the mission." He was ashamed because he knew how asinine he sounded.

This was all bad. If CID allowed the knowledge that I was a Marine in Afghan clothing to leak, the sellers would kill me, or Nawaz and Abed would. If CID did not know I was a Marine, then I was just an Afghan trying to steal rifles from the U.S. and they could shoot me. I realized that I preferred CID did not know my real identity. I believed more in their desire to obey the rules than in their ability to keep a secret; if I surrendered, there was a good chance they would rather arrest me than kill me. It's how they thought.

Jenkins reviewed the timing and location with great precision, trying in his bureaucratic way to reassure me. I pretended he had succeeded, shook his hand, and told him to pull over, and I hopped out of the jeep. I should have just disappeared right then.

31.

Some knockers on Mrs. Colonel, huh? C'mon, admit it, you'd love to get hold of them. We all would. He had to get her out of the military. It was just a matter of time before a senior officer claimed her, and McColl realized he was too ambitious to fight for her." Blondie filled his mouth with eggs as he spoke. We sat in the dining room, having a last meal before heading out to not find the money. Unlike that moment on the base in Jalalabad, I was exhilarated at the prospect of taking this mission to the next level. If help had come, I would have ignored it.

"She's not my type," I said.

"Like you'd turndown," said Toothless, mushing it all together.

"Too expensive."

"Said the man with twenty-five million dollars," said Blondie. The shooter from Camp Pendleton came in with his partner, the tall guy. Their names were Stallworth and

Pitt. They grunted their greetings and helped themselves to the food.

"Money's useless if you don't know what to do with it," I said. "That's why you guys are the right men for this job."

"Whaddya mean?" Toothless put down his fork and tilted his head like a little kid.

"If you were going to steal some of the money, you'd only take a little bit. That wouldn't make you any more honest or loyal than someone who took it all. It's just that twenty-five million is too much for you." It's very hard for someone with no imagination to imagine what that means. For Toothless, it meant I was talking about a dark place at the edge of the earth. He didn't want to go there.

"Whamakesyou think I'mstealing anything?"

"Everyone thinks of it. You have to. Just like what Blondie said about the colonel's woman. I didn't say you were going to steal. Only that you had thought of it. And when you did, you wondered, why not take a little bit? And you did that because you can't think about what you would do if you had it all."

I knew his next line: "I cantoo."

"He'd get a solid gold tooth," said Blondie.

"Shut up."

Pitt said, "Twenty-five million lasts a long time when all you like is fifty-dollar whores and Budweiser."

I asked, "What would you do with it?"

"Yeah, after yagave m'whores twennydollars for seconds," said Toothless. He opened his mouth and showed off his gap to mark his wit. Blondie was staring at me. He wanted his turn.

"Whores and booze. None of us wants the money because it scares us. No one thinking he could open a bar on the beach in Australia? Stake himself to NAS-CAR? Stallworth could buy his own chopper and start a search-and-rescue company."

"I'm not gonna be needing a job anytime soon," Stallworth said. He also deserved to have no teeth.

I looked at Blondie. "What would you do with the money?"

"Money runs out," he said. "You have to get something that keeps the money flowing."

"Bonds?"

"Fear and respect. With twenty-five million, you're a general, you give the orders. I'd do as I pleased and use the money to make people put up with it. Then it would be easy to always get more." He looked around the table from face to face to let each of us know that he was ready to start, money or not, handing out the fear and demanding the respect.

"So Blondie is the only one of us interested in taking all the money for himself?"

"I didn't say that."

"Maybe we'll all be working for him."

"He's alreadygotall the knives hewants," said Tooth-less. The others chuckled to duck away from Blondie's anger. The cook with the white hair came in and started clearing plates.

"I only brought it up because I haven't counted the money or even seen it so I don't know how much there is to start," I said.

Blondie got up. He came behind me and leaned close with both hands on my shoulders. He said, loud enough for everyone to hear: "I hope there's no money." We all knew what he meant. As he started to leave, McColl came in.

"The equipment has arrived. On board in fifteen." I downed the rest of my coffee and got up with the rest of the boys. The equipment amounted to hard hats with LED lights attached, ropes, and APRS walkie-talkies, which I hoped wouldn't work too well under-ground. We were going spelunking in southern Arizona to find the money.

We took two AH-1 Cobra helicopters. Why we needed attack helicopters remained a mystery. Jessica flew one bird, and I rode with Pitt, Toothless, and Stallworth in the other. I could tell because of the way they were quiet and avoided looking at each other that they were thinking about the money. Our bird flew ahead and circled the spot a few times to check for an ambush. The coordinates took us east of Tucson and south of I-10. Pitt hovered over the spot while we all tried to see something meaningful on the ground, but there was no big pile of money and no cave entrance. After circling for a while, Pitt found a flat spit of land between a steep corrugated incline that led to a plateau and gentler-looking, sloping hills on our right.

Dan's hideout was on a boat; mine was in a cave. I was ten years old when Johnny Tully, the brother of one of Dan's girlfriends, asked me if I wanted to come along for a ride to find buried treasure. He was just out of juvie home, where he had come across a map, "a genuine treasure map." The treasure, in that case, being fifty kilos of Colombian marijuana. I never knew what he was hopped up on. He could barely sit still in the driver's seat. The map was my domain. Of course, it was a complete fake. There was no buried dope, but I found a cave and crawled in with a flashlight. Johnny was too scared to follow me, and after all the hiking he was soaked in sweat and his eyes were even scarier than when we started out: an American eagle who blinked a lot. I waited until he stopped yelling at me to come out because I had the wrong cave. I could peek out and see him turning the map around in his shaking hands. It wasn't long before he crumpled the map and sank to the ground and lay there shivering, so I crawled out and gave him some water. It was almost dark when he woke up, but we found our way back to the truck, and he managed to drive home after a quick stop at McDonald's. Dan and his girlfriend made a big fuss about me and acted as if they had actually noticed I was gone. They damned Johnny and took away his truck for a week, even though I swore we had been at the movies and stayed to see a couple of different pictures without paying extra. Johnny got sent to prison almost as soon as he turned eighteen, armed robbery and assault, and I never heard of him getting out. I kept the map.

The cave became my refuge. After my first deployment in Afghanistan, and after Officer Candidate School, I began prepping the cave whenever I had leave. When Gladden gave me a hard time about going to Arizona, I was at the cave, preparing a place to hide out if I decided to go permanently AWOL. I never thought I'd be leading anyone here, but it was the spot that would give me the greatest advantage.

The cave had two entrances that I knew of. I led the group around, missing the smaller entrance a few times to increase their eagerness and impatience. The naked sun bothered McColl. "Are we getting close?"

"I think so."

"That's not good enough."

"They don't make Geiger counters for money, Colonel," I said. Then, to soften it, "It's just been a really long time since I was here."

The entrance required us to crawl in one at a time. McColl and Jessica, who would be waiting outside, would have no good spot to rest there while they waited for us. They would guard it like a mouse hole.

GPS doesn't work in caves, but it was not clear that McColl understood that. He held on to his little tracker as if it were going to save him. Toothless squeezed inside first. I fed him the ropes and extra lamps, then followed him. Blondie, Pitt, and Stallworth came inside next. I warned them all again that I had not been there since I was a little kid so I didn't know my way around too well.

We were in a narrow, rocky corridor about ten yards long. Pitt, Stallworth, and Toothless toted the ropes.

"It's been a long time," I said.

"You go first. Slowly," said Blondie. I crawled forward until the ceiling rose and soon after that the walls widened and we faced a huge room with a soaring ceiling and a floor of sharp-edged boulders sloping downward. We stopped, shined our flashes all around. Blondie gave me the signal to head forward. I moved my light from side to side, making sure to aim toward the walls every so often. The roof had no stalactites in here, just boulders that looked like they might fall out at any moment.

We reached a spot where the floor sloped away more sharply. The lights would not shine far enough for us to see anything. It felt like the edge of the world. I looked back at Blondie for instructions. "I think there's a shaft ahead. There might be a way around it. I'm not sure. Want me to check it out?"

"Slowly."

I edged forward, bracing myself and shining my light back and forth. I slipped, on purpose, but quickly caught myself and moved along. Ahead, I could see pale stalactites hanging like giant shark teeth. The rocks ended in a cliff edge and I peered down carefully and shined the light. The drop was only about thirty feet to a flat surface about twenty feet wide and then a pool of dark water: a beach with no sun. I signaled the others to come forward. We all shined our lights to suss out the task. The water seemed to flow off to a passage on the right. Blondie yelled, "There! Go back!" He shined his light on a spot against the left wall that I had just passed over. Five lights swept back and forth and settled on a dusty backpack tucked in a nook in the side wall. Right where I had left it two days before.

We pounded in our pitons and rigged our ropes. Blondie sent Toothless down first, then Pitt, then me. We stood around the backpack as if it were a magic lantern. Blondie reached out for it, testing the weight with a skeptical look. He found a hundred thousand dollars inside. I watched the others while he counted it.

"What the hell is this?"

"Knowing my father, I'd say it's there so I'll know to keep looking. Or maybe he spent the rest. I don't know."

Blondie put the walkie-talkie to his mouth and spoke: "Found a pack with one hundred thousand in it. Come in. . . ." But he received only static. He tried again. He reattached the walkie-talkie to his belt and shined his light around. "Which way now?"

Three choices presented themselves. To the left, a flat passage with a low ceiling, showing stalagmites and stalactites. To the right of that was a similar passage which, I knew, joined up with the first passage about three hundred yards along. After that, access ended in a sheer cliff. Off to the far right, the stream stretched through beautiful, twisting caverns. I had planted backpacks in all three directions, and weapons, too. I did not care how Blondie divided us up as long as he divided us up. "It could mean go this way. It could be a way of saying the money is not here."

"How could it be that?"

"My father would be prepared for the possibility that I didn't come down here alone."

The others were shining their lights around, hoping to spot another pack of money from where we stood. Blondie studied the walls. The moving lights made the surfaces flare and fade, sucking them into shadows, then spitting them out. "Okay, you two head down this way." He pointed at Toothless and me. "You two take the passage next to us," he said to Stallworth and Pitt. "I'll follow the water. It's fourteen twelve now. Meet back here in ninety minutes. And bring along anything you find." He smiled, but his eyes were mean and dark and they settled on me.

The blackness was complete, vacuuming up our lights and swallowing them so it felt as if we were not really moving forward. We caught snatches of what the cave looked like, strobed moments, none of the big illuminated glories of *National Geographic*. I stayed yards away from Toothless and slightly in front to let him keep an eye on me. It took him a while to notice the next backpack. He jerked his light away from the pack and took a few more steps while he decided how to get rid of me. I turned to him. "You okay?"

"Creepy in here. Are yasureya know the wayback?"

"Follow the left wall. When it curves right, stay with

it. You'll see the water." I shined the light along the left wall, then over to him. He moved farther from the backpack. "Sort of odd, isn't it? All that money just sitting in here, waiting to be picked up? It might have gone undiscovered. What a waste. I still can't understand why my father didn't just spend it."

"You gonnastart thatshit again?"

"Admit you're thinking about it. Admit it and I'll shut up."

"Okay. I admit it. I thinkabout having somemoney." He sounded humiliated by the admission, like a twelve-year-old acknowledging to his parents that he thinks about girls.

"We could split what we find."

"You'renuts."

"You mean you won't split with me? You want it all?"

"I'm notstealing anything, so shut thefuckup."

"What about this? You were planning on stealing this." I had worked my way over to the backpack. I hefted it up and held it out for him to savor. "If you won't take it, I will." And I ran ahead, around a spot where the wall jutted out forming a partition. I took my hat off and placed it on a rock so the light would shine in his eyes when he came around the bend. I crossed to the spot where I had left a Ranger combat knife and a 9 millimeter Browning automatic. The pistol went into my belt. The knife stayed in my hand.

First came the two shafts of light from his helmet

and his handheld lamp. His other hand held his pistol. The light in his eyes bothered him, but he turned away from it too slowly. I had the knife deep in his back before he saw me. I ground it in to make sure. The body dropped and rolled to a flat spot. The beams from the lamps crisscrossed like kliegs against the starless dark.

I went to the body and tore off his shirt. The tracker was sewn behind his right shoulder in the same spot they had put mine. There was no need to be gentle in cutting it out. I extinguished his lights but left the body where it was.

I followed the right-hand wall toward the merge with the next cavern, where Pitt and Stallworth were exploring. Their route was the most difficult and I was certain they had not come as far as I had. I tucked the backpack Toothless had found against the wall as added bait, then went back up the center path to meet up with them.

I wagged my light and called, "There you are. C'mon . . ." They moved slowly toward me. "I think I know where the money is. C'mon."

"Where's Tony?" Apparently, Toothless had another name.

"He went back to get Blondie. The money's this way. Have you found any?"

"Did you?" Stallworth asked.

"One pack," I said. "Toothless took it back with him." They looked at each other. "Well, he wasn't gonna leave it with me. Let's go." I started away. They hesitated. "If you don't want to, then just go back to the rendezvous. I'll find it myself."

Pitt said, "How do you suddenly know where it is?"

"I remembered. I saw a spot that I remembered and then it clicked in. He used to take me to a cavern down that way. The backpacks are marking the way. Suit yourself, guys. I'm going."

We found the pack I had tossed and that bucked them up. Stallworth got to carry it, and Pitt and I made jokes about this being the most money he ever touched and the heaviest load. By the time we reached the next cliff, they were well turned around. We shined our lights into the pit and at the walls.

"I'm sure this is it," I said.

Pitt saw the rope ladder first; I had set it up on one of my visits during leave. From the bottom of that drop, a winding path led back up to the water source that Blondie was following. We waved our lights around some more and Stallworth spotted another backpack at the bottom. "That's mine. I saw it first," he said. Pitt shined the light in Stallworth's face. "You best watch yourself, or you won't be having anything."

"Who goes down first?"

They decided Pitt would go first and I would follow and then Stallworth. I fell the last few feet and pretended that my ankle had twisted. While they attacked the backpack, I hopped around. When they looked back at me, my gun was aimed at them. "First, Pitt, you drop your weapon on the floor."

"Hey, now," said Pitt. "You can share the money."

"Do it. Do it now," I said.

Pitt started to pull his weapon and Stallworth made a move at the same time. I shot between them and they froze. The noise sounded more like a cannon than a gunshot. "I'll get you both before you draw. Now." Pitt tossed his gun on the ground. "Stallworth . . ." He did the same. "Now turn off the lights on your hats and toss them over there. Now." They looked at each other before complying. I herded them toward the rope and I moved in the opposite direction, toward the passage that wound toward the water. Holding the gun on them, I smashed their flashlights with my foot and did the same to the lights on their hats. The only light was from my hat. "Both of you lie down on your bellies."

"What the hell are you planning, man?" Stallworth wanted to know.

"Would you rather I tied you up, drugged you, then beat the shit out of you for days until you died?"

"Oh, man, how were we gonna get him to tell us anything? C'mon," said Pitt.

"Thank you. Get down on your belly while I think about that." They did as they were told. I picked up their guns and the backpack of money. "Stay there. This is going to take me a few minutes." I backed up into the passage, keeping a light on them until I reached the first turn. I took a quick look at what lay ahead of me, then doused my lights and touched the wall and felt my way a few more yards. I waited. Both men yelled,

"Hey." The blackness was complete, a blanket as thick as the universe. I held on to my lamp tightly, then forced myself to relax my grip, afraid I was going to break the thing. Our eyes had been gouged out. Pitt and Stallworth argued in rapidly weakening voices about whether to try to follow me or to climb the ladder and try to retrace their path. Soon, even two thugs as dense as they were would be wondering how long eternity lasted.

The longest I had ever been able to handle the cave in complete blackout was seventeen minutes, which felt like an hour. And I had the benefit of knowing I could end it.

I followed carefully along another bend, then put on my hat lamp and crawled through a tributary, upward, until it opened to the next cavern. Pitt and Stallworth would lose what minds they had long before they fell into a hole or off a cliff. I did not care.

32.

With Blondie, there would be no whining or questions. At each bend, each turn, descent, or climb, I turned off my lamps and listened and watched for lights. I reached a long bore-hole that connected to the stream, opening into a large cavern. I knew the borehole was straight and had no other tunnels intersecting it, so I could make good time, even in the dark. But the lack of turns meant that my light would be noticed far ahead every time I turned it on.

Blondie must have been doing the same thing. Out of the black and quiet, he said, "Just come out. I've found another backpack of money."

It sounded like he was in the cavern. "How much have you found?"

"Fifty grand in the one I just found. How about yours?"

"Haven't counted it," I said. "It isn't mine." Neither of us had to shout. The sound and the smell of the water were all I could sense in the dark. I pulled my gun and crouched. I placed my lamp about two feet to my right and tried to aim it toward his voice.

"I wonder where the rest is." He said it as if he were looking for the potato chips.

"I know where it is."

"Are the others dead?"

"Not yet," I said. "How do we split the money?" I sounded less than halfhearted, not even able to make a facetious offer.

"It's not about the money between us, is it, pal?"

"McColl won't be happy about finding you with no money and no me."

"Too bad for McColl then. There's bigger fish than him running the show. They'll blame him, not me. It was his dumb plan to put the money in the ground."

I could hear him moving slowly to my right. If he went far enough, he would have an open shot at me. I had no shelter. I reached down and flicked on the lamp and jerked away from it immediately. He shot and the lamp went out. I shot. He yelled, "Damn it!" And I heard a soft splash, as if he had dropped the gun into the water. I moved like a blind man, arms out front, across to the other side of the borehole. When my hand jammed against the opposite wall, I flattened myself to the ground, held my breath, and listened: the water was stirring. Was he looking for the gun? I had never tested the depth of the water. I rolled toward the center and sprayed four shots along the waterline. I rolled back to the wall. If my shots hit, Blondie wasn't telling me.

If time, space, and light define each other, when you take one away, what happens to the others? I did not know if time was moving and I struggled to maintain a sense of where I was. My breath was too loud, echoing through the cavern like some insane yodel. My neck creaked, imitating a breaking branch, but brought out no fluttering bats. I waited.

Too long.

The spotlight hit my eyes and Blondie was just two feet away on my left side. The knife exploded out of the light. I rolled to shoot, but he kicked my forearm with his boot and my gun skittered into the cavern and toward the water. He came down with the knife. I rolled far enough to make him miss and I kipped up to my feet. His light faced the wall, bouncing off and showing the water, a pond still as ice, surrounded by thick, pale stalagmites.

I pulled my knife and faced Blondie. He held up his knife. "It's a Gerber Mark Two. You've seen 'em. You'll see this one up close, too. You might even taste it. I like to cut out tongues."

He did not need to show off the knife to convince me he knew how to handle a blade. Under normal circumstances, his remark would have made me stick my tongue out, but I didn't want Blondie to notice how dry it was.

He moved closer to me. I backed up toward the water and went around a stalagmite. Its long shadow ran on behind me like a pipe into the water, where it faded to black. "Hiding? I see you," Blondie said, still sounding relaxed. He strolled forward. When he got close enough to touch the stalagmite, he reached up and turned on his hat lamp. Blinded, I jumped back. His blade nicked my chin. He came forward in one hop and made a large sweeping try across my body. His momentum carried him to his left, leaving an opening. But if I had attacked the opening, he would have spun and caught my arm. "You gotta try, pal. You can't kill me by hoping. Say aah." He came forward and I backed up over a rocky patch. When he reached the uneven rocks, I stopped and slashed at him a few times. He stumbled but righted himself quickly. I stabbed at his gut. He cut my forearm and the blood ran down to my hand, making the knife slippery. I shifted it to the other hand. And in that instant, I spun and kicked him in the gut. He doubled over. I kicked again, getting him in the jaw. His helmet flew off and the light danced across the water like a romantic trail of moonlight over a summer lake. Time to run.

Blondie had to keep his light on and that was all I needed because I knew exactly where I was going. To the right of the pond, a narrow opening stayed narrow through a dozen, exactly a dozen, twists and turns. I counted carefully. At the fourth turn, the ceiling hung low and I had to duck. At the end, the path widened and a column stood about twenty feet high, giving the circular room the feel of a Greek rotunda. To the immediate left was a small room. This is where I stored my gear.

"Ready or not, here I come . . ." The faint reflection of his lamp bounced off the wall of the last turn. The light spread as he moved forward. It disappeared while he waited and listened. This wait seemed brief. But I noticed that my shirt felt sticky. I put my fingers on it. Then found the gash in the shirt and the gash in my chest beneath the shirt. I wiped the blood from my right hand onto my jeans and grabbed a Colt revolver. In my left hand, I held a high-powered LED flashlight that throws out more than seven hundred lumens. Blondie's light came on again and he moved forward into the rotunda. "Come out, come out, wherever you are . . ." As he turned, his light moved around the perimeter of the chamber. He never saw me. My beam blinded him. He groaned and moved back. I shot his hand. The knife flew out with pieces of flesh. One hand and one stump jerked to protect his eyes.

"Now," I said. "Back up."

"Turn that off."

I admired the way he handled the pain. The light bothered him more than the loss of fingers. I held the beam against his face and stepped in to knock the helmet off his head again. "Back up."

He backed up three steps, then dived at me. I side-stepped easily and he crashed to the rocky ground, his groan echoing around the chamber. I kept the light on him. He stayed on his knees, one hand down, the injured hand pulled in to his chest, with his head hanging down. I could tell he expected me to kick him. But I did not kick him.

"Get up."

He tried to grab my legs, but it was a blind gesture. He pushed himself up. "What do you want, pal? You want the money? I told you I don't care. Let's have a straight go of it, though. One-handed. I don't mind. Put down your gun and your damned light. Have some pride, pal."

This was too messy to take any pride, and too satisfying. My complete dedication to revenge was not a revelation. The absolute lack of mercy did not cause me any guilt and would not later, but I was sure pride wasn't going to fill the vacuum.

"Get up. Get up and face me." He did. Even in his posture of pain, he was getting ready for the fight. I used the light to maneuver him where I wanted him. "Back up, three steps."

He held his damaged hand in front of his eyes as he staggered backward.

"Stop, look behind you. Look!"

He turned and I moved the beam so he could get a glimpse of the pit. I had never seen the bottom, wasn't sure it had one. He looked back to me and I got what I wanted at last: his expression of utter terror.

"Your choice," I said.

He barely took a breath before lunging at me. I emptied the Colt into his chest.

33.

I imitated Toothless mumbling into the walkie-talkie. "Fund the mney . . . prblems. Ned your help . . ."

McColl came crackling back. "Roger. Got you. We'll be there."

I muttered something unintelligible and slumped down in the shade of a boulder. The sun was calling me to lie down and relax. The wound on my forearm had dried, but the slash across my midsection was still oozing blood. I let the M40 rifle from my stash and the backpack of money slip from my hands. The bottle of water was too small. The sun was too exhausting. Hibernation obsessed me, and I knew just the cave for it. But the entrance kept moving away and the sun dogged me the way my light followed Blondie. The walkie-talkie had irritating habits: "Come in, come in, we're nearby. Can't spot you."

They were thirty feet below me, just visible beyond a crease. I must have been sleeping for half an hour. I tossed the transmitter I had retrieved from Toothless away from the cave mouth, then retreated inside. Mc-Coll directed Jessica to a ledge where she could get a good view and cover McColl as he worked his way up, obeying his trusty GPS. In his other hand, he held a Beretta M9. He stopped when the GPS told him he had reached the transmitter. He was confused.

I spoke into the walkie-talkie: "Put your gun down, Colonel, or I'll shoot Jessica. And I won't miss."

He couldn't find me in his GPS or the walkie-talkie, so he looked down toward Jessica. She was scouring the hillside near my hiding spot. I fired at her feet. She dropped, rolled, and fired four shots in my general direction. "I still have her in my sight, Colonel. Both of you throw down your weapons."

McColl spoke into the walkie-talkie: "Stay calm, Lieutenant. I don't know what happened in there. Have you found the money?"

"First the weapons, Colonel." I did not need to shout to be heard. He spun, but I was still in the shadow of the cave entrance. I fired between his legs and he dropped his gun. "Now Jessica," I said.

McColl yelled down and she followed orders.

"Walk up here." I stopped her about halfway up, far enough from her rifle. I stepped forward. The sun felt so close I thought I could blow out its fire. "Your men are dead, Colonel. You won't be getting any help." I paused to let that sink in. "Tell me who you're working for. Who runs the operation?"

"We're in this together. You signed on and for the right reasons. This is a great opportunity for you. Stay on course. Complete the mission."

He made a terrible mistake saying "great opportunity." Not only did it sound like he was touting a mattress sale, it reminded me of the wrong turn the world took when this guy lived and Dan died. When Dan sold a job and wanted it to stay sold, the words he would be careful never to mention were great and opportunity. Instead, he would highlight the great opportunities by nakedly trying to disguise them. And after the prospect accepted the job, the deal, the mission, Dan would make sure he believed Dan secretly wanted to weasel him out of it. This colonel ate his own baloney, and it was making me sick.

"I'm very excited to be part of this venture, Colonel. But I noticed in the cave that some of my new partners were not eager to have me join. Before I go forward, I want to make sure I'm wanted. I never want to go where I'm not wanted. Who is the General? Who's in charge? Is it Remington?"

"Stand down, Lieutenant! That's an order!"

I looked to Jessica, but she showed nothing. Sweat dripped into my eyes. My strength was fading. Impatience surged through me like lust. My sense of humor had evaporated.

"Colonel, I lied. I'm really asking because I want to know where to send your remains."

"You're not thinking clearly," he said, and he took

off his sunglasses to give me the eerie stare. "You have nowhere to go except with us. You don't care about the money and we offer you all the things you could never buy anyway. The things you really want."

"Could you give me an example?" He looked at Jessica for support. She shook her head slightly to warn him off. McColl stared at me, hoping I would forget the question. "You mean," I said, "the chance to kill. You think I'm a homicidal maniac like Blondie."

"You need orders, structure . . ." I shot at his feet to shut him up. He went on. "Without me, your career as a Marine is over. Without me, you're all alone."

"You have it backward, Colonel. Without me, you're done. Tell me who you work for. Last chance. Who is the General?"

"You can't kill me." He was matter-of-fact, confident, and wrong. "There are five stashes of money like the one your father stole. And I'm the only one who knows where they all are. You can't kill me."

I looked at Jessica. "Is that true? The first part about being the only one who knows where the rest of the money is, not the part about me not being able to kill him."

"He's the only one who knows," she said. "Please. Don't kill him. You don't have to." She didn't know me too well.

"Just do as you're told, Lieutenant. Go back to taking orders." I must have looked really shaky because he started to bend down for his gun. I shot him in the groin. He yelped and fell backward, half propped against a boulder. He kept moaning. I distracted him from that pain in his groin by shooting him in the gut. The blue eyes stared at me with real expression for the first time. He was astonished. I went close, bent down, picked up the tracker. Then I put a bullet through his left eye.

Jessica was scrambling down the hill. Too tired to chase, I fired near her and shouted for her to stop. She held her arms up while I trekked down the hill, slipping twice and trying to hide my difficulty in getting up. When I came near, she said, "Don't shoot me."

"Why?"

"Because I'm with the Treasury Department."

I didn't have the strength to chase her and I didn't want to shoot her. "Are you hungry?"

"Yes."

"I'll share my food with you if you stop lying to me."

We shared the energy bars I had brought out of the cave with me. Colonel Logistics had neglected to pack any food for this outing. Maybe he planned to eat the money.

"I'm not a Treasury agent. I don't want to give you the wrong impression," Jessica said, and she sounded like someone asking for a loan that would be paid back in companionship. We sat protected by the cave mouth, though the sun had slid low enough to spread the shade over the mountainside. I offered to move back into the cooler depths, but Jessica was nervous about that; she wanted to make sure Shaw could find us. My only goal was to keep her close until Shaw arrived. Her lies would have to wait for my strength to return before being dissected. "I just saw what was going on and I thought I had to do the right thing."

"So you approached the Treasury, told them about the conspiracy."

"Well, Steve . . ."

"Shaw?"

"Yes. Steve approached me actually. It took me a while to get my head around the idea of informing . . ."

"Must have been tough. Undercover for how long?"

"Three years."

"I've been undercover, but no way I could have lasted three years. It gets tense."

"It does."

"And lonely. Communicating is the worst. That's when you get caught. You must have had to see Shaw in person, given the updates that way. Sneaking out. Bad as it is, it's better than anything electronic. The horses . . . Is that how you did it? Does Shaw ride?"

"I really shouldn't be talking about this," she said. She took a long chug of water. "How did you discover the cave?"

"And most of all, you really need the boost you get from the meeting. At least I did. Because you get lonely, so damn lonely. You really start looking forward to those meetings. Looking forward to seeing Shaw. In this case."

She did not answer, just fixed her eyes on the entrance and clutched her satellite phone. Sitting fed my fatigue. If Jessica would have argued or complained, I could have stayed awake. "You and Shaw," I said. "That must have been the engine that kept you going. Not undercover really. Just sneaking around." She walked outside without saying a word.

I moved a little deeper into the cave where I could feel relief from the heat. But I was burning up from something else: if Shaw didn't kill me, I was entering the final turn on this mission. Exhaustion mixed with obsession and I gave in, let myself drift back to the hills outside Jalalabad.

34.

I drove the pickup, one of the rifles beside me, GPS tucked under the dash. Nawaz and Abed led the way in their jeep, off the highway, down a curving slope, through a valley thick with trees, up a winding, crumbling canyon road, and off that road into a hidden dead end boxed by craggy hills of rock with trees and shrubs fighting through to hold it all together. They turned their jeep to face the way out and I did the same with my truck, parking about ten yards from them. The Americans had not arrived yet.

Major Jenkins had given me crisp, newly wrapped hundred-dollar bills. I spent about ten seconds working on my explanation for Nawaz and Abed of how I got hold of new money like that, then went out and bought a truck, sold it across town, bought a second pickup, sold that, and bought a third. That amounted to less than twenty thousand dollars of nice dirty money. I soaked the rest in water and gasoline, wrung it out, and stuffed it in a bag. It was still damp and smelly when we arrived at the spot.

The Americans were late. Nawaz wanted the money. He asked for it back in Jalalabad and I told him I would hand it over at the rendezvous, though I had to count it in front of him on the spot. Now I said I would give it over when the Americans arrived.

"We will leave if you don't trust us," he said while Abed nodded and shrugged behind him.

"You might leave if I do." We all laughed. I sounded so false I was sure I had given myself away, but they were tense, too. Abed kept an automatic in his belt. Nawaz always had knives. The canyon was quiet except for chirping birds, the kind of quiet that usually makes people calm. None of us was calm.

The Humvee raced in and drove a fast circle around us, filling the air with dirt, before pulling to the front of the canyon to block our exit. The Americans popped out before the dust settled and came forward fast with hands extended and smiles flashing. "Howdy, boys, sorry to keep you waiting. Ready to do business?" Junior said it too fast. He was nervous, too. The lieutenant opened the back of the Humvee.

I went to my truck. Junior asked Abed, "Where's he going?" Abed did not answer him. I came out with the bag of money and handed it to Abed.

"The money," he said.

Ten long heavy cardboard boxes were stacked in the rear of the Humvee. Everyone gathered around while I took out the top box. Nawaz handed me a knife to slit it open. Two brand-new-looking M107 .50 caliber rifles. I lifted one out of the foam casing and unwrapped it so I could admire it in front of everyone. "That's it," I said to Abed and Nawaz. Remington and Nance understood.

"Okay, let's pay up and we can be done."

I said in Pashto: "I want to check other boxes before you pay." Nobody liked that. They barked at me, but I could still hear the birds; I wanted to hear the cavalry. Abed yelled at me. I yelled back: "Are you with them?" That steamed him. Nawaz had to try to calm him down while Junior started yelling, "Calm down, calm down. What the fuck is going on?" I agreed to check only one more box. I dumped four boxes on the ground and got Nawaz's knife back to open the fifth. All was okay.

"You got a suspicious friend, Abed buddy."

Abed counted out the money for the Americans while I loaded the boxes into the pickup as slowly as I dared.

Lieutenant Nance said, "What's the story with this money? It's so dirty."

Junior said, "If you don't like dirty money, you shouldn't have joined the Marines." And he thought that was the funniest thing he ever heard. At last he came up for air and said, "Pleasure doing business with you, Abed. You know where to find me." Junior and Nance shook hands with each of us, got into the Humvee, and roared away.

Now I was going to drive away with twenty rifles stolen from the Marines. Abed and Nawaz were joyful, patting me on the back and discussing when we might meet again. I understood their joy at the completion of a perfect caper: guns to fight the invaders, supplied by the invaders, and paid for with the invader's money. They were murderous cutthroats but likeable rascals compared to those Marines.

To Nawaz and Abed, I said: "When will we meet again? Will you honor me with a visit? How can I thank you?" To myself, I was saying: Where will the road-block be set up? How far would I get? Was it worse to be arrested or shot?

They drove off quickly and the shots, two of them, came only a few seconds later. Luckily, Junior was stupid enough to expect me to follow the others. I scrambled up the flaky hillside, not caring about cover or leaving a trail. The top was all I had in mind.

The Humvee came in slowly this time. It stopped next to my pickup long enough for them to consider taking back the rifles. Though I would have loved to get rid of them, they were the only evidence I had of the crime. The money would be easy to hide or ditch. Stupid and greedy, they opened the doors to get out. I fired a few shots close enough to scare them back inside and they tore off without bothering to shoot out my tires.

From the top of the mountain, I had time to test the rifle's sight with a few long-distance shots before the

Humvee came around a bend. I hit two of their tires with my first three shots. When they stopped, I shot out the other tires and went after the gas tank and the radiator.

Leaving the pickup and the rifles, I scrambled down one hillside then another so I picked up the road ahead of them. They were hiding below the road like two dumb muggers waiting for a passing old lady. I came up behind them and jabbed a handgun into Captain Remington's ear, hard, so it hurt.

I spoke English. "Drop your guns and hand me your cell phone." They didn't understand at first what they were in for. I made an ass of myself explaining. "Treason, guys. Life in the penitentiary."

"What're you, some kind of MP? You got nothing on us."

"We have video, we have recordings, we have the evidence." Junior was not half as scared as I wanted him to be, though the lieutenant was trembling.

I called Major Jenkins and explained that he had twenty minutes to deliver the CID. "If I sense any threat to me, these guys die immediately, then I'll go after the rest. You come last." Jenkins started to babble about how they should have been there before, how he had set it all up. I hung up on him.

CID arrived in ten minutes. I was dressed as an Afghan and was aiming a rifle at Americans. Junior said, "We've been tracking him for weeks. He's a traitor. Arrest him."

They told me to put the weapon down and I did, and before they could arrest me I jumped on Junior and started beating him, figuring that would be my only chance. I got hit pretty hard by the CID, but it was worth it. "He was selling guns to Taliban," I yelled as they carted me away. I heard Junior say, "He killed a Marine captain."

Major Jenkins got me released immediately, though I was restricted to Kabul. I shaved and put on my uniform, but I could not blend in. I spent endless hours being interrogated.

"Why did you target these two officers? Who told you to request those particular weapons? What happened between you and Captain Ballard?"

"Nothing."

"He's dead. You were the last person to speak with him. The last American. Captain Remington did not know Captain Ballard. They have no connection. We checked."

"Junior fingered him. He recognized him."

"Captain Remington did not know Captain Ballard. You are the only person who knew that Captain Ballard was posing as an Afghan. You are the only person who could have killed him for that reason."

"I had no reason to kill him."

At last they brought in the expert, the major with the psychology degree. "When you prayed as a Muslim, what did you think about? What did you wish for?"

"A new bicycle."

"I don't believe you." He stared at me. "What are you hiding? Maybe you prayed for a sniper rifle. You're a good marksman. High scores. But you're not a sniper. Do you resent the Marines for not making you a sniper?"

"No."

"What do you resent the Marines for?"

"I don't resent the Marines."

"Then why did you embarrass them?"

Suddenly, the interrogations ended. Major Jenkins came around to visit and bring news. We took a stroll past the presidential palace. Two Army specialists followed us.

"You're going to join a Marine outpost in Nuristan Province," said Jenkins.

"Why is that bad news?"

"They've been released. No charges. The story will be that they were on an intelligence mission, too secret for any details to get in the way. They're being transferred. Captain Remington is going home. I don't know about Nance, but it won't be anywhere as dangerous as where you're going."

"Junior's father intervened?" We had to stop because a motorcade pulled up in front of the palace. No one got out. We turned and walked back. The followers moved across the boulevard. It would have been easy to lose them, but I could not think of a reason to do it.

"No one tells me. The talk isn't going your way."

"Do they believe I killed Captain Ballard?"

"Not at the moment. But the idea will live on. I'm being sent home."

"Congratulations."

"Not in order. Here I run intelligence operations. I deal with men like you and Captain Ballard. There I order fourteen-year-old boys to tie their shoelaces and watch them fondle their zits. You did the right thing and you did it well, but . . . be careful, Lieutenant."

We shook hands. He crossed the boulevard, right toward the followers. They moved aside to let him pass.

35.

The outpost was a line in the sand. As I stood in the trench along the perimeter, I would contemplate whether the line came first: Draw a line, then pick a fight over it; or the fight came first then the line was drawn to give some structure to the fight. We could not have been more accommodating to the enemy if we drew a target. Captain Overton was in charge. He was tired, scared, and endlessly responsible. Only thirty years old, he looked forty-five. Every death killed him a little bit more, but he followed orders, bombarding the enemy with our howitzers, sending out patrols to the clusters of buildings that constituted villages, and seeking out engagement with the enemy. In the few weeks I was at the outpost, I never saw him rest, never saw him give anyone short shrift, never saw him curse out a lying villager. Some of the men understood their commander was a hero; the rest would figure it out someday.

The worst beef the men had with Captain Overton

was about me. The story of me stealing arms and wrecking the careers of two brave Marines had beaten me to that hillside. I was shunned. That was fine. I was eager for the clarity of combat after weeks of intrigue. Camaraderie was not essential. One tough guy handed me a jammed rifle while we were in the trench. I jammed the butt into his groin, which ended that kind of behavior.

Captain Overton asked me if I wanted to address the men. I declined. He said, "It might help." Then I knew he was a true believer in futile gestures, which is what made him the perfect man for the job. It began to dawn on a few of the men that believing I was there as punishment meant it was a place of punishment and since they were there, too . . . It did not make them change their minds about me, but doubt crept in. A sergeant sat down next to me with his dinner and said, "So, what did you do to deserve this, Lieutenant?"

"I requested it," I said. He couldn't curse me out so he walked away.

So many opportunities to kill me by accident passed by that I stopped trying to guess when the mistake would happen. An Afghan National Army sergeant and I were working our way up the back side of a steep hill to get an angle on enemy fighters who were bombarding our patrol as it passed through the valley. Our 120 millimeter mortars were set up on the opposite hillside, but they were having little effect. The sergeant and I moved into position almost level with the enemy, only fifty yards from them, and the trap fell quickly. By the time I spun around, the crossfire was thick. The first mortar hit near us and I was thrown about five feet. My helmet blew away and my radio was crushed. Somehow I held on to my weapon, but it only accentuated the futility of my situation. Instantly, the enemy spotted us and turned their fire our way. I crawled to a spot between two large rocks. One faced the enemy, one faced the Marines, like bookends. The mortars kept coming from the opposing hillside and then they started coming from down below, too. All of it directed at us. Except there was no us anymore. The ANA sergeant was on his back, eyes open. He wasn't bleeding, but it wouldn't have mattered if he were: he would not need the blood anymore.

The enemy slowed down their firing after a few minutes. They didn't have ammunition to waste and must have noticed they weren't being fired on. I turned my back to the Marines so I couldn't see the fire coming in. The mortars and tracers continued and all the fire was friendly. And relentless. I had nowhere to run, nowhere to hide. No one to fire at. No thinking to do. No tricks to play.

I'm often scared. I assume everyone is. It would be inaccurate to say I like it. I don't crave the rush the way some people do. But I do seek fear, test it, tease it. Stuck there between the rocks, something else happened, something I wish I had never experienced. When I'm afraid, I can try to be smart. I can be aggressive or unpredictable. Even reckless or defiant. I can try things that push the fear away, make it secondary.

None of that was possible on that hill with the shells and bullets falling like lethal raindrops, marking a mysterious pattern too quick and dense to comprehend. The betrayal that launched the onslaught wasn't important because it was only the fulfillment of my expectation. This was far worse. I lost hope, so nothing was left to hold my veneer in place. My guts burned with a concoction of helplessness, fear, and rage. The sky was a giant mirror: all I saw was myself, stripped. And it was no consolation that I was the only one seeing it. I had always held a disdain for hope and the people who clung to it. Hope is what Dan used against them, slathering on the false kind, and since no one could tell that from the real thing, therefore it must all be false, I thought. But I learned that hope had one important purpose: it protects us from hell.

There was no decision, none that I am aware of. I was standing, facing the fire, back to the enemy. I remember my hands being clenched. Shells burst around me, though it couldn't have been too many. I walked down the hill, steadily, slowly, oblivious to the shells. The firing stopped. None came from behind me. The enemy must have slipped away. I didn't turn to check on them. If this was bravery, I never want to be brave again. It felt more like surrender.

Captain Overton said, "I'll find out who gave the wrong coordinates. I'll find out how it happened. I think it went on so long because they didn't know. They genuinely thought they were shelling the enemy position."

"How long did it go on?" We were in a corner of the trench where we thought we could have an absolutely private conversation.

"Forty minutes." He looked away.

"It doesn't matter," I said. "It doesn't matter who said what or who got fooled or who wanted to be fooled. Someone else is behind it. Everyone has to follow orders."

"No one ordered that you be murdered."

"There's all kinds of orders. We know who is behind this. Don't blame the grunts." My thoughts turned to revenge and General Remington. Maybe I should have been thankful to him for the knowledge gained, but I wasn't.

"The supply helicopters are coming in at oh nine hundred hours. You're going out with them. I can't protect you."

"I can protect myself. Please let me stay."

He was a good man and I knew I was pushing him to a place he did not want to go. He nodded and walked away. But three hours later he called me in.

"You're going home."

"I thought, sir . . ."

"New orders came through. Seems you're the subject of an inquiry. There was a questionable death. A Captain Ballard."

I didn't know I would see General Remington at

Camp Pendleton. It's odd that we didn't embrace, because he must have been happy to see me there, within his clutches, and I was even happier to see him. He was a big-deal general, but he looked out of place. Smart, dumb, selfish, vain, proud, lazy, foolish, cruel, timid, or bold, you could find every trait and more in any company, even most platoons. Marines might hate one another, screw each other's daughters or wives, hate someone's race or religion or who someone liked to go to bed with, but we all shared one trait: we all fought the enemy, all put ourselves aside when facing the enemy. But not Remington and not Junior. They were fighting their own war in their own corps. The general was another kind of enemy. He had to be defeated. Junior, too.

36.

At last the exaggerated, loud whisper from a woman, "Up here," woke me. I jumped up and grabbed my rifle. When Jessica saw me, she started to scramble down the hillside, but she stopped when I told her to.

Shaw was on his way up, moving casually, as always. He looked like a golfer strolling over to get a better view of the pin position. "Hey, Rollie."

"Stop there." He stopped and raised his hands about shoulder height. Jessica was between us.

"Thanks for not killing Jessica," he said. "And congratulations. You got what you wanted. Found the money and killed McColl and his gang. Not what I wanted, but good work. What do you plan now?"

"I'll give you the money. No tricks, if you'll tell me who is involved. I want to know how far the conspiracy goes."

"It's a federal investigation. I can't reveal that information."

"Okay. No money. You can leave now."

"Not that simple, Rollie. Now that we have proof you have the money, we'll go to court. You'll go to jail until you produce it."

"I'm a Marine. They'll have me. Not you."

"You don't want that."

I screamed: "'You don't want that. You don't want that.' Why? Who's involved? I can get him. He'll want me. I'm the bait. He'll believe I'm coming after him. Let me do it. I can bust him."

"Who are we talking about, pal?" Shaw said. His voice was low and cautious, as if a mistake would ruin everything.

"You know damn well. Remington. General Remington." I wish I could say I was faking the anger for show or to trick Shaw, but it was real and I did not like it.

Dan said, *"Calm down."*

Shaw said, "Put the rifle down and we'll talk about this." Which meant the same thing. I wasn't going to shoot him, so I put the rifle down.

"Let's get out of here before dark," I said.

I wanted to fly, but Shaw reminded me that the choppers were easily traceable.

"By whom?"

"You've already decided."

We ate in Tucson at a diner on Speedway. There was no use rushing up to Arrowhead; the bakery would be closed by the time we got there. Shaw relaxed next to

Jessica in the booth. He ordered coffee, but he should have had a martini. He had the posture and manner of a crooner. Jessica ordered a steak and I asked for a burger.

"I'll try a piece of that pumpkin pie," Shaw said.

"Ain't got no punkin pie," said the waitress.

Shaw smiled at her. "How about a piece of that pie smiling at me in the mirror, the one that looks like pumpkin pie?"

"Ain't got no punkin pie," she repeated.

"I bet you say that to everyone who asks. I bet you do it just because you like saying it."

She loved him. Her smile lit her face, making her attractive, probably for the first time in a while. Shaw sipped his coffee and looked at me. The waitress scooted away. "We know of eight active and retired senior officers involved in the plot."

"All great fighters, I'm sure, but not enough to take over Kurdistan."

"They have promises from many others. For when the time comes. But they haven't done anything but talk up to now, so the money is a big deal. It gives us a crime."

"So you're going to bust them for receiving stolen goods?"

"Right now, the only person who is going to be busted is you. You still haven't given me the money."

"Remington was McColl's commanding officer in both Iraq wars. Remington is one of your eight."

"And you killed all the main witnesses against him." I looked at Jessica, indicating that she should have the goods. He shook his head. "We need more. A lot more."

"Let's give him the money," I said, and I watched Shaw closely. "Then you can bust him for having it. He's not going to say no. You can use that to get him to lay out the whole plan and everyone involved."

The waitress brought our food and waited to make sure Shaw liked the pie. "You're right," he said. "It's worth bothering about." I moved my water glass out of the way because I was sure she was going to launch herself at him. Even Jessica, who rarely found a worthy rival, and certainly couldn't be threatened by this woman, snarled a bit. Shaw said to me, "Keep going."

I looked the waitress off while Shaw savored the pie. "I'll take the money to him. All you have to do is find him for me."

"Sounds so simple. Why is Remington going to see you? And why are you so charged up to see him?"

"It was his son I busted in Afghanistan. Remington has been after me ever since. He'll see me."

"So we find him, send you in there . . ."

"You don't have to find him. Let him know where I am, with the money, and what I've done, killed McColl and his gang. He'll find me."

"He'll bring reinforcements. Better if you surprise him."

"Where is he now?"

Shaw turned to Jessica. She said, "If I told him to meet me at the ranch, he probably would."

"He has a crush on you." I said it as a statement and she did not refute it. This was her burden and she bore it the way tall guys bear remarks about the air up there. Talk of Remington and his vulnerable spot made me ache to get out of there, get moving. We still had to go all the way to Arrowhead for the money and my mind raced for ways to get Remington without the money. There were none. Dan was bothering me, but I shut him out and gobbled my burger and thought about how I would handle General Remington.

Shaw was taking forever with his damned pie. If that waitress poured him any more coffee, I was going to dump it on him.

Dan rode in the back of the car with me. He wanted to discuss Shaw. "*Smooth,*" he said. I did not want to discuss Shaw. He had let me slug him and escape, and had talked the cops in Phoenix into letting me out. Incompetence usually included some measure of officiousness, or at least formality, but Shaw had neither.

"*He's matched every move you've made,*" Dan said.

"*He's giving me what I want,*" I answered.

Jessica shook me awake just as the first pale light was sneaking around the mountains. "Are you okay?"

I nodded.

"Where to?" Shaw wanted to know.

The town was asleep, as still as Christmas morning.

A fisherman flicked the end of his cigarette out the window as he went past us. One old car sat in the lot at the Miracle Diner. As color seeped in, so did activity. I was glad we arrived before the place filled up, before Loretta would be there. From inside the bakery, a woman unlocked the door and took down the "Closed" sign.

Outside I paused, remembering that first day, before meeting Loretta and wondering if I could deal with the smell on empty pockets. "There's a key here for me," I said when the woman came out from the back.

"What name?" she asked as if she had rehearsed it, expecting a wrong answer.

"No name," I said. Her jaw fell and her face jutted forward as if she could not believe I gave the right answer. She hustled to the back and returned in a moment with the envelope containing the key. I ordered muffins and three coffees to go.

We parked outside the self-storage facility. "All together? Or you want me to wait here?"

"No, pal, you come along, too."

If he was going to kill me, this was the best place for it. He could stuff me in that locker and it would take days for anyone to notice the smell. I led them down the walkway to my locker, number seven. As I put the key in the lock, I started to smile because it occurred to me that Loretta could have taken it all.

"This is not another trick, is it?"

"If it were, I wouldn't give it away with a smile," I

said. And I held the key but did not put it in the lock. "And I don't see you smiling."

Shaw shrugged. "We came this far, might as well find out."

I opened the door, flicked on the light, and stood aside. Shaw waited for Jessica to enter, then followed her in. He kneeled next to the body bag and unzipped it and pulled it open wide for Jessica to get a look. "How much is it?"

"Never counted it."

"Mind if I do now? They're going to ask me someday."

He counted the money. There was $23,990,000. Shaw looked up at me.

"Expenses," I said. "If you want to take a cut now, I'll never tell."

I watched him carefully as he zipped the bag and hoisted it on his shoulder. I didn't see where Jessica could be hiding a gun, so it had to be Shaw's move. I went out first. Jessica followed. I held the door for Shaw. But there was no move. We loaded the money into the trunk and headed down the mountain to make our move on Remington.

37.

handed Jessica my knife. "Tear your jeans, too," I said. The plan was for her to rush back to the ranch, torn up, breathless, and helpless, and inform Remington that I had killed McColl and company and that I definitely had the money and I was headed for the ranch. Then I would go in and get Remington, distracted by Jessica, to confess on the digital recorder we had stopped to buy. Shaw would secure the outside.

Shaw and I huddled low in the backseat while Jessica drove up to the gate and punched in the code. Cameras covered every angle. There were no lights along the driveway, which curved left through sparse pastureland for a half mile before the house came in sight. Jessica slowed and we tumbled out. The wind was strong and after a moment the sky showed the glow of the security lights that switched on when Jessica's car pulled up to the house. We hustled to the far side of the corral and crouched against the posts.

We could see Remington comforting the distraught

Jessica through the living room window. He sent her to slip into something easier to tear and he strode out to alert the troops in the barn. A few moments later, three men carrying pistols raced out of the barn. Two took the driveway toward the gate. The third man was the cook with the white hair. He drifted toward the front door of the house and slunk away from the lights near the bushes and waited there.

We waited. Shaw, propped against the post, looked like he was missing a guitar and a piece of straw to chew on while he sang about the moon over the desert. I watched him, then turned to the cook tucked into the shadows next to the house as if it were shade. Shaw still puzzled me. I could not fit him into any mold, no matter how much I altered it. Not cop, not soldier, not conspirator. I felt disappointed that he had not tried to kill me at the locker. He confused me by seeming to be just what he said he was.

"Only three of them?" As soon as I said it I was sorry. I knew the answer. I just asked so I could hear his voice, search for something new in it. I hoped he didn't sense my intention.

"If there are more, you'll hear the shots. Just send Jess out when you're ready for me."

"*He's in your head now,*" said Dan. "*Get him out of there.*"

"*Look who's talking.*"

The door of the warehouse opened and General Remington strode out toward the house. A moment later another man, younger judging by his gait, joined him. The second man was partially blocked by the general. They marched in lockstep past the stable, where a light burned, then into darkness. "He's got someone with him. I'll go with you," Shaw said.

"I need you out here."

"Plans change. You didn't count on him having help."

"I got it." I was too sharp, too eager.

"Who is he?"

"The general's son. Junior."

The cook saw them approaching the front door and stepped out to show he was on guard. Remington and Junior ignored him with the casual arrogance that was infuriating but earned in the general and just comical from Junior. By that time, I was on the side of the house so that the cook's back was to me as he watched Remington enter. I hit him hard on the back of the head with the butt of my gun and yanked his long hair to take him down faster. I kicked his head a couple of times for good measure. When he had a chance to think about it, he would probably decide it was better than dying. I peeked through the big window. The living room was empty.

The money was in the trunk of our car. I slung it over my shoulder so it sat in two fat lumps like engorged saddlebags, and gun in my right hand, I slid through the door. A half-filled glass of scotch or bourbon with ice almost melted sat on a coaster on the coffee table in front of the cowhide couch. I set the money down in front of the couch. The dining room was also empty, clean and in order. I pushed into the kitchen. A pan sat on the electric burner, but it was empty and cold.

I did not have to wait long back in the living room. Junior came in, spotted the body bag, and just as he touched the zipper, I put my gun into his ear, again. He was not armed.

"Hello, Junior."

"You keep putting guns in my ear. How'd that go for you last time?"

"Last time isn't over. Call your daddy. Nice and calm."

"Well, that's just what I had in mind." He started to rise, but I pushed him back to his knees. "General," he yelled.

I stepped back. "Sit down on that chair. Facing away from me." Junior complied. He did not seem worried at all.

The general came in, saw his son's back and the body bag and turned to face my gun. He was wearing his Marine utility camo uniform, the brown desert version, but I could see him anyway. He was armed. His hand edged that way.

"Keep your hands still, General." I tried to make my eyes look wild and I jumped forward to scare him a bit, but he did not seem too scared. I turned him around and took out his gun, a Beretta M9, the standard issue.

The general was a hotshot "one in the chamber, fifteen in the clip" kind of guy. I held his gun low, flicked on the safety with my thumb, and set the gun on the long table behind the couch. Maybe his arrogance would combine with my luck and he would make a move for it. Junior sat in the chair; his only movement was to cross his legs.

Remington was a trim fifty-five-year-old man, short neat hair going to gray, parted on the left side. He had fine, little-man features. He could have had a career as a character actor playing corrupt corporate executives, but that would have meant quitting the conspiracy business. He wasn't ready for that.

"Put your gun down, Lieutenant."

"Well, sir, one of us is going to hold a gun on the other, and considering the way everyone has been treating me lately, I prefer to be that one."

He sighed, like a teacher dealing with an especially dense student. "I'm going to pick up my drink. I won't throw it in your face." He moved toward the coffee table, but I stood in his way and shook my head. I liked the idea of him wanting something he couldn't have. He stopped, quite close to me, then pushed me. Generals don't take no from lieutenants. How much harder would he have pushed if it were Jessica instead of a drink on that coaster?

I slapped him back and forth with my left hand. He was not a coward. He stood his ground and inhaled deeply, as if he were going to huff and puff and blow me down. The more he wanted that drink, the more I did not want him to have it. "You didn't come here to kill me, Waters. That's clear. So what do you want?" His breath stunk of booze.

"He wants to kill me. Or put me in jail," said Junior.

I wanted a different start to this. I wanted him to believe I was here to make peace.

"What do you want, Lieutenant?"

"You've been after me since Afghanistan. Here's your money. I want it to stop. I want to be left alone. Junior is free, and that's what you wanted."

"Is that all?"

"Let me go back to Afghanistan. Or work for you in Iraq. In Kurdistan."

Junior laughed and stood up. I had to back up to keep them both in sight. "He wants to go back and pretend to be a raghead again. You can get stabbed that way, pal."

"Shut up!" The general knew how to say that in a way that made people obey. Junior sagged. The general stared at him for as long as it took to make sure he had perfect control of the situation. It didn't take long, and in that time, he also managed to convey a good measure of anger with Junior. Done with that, he turned his talents on me.

"Drop the act, Lieutenant. You interfered in an intelligence mission in Afghanistan, wrecking months of work and the reputations of good Marines, one of whom is my son. Now you're doing it all over again stateside. You killed I don't know how many men, good men, including Colonel McColl. I won't be sending you anywhere."

Where was Jessica? She was supposed to be my witness. Where was Shaw? This was a bad plan and I should have known it, but I was too angry, too eager to nab Remington. Record his confession? That's just a bad movie idea. Remington was a lifetime intelligence officer. It wasn't that he might think I had a recorder, it was that a confession, or the truth, was hours and hours away from his mind. With a paint scraper, a mask, and two weeks, I might have been able to get through the layers of lies, but the batteries on the recorder would be long gone by then. But my fury stoked my foolishness. Retreat wasn't possible anyway and playing innocent was just a waste of time.

"Your son is just a greedy pig. A selfish, spoiled, incompetent crook. But you know that or you wouldn't have tried to have me killed. He didn't care who died, as long as he made money on the deal. He was fighting for his own side. Just like you are. This money is for you. There is no intelligence mission. It's all just a two-bit conspiracy that will never go forward. You're not taking over Kurdistan. This money is for you."

"What happens to the money is none of your business." Junior couldn't control his mouth.

"Why didn't you have him kill me, General? He's been following me, at least some of the time. Why not order him to kill me? He's killed Marines before. The money. You wanted the money."

"I do have orders for after I recover the money." Junior was looking at the gun.

"Shut up."

"Listen to your father, Junior. He's got good advice."

"Oh, what the hell, no one is gonna believe a word from you. If my father had it his way, you'd be dead and we wouldn't have found the money."

For a moment, the general's shoulders sagged and his jaw went slack. I thought his eyes darted longingly to his empty glass. But he straightened up quickly and shook his head at his foolish son. "Your orders are to keep quiet."

Where was Jessica? Where was Shaw? Remington's eyes told me I was right about him, but that was not any help at all. He stared calmly at me and focused on delivering his message. "Maybe we should let lieutenants from combat units run our intelligence missions. Maybe you should be in charge. You're ignorant and untrained, which makes you dangerous. You have no idea what it means to follow orders. You never should have been accepted into the corps, much less promoted to officer. Colonel Gladden allowed you to help the civilian government find this money and the result is that you've turned it into a crusade against me. We should have kept you in the brig where you belonged."

As a summary of his defense and explanation of why

I deserved court-martial and life in prison, it was not bad. Every officer would buy it. Every desperate criminal claims his crimes are important government business, so important that no one else can know the details, but this guy would be believed because he had the great reputation. He would get away with it. I had certainly busted up the operation in Afghanistan. The torture of Dan would be laughed off, especially since his own son had burned the evidence. What else was there? Dan stole the money. I recovered it but refused to hand it over because I wanted to drum up accusations against a Marine Corps legend. He had one thing exactly right: my crazy hatred of him had brought me here into a trap of my own making. My lie of innocence, wanting to join up, was blown. No good or useful lie occurred to me and all generals are immune to the truth so that was out.

"Jessica," I called out. "Come in here. I need you in here."

Remington's eyes flared while we waited for Jessica's reply or appearance, but I knew she would not appear. Junior smiled. I stepped beside the window with the childish idea that I would see Shaw on his way in. No one was there. Then a light flashed from far up the driveway and two shots rang, quickly followed by one more.

Remington was eyeing his gun. I moved behind the door. "Stand still, General."

And as I glanced out, Junior raced into the hallway toward the bedrooms and disappeared. Remington saw him go. "Junior . . ." It came out soft and halfhearted, unlike anything I had every heard him utter. Then he looked at me and his eyes met mine, and for one brief moment we shared a feeling: disgust. We quickly averted our eyes, as if ashamed of the moment, neither of us having the strength or will to acknowledge any mutual feelings. Lights arced across the window and into the room, sweeping across Remington. Tires crunched the gravel and the lights went out.

Gladden entered with Pongo and Perdy, guns drawn. Maybe the realization that having four tigers by the tail might make my next steps difficult made me hesitate. Gladden read Remington's expression and turned to face me. We held guns on each other. I kept glancing at Remington to keep him still.

"Put it down, Lieutenant. That's an order," Gladden said. It was the kindest he had ever sounded. Pongo and Perdy pointed their weapons toward me, but they eyed the general, in case Gladden forgot to.

"His son just ran down the hallway," I said. "He wasn't armed, but he might have weapons back there."

Gladden pointed to Perdy to check it out.

"He's behind it all," I said. "He's running an operation to take over part of Iraq. That's what all the money was for. This ranch is one of their bases. I know it's hard for you, but think about it." Maybe this was not the best time to insult him, but how would he trust me if I suddenly changed my tone?

"I'll think about it when you're in the brig."

"I'll never make it there. He doesn't want me telling this story. And he won't like it that you've heard it. Not any of you."

Gladden looked at the general. His gun stayed on me, but Pongo shifted his focus enough for Remington to think the outcome was in doubt.

Remington said, "The lieutenant has some wild theories, Colonel. Some of them have to do with ongoing, classified intelligence operations." He moved sideways to the coffee table for his drink and hesitated, as if he didn't care about it, before pouring it down his throat. I could tell it wasn't enough. He held the glass for a few moments while he considered whether refilling it was possible.

Everyone watched him. Even me, when I should have been paying attention to the guns. Gladden said, "We've been following him, sir. We're going to take him back to Camp Pendleton and get to the bottom of it. He found the money. We know that."

"Oh, hell, it's right there behind him. In the body bag. The general's as guilty as a bull in a barnyard, and you know it. It's all about guts now. Yours. Do you have any?"

"Arrest him and be done with it, Colonel. I don't have time for this."

I said, "Arrest him and your career might end. He'll use all his juice to get out and when he does he'll come after you, worse than he came after me. Much worse because you're a cop and he knows you'll always be suspicious of him. So this is your big chance, Colonel, to find out if you have it inside you. Are you a guy put on earth to arrest drunks? Or are you a real Marine? Can you risk it all knowing your chances are slim? This is so much fun."

This time Gladden did not glare at me. His lizard eyes were turned inward. The soft light made the crags in his leathery face seem deep as incisions. Remington was dismissive. "Cuff him, Colonel, and take him back to the base." He moved to pick up his gun. Gladden stiffened.

"Stay right there. Don't touch that gun."

"You let him intimidate you, Colonel Gladden. I'm shocked. I had you as a hard-nosed Marine. You know better than to stick your nose where it doesn't belong."

"It's about the only thing he knows."

"Shut up."

Perdy came back in. He shook his head: "No one back there." He took a position next to the hallway, behind Remington.

I liked this, liked watching Gladden have to face the truth. "Why is he here, Colonel? It's impossible that I started it. You sent me. Either you sent me as a patsy or you sent me to get him. There's no other way."

"Where's Shaw?"

"I don't know. Didn't you run into him outside?"

Pongo and Perdy shook their heads.

"If you don't arrest him, I will," said Remington.

"Why are you here, General?" Gladden tried to sound

calm and sincere and concerned. He had no practice so he was no good at it. He sounded like a straight man feeding lines to a forgetful star.

"That's classified, Colonel. Don't ask again."

"When he kills you, that will be classified, too," I added for clarification. That brought out the old Gladden. The eyes bulged and he leaned toward me and snorted.

"You're making it worse, Waters. General Remington, I have to ask you to accompany us back to Camp Pendleton."

"Are you arresting me?"

"I'd rather not."

"Well, you're gonna have to," I said.

"Shut him up," Gladden said to Pongo and Perdy.

"You're going to have to arrest him, or none of us will make it back to Pendleton. There'll be an accident along the way. Or it will look like I got hold of a gun and we all got shot." Pongo moved behind me and gave me the baton-across-the-throat treatment. Perdy came over to help, though that was not necessary.

"Let me speak to you alone, Colonel," said Remington quietly, conspiratorially, like an old friend who doesn't want the kids to hear what he has to say. Gladden nodded to Pongo and Perdy. They hesitated, as if questioning him, but he glared for an answer and they pulled me outside.

I managed to say, "Keep an eye on him." The baton was eased. "I won't run. I promise. But we better watch." We stood looking through the big front window. The motion detector had turned on the outside light. We all stood still, positioned out of direct sight. The white-haired man was still unconscious in the bushes near us.

Remington spoke and Gladden holstered his weapon. Remington was doing most of the talking. He wandered to the bar and filled his glass and took a deep draw and kept talking. We could only see Gladden in profile, or his back. As Remington roamed the room, drink in hand, Gladden held his spot, just turning slightly. He shook his head. That infuriated Remington, who was barking at him.

Gladden shook his head again, but now Remington was near the couch, around the back of it, next to his gun. He stood there talking and it was clear that Gladden saw it. He tensed and bent his right arm.

I looked at Pongo and Perdy. They saw what I saw and they were ready. Still. Weapons out.

Gladden shook his head again. Remington shrugged, guzzled the liquor, put the glass down on the long table behind him, and his hand came back holding the Beretta. His arm tensed as he squeezed the trigger. We couldn't hear the click, but we could see it. Nothing happened because the safety was on.

Remington's eyes fell and he froze. His mouth hung open in wonder. Gladden pulled his gun and pointed it at Remington. He was ordering Remington to drop the Beretta, but Remington did nothing for a long moment. I wanted to see Gladden's face and knew I would regret forever not having that chance.

Remington suddenly raised his gun. Gladden fired. Remington fell back. We were inside by the time he tumbled over the back of the cowhide couch, spreading red over the splotches of brown and white. Gladden turned on me.

"You goddamn fucking sonofabitch . . ." And he slugged me hard in the jaw with his left fist.

38.

The cell was still ten feet by ten feet by ten feet. One thousand cubic feet of stale, thick, lethargic air. I sat in full lotus and brought up my vision. For two weeks, it had ceased to be a refuge and become a hangout which I wanted to avoid but couldn't stay away from. Dan had infiltrated. A virus dressed as my father. He acted as host and honored, but uninvited, guest dispensing his unwanted gifts. I could change the venue, but he always found me. Two of us stuck in one thousand cubic feet. I brought up the Buddhist retreat and there was Dan. On the boat with Kate and Scott and the Big Boys—and Dan. Dan asked if I liked the boat.

"Haven't you had enough with boats?"

"Good point."

He ran through his entire repertoire of stories, charming asides and compliments, and wisdom. The laughter must have had the guards thinking I was cracking up. But I was just working my way to the question that had hung over me since I first heard why everyone was after him.

"*It was too much,*" he said.

"*Liar.*"

"*It was too much.*"

"*That wasn't why you didn't touch it.*"

"*It was so much. So much . . .*"

"*So what?*"

"*So much that it would never run out.*"

"*So what? That's not a reason to ignore it.*"

"*It is. So much that life would be over. The chase would be over. No more deals to make. I'd always be on the other side of the deal. . . . I'd be the mark.*"

"*You?*"

"*See what happened when you got all the money? You got played.*"

"*That's not over.*" But the comment stung. I turned it back to him. "*So you hid it. Forever?*"

"*For someone who would know how to handle it. For you.*"

I did not want to hear the rest. My training told me Dan in giving mode was a dangerous man. Being dead was only a minor safety factor. Dan gone sentimental was no use to me. Worse. The thought was unbearable. Unallowable.

We changed the subject many times for many hours. Dan told me stories from before I was old enough to remember. He once trained me to burst into tears and beg him not to sell a desert shack and the surrounding property because I loved living there so much. Of course, he never owned it. He made me hide one time so he could get my teacher to help look for me. He wanted to go to bed with her and he did.

I could enjoy his lies in that cell. I thought this might be good-bye. A farewell trip to the land of Thorough Deceit. Dan offered to go. *"I'll be back,"* he said, which meant he would not be back. I stopped that. I could throw away the money but not the lies, not the tricks, not the charm. Dan was baggage, baggage filled with air.

The clip-clop of Sergeant Matthews broke in and Dan vanished. I kipped up and stood close to the sergeant so my sweat and odor would bother him and he could hit me. But he didn't do it. That meant the Marines thought this part was over, though I knew it was not over.

As I crossed the quad, no general stood watch.

Gladden's paws rested on the arms of his chair so it looked like he was ready to spring forward, but it might have been that the suction cups were holding him in place. "Siddown, Waters." That was it.

A major sat across from him in the chair Shaw occupied the last time I was here. He was about fifty years old, dark, and puffy. He looked like he spent his days behind a desk and then went home to read books.

"You're cleared, Lieutenant. Charges dropped."

"Cleared of what, sir?"

"You're out of jail and back on active duty."

"I think I deserve to know more, sir. I mean, I'm not asking for any kind of commendation or recognition, but I did go to considerable lengths to do as you ordered, sir. And along the way I lost my father, scumbag though he might, or might not, have been."

He stared at me a while, his lizard eyes waiting for me to make a wrong move, and disguising the fine calculations he knew how to make. The man next to me watched me but did not say a word.

"What do you want to know, Lieutenant?"

For a vicious cop, he was a real softie. I was torn. I wanted to needle him, ask how it felt to kill a senior officer; I wanted to thank him for killing the senior officer. I decided to shut up.

Gladden started in without warning. "I was a major . . . past the time I should have been. General Remington had a hand in that. Two weeks ago, he asked me to assign you to cooperate with Agent Shaw, and he, General Remington, hinted that if I played along with him on this, he would help me with the next step in my career. Knowing some of the history between you, I found that peculiar. That's why I sent Patterson and Pruitt along with you. For your protection. So the answer to the question you want to ask is that I didn't care whether he was a senior officer or not. That didn't make me hesitate. I did not like killing a man who I had a gripe with, and more, I did not like killing a man who had insulted me and questioned my integrity. I tell you this so you can think about it while you're wondering how you lived through it all."

I was quiet for a moment. His flat gaze never left me. "So you're saying, sir, that my insubordinate attitude toward you might have helped save my life."

"So far." He looked away before I did, but I was not going to last much longer.

"Well, I'm glad you two have worked that out. We can get on with business," said the major. His voice was soft, calm, and commanding.

"This is Major Arthur Hensel. You'll be working for him now. Any further questions you have should be addressed to him."

Pongo and Perdy were waiting outside the office. We all shook hands. I thanked them and one said, "Stay in touch, Lieutenant."

"You're good guys. You'd have been within your rights . . ."

"We knew we could have had you anytime, so . . ." the other one said.

Major Hensel kept walking. I caught up to him outside.

"We've identified a number of active-duty officers involved in the conspiracy to separate Kurdistan from Iraq. The computers gave us enough information to make arrests of six senior officers and a number of retired military. We think there are other cells out there, but we aren't certain. It's clear that some of the conspirators took the plan quite seriously. General Remington was not a central player in the conspiracy. They had approached him and he let them believe that he was sympathetic. He might have been planning to join; he might have been planning to bust them. When he saw that the conspirators wanted you, he was glad to up his cooperation. The ranch belonged to him. He let McColl use it as a way of keeping an eye on him. As for the money, we don't know. It may be that he just saw it as a side benefit in getting rid of you. McColl was his connection to the conspiracy. With him dead, Remington probably thought that was over." He paused while we walked toward the parking lot. "Everything I've told you is classified. We don't want the conspirators to know how deep our knowledge goes. And we don't want the public to know about a possible military revolt of this scale."

That was the first time an officer ever explained to me the reason for classifying information. And admitting a large problem was way out in the land of unusual, too.

I had other information in mind. "What about Junior?"

"You mean Captain Remington? He's back on active duty. We have no evidence that he was part of the conspiracy. We have no evidence that he was involved in any crime. The few sentences he speaks on the recording don't give us much. He claims he was acting under orders from the general. We can't refute that. He's an active-duty Marine officer, Lieutenant. Do not go after him."

"And if he comes after me?"

"I've given you my instructions." He stopped walking and looked at me to make sure I understood.

"Will I be going back to Afghanistan?"

"The Defense Intelligence Agency, with whom I believe you have a gripe, a justified gripe, I might add, has asked me to form a unit drawing promising candidates from all services to deal with national security issues that involve the military."

"What does that mean?"

"For now, it means I can stick my nose in where I want to and you work for me and do as I order you to do," he said with a calm assurance that left no room for an answer, or a question. "We're called Shared Defense Executive."

"Shared Defense Executive. What do we call it for short?"

"What makes you think we call it anything for short?"

"Because it's the military, sir, and no one ever named anything without thinking of a shortened version."

"We've been calling it SHADE. Don't like it much, but it seems to have caught on." The part about not liking it was the first lie he told me. It made me more comfortable with him. "You have two weeks off before you start."

"Thank you, sir."

"Where will you go? Arizona?" I didn't answer. "The money left in the cave . . . Leave it there for now. Out of the system. We might need it later."

"Yes, sir."

"But try to give me an accurate accounting."

"Yes, sir."

"And, one more thing . . . Her real name is Teresa Boyle. Shaw, apparently, used his real name. He was CIA. Met McColl in Iraq and hooked up with the gang from the start."

"How much money was missing?"

"There was twenty million in the bag. You tell me."

"I never counted it."

39.

I bought a gun in Hermosillo. I'm pretty sure it was
older than me. The kid swore it worked and had
not been used in any crimes to which it could be
traced. No murders. I took his picture with my cell
phone and told him I would give it to the police if possession of the gun got me in trouble. "Chingate, ca-
brón! Dame la pistola si no la quieres," he said, trying
to show me how much he didn't care.

"Probablemente ni dispara." But I took it anyway.
Maybe because I never wanted to use it.

My search criteria went like this: horses, Western
riding, away from military bases, drivable because they
would not want to board planes with all that cash. And
believable—they would have to be able to sell their
story to the locals and any other Americans they met.
They had a two-week head start and likely would have
new names and identification.

For three days I searched for Steve Shaw, Teresa
Boyle, Jessica McColl. I was able to access credit card

transactions, so there were plenty of false leads. I threw out everybody who made purchases outside Arizona, Nevada, and California for the period of the chase. I knew Shaw had been in Tucson waiting for me, and Jessica/Teresa had been at the ranch, so anyone who made a purchase on that day was thrown out. I was left with nobody.

Before I closed down the database, I checked on some other names: McColl, Remington, Pitt, and Stallworth, and I saved Peter Stenson, Blondie, for last. I found a Peter Stenson who received mail at the post office in Blythe. Two weeks earlier, he used his credit card at a Pemex station in Nogales. That was two days after I had put five bullets into him and dumped him down a shaft with no bottom. I couldn't figure how Shaw would have gotten the card. Teresa must have lifted it from Blondie.

The rest fell into place. Guaymas is a seven-hour drive from Tucson and has a harbor busy enough with shrimpers and pleasure craft to allow for unnoticed arrivals and getaways. There is also a large American expat community in San Carlos, just north of Guaymas, in case someone felt the urgent need to scam. I called everyone I could find who had horses for sale. Pedro Nunez at the Ocampo Ranch apologized: the horses I was asking about had sold last week. Yes, it was a blond lady and her husband. "Que me hayan podido superar de nuevo," I said.

Before I left, I stopped by the depot. In spite of the

air-conditioning in the shed, Sergeant Comeau glis-
tened with gooey beads of sweat.

"I need a car, Sergeant."

"Yes, sir." He unstuck himself from his chair.
"Haven't seen you around."

"You, too."

"I've been here. Thought maybe those guys who
were following you might have kidnapped you or something." He wasn't being coy or implying that he knew
something. No one gave Sergeant Comeau information
because everyone knew he was likely to repeat it. He
was Head of the Office of Comings and Goings.

"Give me something reliable. I'm going to Mexico."

"Oh, sir, I'm sorry, sir, no vehicles can leave the
country."

"Did I say Mexico? I meant New Mexico."

He wiped drops of sweat above his eyebrow. "Please,
Lieutenant. It'll come back at me."

I hemmed and hawed a little to make sure he would
know I really meant Mexico, and I mentioned Guaymas so he would have a good story to tell. Then I
made him assign a private to drive me to the Avis in
Oceanside.

How many came to Dan pleading for a refund, a repeal,
just plain mercy and left befuddled? How many brought
threats and guns and just missed him around the corner? I was eleven, playing soccer at the schoolyard in
Phoenix, when Dan pulled up in an old Mustang.

"Hey, tough guy," he yelled as if it would make me come running. I waited until the game stopped and walked over. Dan had been away for more than a week. He took me for ice cream, then to the sporting goods store for new shoes. He was filled with stories. He had been on a cruise, he said, and had caught a shark. He pulled out something and tossed it on the table. "Here's one of his teeth. It was tough to get out, tough as it was to catch him. Don't lose it." We stopped at the bank next.

"You wait here," he said. "I have to go into the vault."

"Put this in there," I said and held up the shark's tooth, or whatever it was. "So I won't lose it." I waited on a couch in the lobby. Dan came out with a soft leather briefcase that looked like it was stuffed.

The Mustang was parked in the grocery store lot. It didn't start. Before we could get out, a man materialized next to each door. Dan put the window down. The man at his window did not say a word. He just put out his hand. Dan looked at the other man, the one at my window, then back at the first one. "The kid," Dan said. The man shrugged. Dan handed him the briefcase. The man looked inside, nodded to the other man, and they started away. Dan said, "The distributor cap?" The man pointed to the car behind us. It was on the hood.

I knew this was a big defeat for Dan. Worse than having to skulk away in the night or being kicked out by a screaming girlfriend. I had never seen him so low. I thought about it for a long time and the lesson I took was that to turn the tables on him, you had to reduce the whole thing to one move. If Dan could have convinced them that the money was in the bank, he would have gotten away. If he could have worked out any room to maneuver, he would have disappeared, probably leaving me as collateral. We never went back to that bank. I never saw the shark's tooth again. Eventually, I decided that it was in the briefcase anyway.

I had to reduce the moves Shaw could make or risk having him slip away again. I found him at a golf club, watched him tee off. That night, he and Jessica had dinner at a beachfront restaurant in San Carlos. He was using the name Steve Salter. I called Major Hensel and asked him to check the local banks for accounts opened in that name. Banco Nacional de México had the account with about 280,000 pesos in it, about $24,000. The millions were not in the bank and I discounted the idea of a safe-deposit box because it inhibited quick getaways.

If ever there was a moment when I was thankful for my advanced degree from University of Dan, this was it. He was so eager and excited next to me that I found myself shushing him at times. I parked the Avis car in a secured lot at my hotel and walked to a local rental place so I could have a car with Mexican plates. Dressed in a suit and wearing five days' worth of mustache, I inquired about the couple at the golf course and at the restaurant, and at the harbor, where I was certain Shaw had made some just-in-case arrangements. Without saying as much, I let everyone think I was with the PFM , which is the Mexican FBI. I spoke only Spanish. All this was just a distraction, something for Shaw to concentrate on. I wanted him debating how big a bribe would be required for the mysterious PFM agent. And then, when I came into the picture, he would discount the idea of killing me immediately because police were hovering around him.

Done with my inquiries, I was on my way to the motel to shave and ditch the suit when I saw the shiny black Dodge with California plates for the second time that day. I crossed the street to a taco stand and waited in line and watched, even though I knew who was going to get out of that car. Junior looked like a guy who lost track of what planet he landed on. He stretched his legs and gazed all around and shook his head. He didn't try to hide, so he had not spotted me. Two fishermen walked past him and Junior accosted them. One of them bothered to shrug his shoulders, but they never broke stride. Junior did not speak Spanish. I made a quick decision to let his arrogance go to work, set up barriers for him, and hope that gave me the time I needed to work out my plans for Shaw and Teresa.

They were living in a hacienda on the bluff between Guaymas and San Carlos. Before dawn, I was in the woods behind the house, Dan chuckling on my shoulder: *"This is going to be fun."* I agreed. It was fun already. The soft acacia scent mixed with something sweeter, a small red flower with yellow fruit and the dirt moist with dew. The sun drew up behind me, pierced through the trees, and tore the darkness to shreds.

Shaw left with his golf clubs at seven. *"Wait here,"* I said to Dan.

"You're selfish."

"I'll tell you all about it."

I did my cop act for the servants and gave them two thousand pesos each to take the rest of the day off. They pointed the way to the bedroom.

"Coffee for you, and a mango."

Her eyes were still closed. The blanket pulled high. She mumbled, "I thought you were playing golf."

"Cream, no sugar. Right?"

She didn't need even one sip to be wide awake. I put a finger to her mouth and handed her a cup. As she straightened herself, the blanket fell forward. She was wearing a T-shirt. Her blond hair, tousled a bit, made my fingers itch to run through it. "He is playing golf. I waited until he left. It's taken me two weeks to find you. Have you been here all the time?"

"No. I mean yes. It took a few days . . ."

"Don't be afraid. Just the opposite. I . . . I . . . Well, I'll just come out and say it. I got away with the money. All of it, except what Shaw took, but I realized immediately there was something missing. Not something, someone."

She had heard it all before, probably since she was ten. And she was a quick thinker. "I didn't want to leave you there."

I sat next to her. "I know that. If I weren't sure of that, I would not be here now. I have the money with me. Let him keep what he took. I don't know if he'll even look for you. I know he won't look as hard as I did."

"You're lovely," she said, and stroked my cheek. "But this is a little sudden."

"As sudden as it is, that's how strong my feelings are for you." I kissed her and she responded.

"Give me until tomorrow."

"It's hard to leave you right now." I'm sure I'm the first guy to say this: I did not want to make love to her. But I had to. I did not want to do it, but that is not the same as saying I didn't enjoy it, or that I regret doing it. And I admit that the delight went deeper than just the physical exploration of the delightful Teresa Boyle. She was Shaw's woman.

She quizzed me gently about how I got away with the money and moved on to where I was staying in Guaymas. I avoided answering that. She said, "It's got to be dangerous traveling around Mexico with all that money."

"I have someplace for us to go where we'll be safe and happy. What time tomorrow? Should I come up here to pick you up? You might have to dye your hair."

"You think of funny details. I thought that the first night we met at the ranch." She kissed me. We talked about how to make the getaway, eventually settling on a dirt road that ran to a beach at San Carlos. She would tell Shaw she needed the car to go shopping, drop him at the golf course, then meet up with me.

I did not want to go back to my hotel room on the chance that Junior might find it and did not want to check in to another room for the same reason, so I settled on a house for sale in San Carlos, not far from Shaw's, and broke in to spend the night. It was partially furnished and the water was running, so I was comfortable. Though I had done this kind of thing plenty of times before, it had been many years, and it gave me a good feeling, probably because I knew I didn't have to do it. I spent a little time sussing out how necessity negates pleasure and what that means, but I couldn't reach any conclusions worth sticking with. It couldn't be nostalgia: my days of homelessness were bad. I would be the worst kind of liar to romanticize them. The thing I liked, at least that night, was doing something I was not supposed to, something wrong and illegal. Doing something wrong and illegal should not have been a big deal to me, and should not have given me the sense of relief and release the way this did. I studied a lot of flickering lights before I admitted the cause: Major Hensel's orders were weighing on me.

I relaxed on the terrace for a while, watching the flat bay and the lights of the resort below me. Then I sat in full lotus and brought up my vision, complete with Dan sticking his head out the window. He wanted to review the plans for the next morning with Shaw and Teresa, but I wanted my mind blank so I closed the window on him.

Later, on the couch, I let Dan calculate the full matrix of possibilities. Whenever my mind drifted to Junior, I could hear Major Hensel saying, "Don't go after him."

40.

Shaw knelt behind bushes on the sand dune, peeking out at the dirt road where Teresa stood beside the car, waiting for me. A small blue nylon duffel sat beside him. "Hey . . ." I said it softly, but he heard despite the noisy wind. He held a small automatic in his right hand. My gun was in my belt behind me. I left it there.

"I knew. I knew it . . ." He was shaking his head like a guy whose putt broke the wrong way. "You don't have the money, do you?"

"You walked away from it before. I didn't think you could do it twice."

"It's too much." I wasn't sure if he meant it the way Dan did: too much to do anything with, or too much to resist? "Did you have to nail her?"

"You wouldn't have trusted me if I hadn't. It was a matter of credibility." The wind blew his curly hair around and rippled our shirts. The sun had us squinting.

The high dunes blocked the view of the beach and the ocean, but I could smell it and hear the waves.

"How did you find me?"

"Teresa told me where you were going." He knew it was a lie and it was all he would get. "But I don't know when you took the what? Three million nine?"

"When you and Teresa went into the store to buy the recorder."

"You were the inside man from the start. You were there when Dan was killed. It was your idea to give me the jeep and the money and to turn me loose."

"That's right, pal. You can thank me for that. McColl had different ideas for you."

"But you let them kill Dan."

"Not even Dan wanted to stop that. There was nothing I could do."

He was right. The only thing he could have done was not played the game, and that wouldn't have saved Dan, either. "You were good. You took the punch. Stayed out of my way, let me do the work. I got rid of all the barnacles. Except Junior. I can't figure how he fit with you."

Shaw smiled. He wasn't going to tell me that and I felt foolish for asking. It was probably as simple as Junior sniffing around the money and Jessica drawing him off the scent.

"And then once I had the money, you set me up to get killed by General Remington."

"I was just giving you what you wanted. You kept

bringing him up. I sure didn't. Every sucker wants something. C'mon, you're Dan's son, you know how it goes."

"What do you know about Dan?"

"I knew him in Iraq. Great guy. We worked some projects together. Dan knew his stuff. He talked about you, too. Very proud father."

I let that one pass. "Here's what I think you should do. Take about one hundred thousand out of the duffel, then join your girlfriend, get in the car, and go anywhere you want. Stay around here if you want."

"I'm holding the gun."

"Then use it. You're not stupid enough to do that. My offer is the best one you'll get. I found you. Kill me and someone else will find you and they won't be as generous. You'll spend all the money hiding and it won't work anyway. This way, you walk away with a little working capital, plenty of suckers to fleece, and no one on your tail." His shoulders sagged. He knew he should accept, but no one likes being outmaneuvered. His phone rang. He ignored it while he tried to find a winning angle.

Behind him, Teresa came over the dune. She yelled, "You bastard." Shaw turned. With my left hand, I pulled his right wrist forward, around my left side, and slid my right arm around his elbow. Maybe his arm didn't break. The gun fell and he fell. I picked up the gun and then the duffel.

From the ground, he looked at Teresa moving

toward us, and for a moment, he looked like a guy checking out a babe at the beach. What a gift. He got up and used his left hand to brush sand from his shirt. "For Gladden? Remington? Who you doing this for? I figured Dan's son would be looking out for himself."

I took out a handful of bundles of bills and tossed them on the sand. "That's enough to keep you going." He did not bend down for them. I knew it disgusted him to be on the receiving end of that move: the cheap payoff to mollify the mark. "It'll blow away," I said.

"You bastard," Teresa said. I think she was talking to Shaw.

I had taken only about ten steps when I heard the shouts: "Dammit!" Both of them were yelling. I didn't have to turn. Hundred-dollar bills were swirling in the air all around me.

41.

Suddenly Guaymas looked like a wonderland to me. Every cliff was a perfect spot from which to launch a body. The ravines were just natural, impenetrable graves. The desert was filled with nooks and crannies, dining rooms for carnivorous vermin. The harbor was deep with potential; even the garbage in the alleys sent my imagination on fire. I felt no shame at this exercise because I knew I was just one in a long line of Junior's acquaintances to fantasize about dumping his dead body somewhere. How many had explicit orders not to go after him?

The duffel of money went into my American car, parked in the hotel lot. I took five thousand dollars to the bank near the plaza where I had seen Junior and changed it into pesos. It didn't seem that Junior had located me so I went to my hotel, hoping he had staked it out. I didn't spot him outside and he wasn't waiting in my room. I showered and took a nap, telling myself that if, when I woke up, Junior was not to be seen, I would start back to Pendleton; if Junior was around, I would have to deal with him. When I went outside, around six P.M., the black Dodge was parked at the far end of the lot.

I tried out a small lie: *It would be useless to run; he'll just keep tracking me; I must deal with him immediately.* But that always ended with: *But he came after me; I had to kill him; it was essential, defensive, prudent.*

If Major Hensel bought that story, it would mean he was either corrupt or stupid and I would have to quit SHADE before I started because, either way, it would mean failed missions and wasted effort, at best. For the story of Junior's demise to pass Major Hensel, I would have to be left out. Completely.

South of the harbor, a row of low-down bars serviced the sailors and fishermen. A few enterprising, optimistic prostitutes hung around: early-bird specials. After parking, I circled around so I could see where Junior left the black Dodge. I picked a tavern away from the cars and sat at the bar and nursed a few beers, talking baseball with the old guy to my right and the bartender who was missing one eye. We spoke Spanish, but I did not want them to worry that I was a cop so I let them know I was a gringo. Fishermen drifted in. The jukebox played a mix of Mexican and American rock and roll. Somebody especially liked Freddy Fender.

"*Come in, Junior. Confront me. Threaten me. Pull a weapon.*"

"Hey, buddy boy, hand over the money. It's mine."

"Nothing is yours, Junior. You're a . . ." A what? A scumbag? What would be the use of calling him anything? Of talking to him at all? Junior was beyond words and he thought by now, he was beyond punishment, beyond shame. Punching him out would not bring enough pain for him or enough satisfaction for me.

I looked at the old man next to me and said, "My father is a big-time general in the Marines, very powerful and very much feared. So no matter what I do, I can get away with it. Okay?"

The old man got up quickly and left. No one around here would care about Junior's connections. Junior did not come in so I drained my beer, and leaned toward the bartender, and told him I wanted to buy cocaine. He rolled his eye. I gave him two thousand pesos. "Para usted. De buena fe."

I followed two friendly, happy-go-lucky, south-of-the-border dudes down to their boat, where they sold me twelve thousand pesos' worth of cocaine, which I asked them to divide into three bags. They were happy to do it. "Are you sure you don't want to try it? We want satisfied customers. You can send your friends."

"There is something else," I said. "Someone is following me. I'll pay you an additional five thousand pesos if you'll just delay him. Don't hurt him, please. I need about ten minutes."

"You bet, amigo. No problem. We know a lot about hassling people."

We started walking back to the bar. I was about to say good-bye, have them deal with Junior, but I had another problem. "You guys know where I could pick up a coat hanger and maybe a screwdriver around here?"

"How about just use a slim jim, amigo?" We walked back to the boat to fetch the tool. They refused to accept money for it. "We have a bunch of them. Come back if you need more blow, okay. And we'll look after your friend." But Junior was not following me. I wandered around for a while, then signaled to the dudes. I paid them for their trouble and called them off and headed toward the bar.

A young prostitute fell in beside me. She spoke enough English to get her job done and I let her go on with it. "You very handsome hombre. I love you. Come with me."

"And you're very beautiful and I love you, too. Very much. But not right now."

"Now, okay? Cheap deal. Cheap deal special for you."

"How cheap is cheap tonight?" She didn't understand or wasn't sure. She looked back at the small Ford trailing us, driven by her pimp. "One thousand pesos," she said.

That was pretty cheap. But I wanted to find out just how much in love with me she really was. "Two hundred," I said.

She looked back to the pimp in the car and held up two fingers. He held up one. She shook her head and said, "Doscientos pesos. Doscientos." He paused, then shrugged and nodded. Maybe he was in love with me, too. Maybe they did not love me at all and someone else was subsidizing the difference.

I paid her on the spot and took her arm, and she led me to a crumbling three-story building where two sleazy guys hung out at the door. The pimp followed us. He called out to the sleazy guys and they moved aside to allow my new love and me inside the courtyard. A concrete staircase ran up the right side to an outer walkway. Flaco Jiménez and his accordion, or someone who did a good imitation, was playing from two different rooms with competing songs. In the courtyard, a disused molded plaster fountain was half filled with still, fetid water and cigarette butts. I threw a coin in and smiled at my love. "Which room?"

She pointed to a room on the left side of the second floor. The lights were out. She glanced back toward the gate. I could see the tail end of the pimp's car idling. My love marched for the stairs, but I stood still. She stopped at the bottom and turned back and smiled at me. She shifted her pose in a way she thought was enticing and gestured for me to join her. I moved away from the staircase, under the left-side walkway, so I would not be visible from the room. "Ven aquí, por favor," I said quietly.

She was scared. She looked toward the gate but no help was coming from there. I held up a bunch of pesos. When she came close, I held out my hand. "The key. La llave." I rustled the pesos in my other hand. "Give me the key, then go. Don't hang around. He won't find you."

She understood.

I moved deeper under the walkway, deeper in the shadows. When the sleazy guys glanced in, they didn't see me, so their eyes rose up to the room on the second floor. They shrugged in unison and retreated. Flaco stopped playing in one room. And a moment later, he stopped in the other room. The only sound was the scratching of the rodents near the stairway.

Junior was making it easy for me. I could burst in and shoot him; he would be hiding, probably in the closet, waiting for me to get in bed with my love. I had the cocaine to leave with his body: another gringo drug casualty. Or I could wait right where I was and shoot him when he came down, frustrated and angry, ready to take it out on the pimp and the whore.

"Don't go after him."

There would be no witnesses. If there was an investigation, it would not lead to me. He had caged himself and no one could make an argument for mercy. I took out the gun and spun the cylinder to make sure it was loaded, and I started for the stairs. Two steps were all I could take. I knew I could kill Junior and come out alive, but this felt like a trap, a trap made of crumbling concrete and rusted iron and the foul stench of the fountain, which would cling forever. Flaco started playing again at once in both rooms. I put the gun in the backpack and walked out.

Two fishermen and their wives or dates watched me open the Dodge with the slim jim. I put my gun in Junior's glove box along with one bag of cocaine. Another bag went under the driver's seat and the last in the bottom section of the trunk, tucked in with the spare.

I asked for an outside table at the restaurant down the street from the car, ordered a beer and arroz con camarones, because camarones are a big specialty in Guaymas and I didn't want to leave without having any. Using the pay phone inside, I called the PFM, the local police, and even the uniformed federales, giving them all the details on Junior's car. I spoke only Spanish and gave no hint of my identity. Having been burned twice with authorities letting Junior off the hook, I thought that if multiple agencies were in on the bust, there would be a better chance of the charges sticking.

I forced myself to eat slowly. Everything was control at that point. The cops were in place within twenty minutes. I don't know which organization arrived first. I paid my bill and waited. Ten minutes later, Junior strode into the square, heading for his car. I looked away, and when I glanced around a moment later, he was gone.

He could not spot me sitting out in the open cafe, but I knew where he would go to look for me. I strolled down to the bar where I had sat before, came out, and walked to my car, taking my time. Inside, I watched in the rearview mirror as Junior hustled back to his car. It was easy as leading a dog on a leash.

I started the car. And I let the thoughts of confrontation drift away: pleasing fantasies of indulgence vaporizing, as they should. I was following Major Hensel's orders, Colonel Gladden's example of restraint, and Dan's lifetime of lessons: a line so crooked that toeing it required a crazy dance. I pulled into the street to get a better angle in the mirror.

Junior put the key in the car door and sprang the trap. Cops came at him from all directions. I drove away.

42.

Kate's office said she was on vacation. Scott's boat wasn't in the slip. Maybe they were honeymooning. Major Hensel met me at Air Station Miramar. I handed over the money I took from Shaw and gave him the accounting he asked for of the money left in the cave. I neglected to mention the money I gave Loretta. He didn't ask about Junior.

"What do I do now?"

"What do you want to do?"

"That's a lousy question to ask, sir."

"I know the answer. I just want to see if you know it, or will admit it."

I knew the answer, too. And I didn't want to admit it. This guy was good. He could even read my expression.

"The other graves full of money."

"Where do I start?"

"Start at the beginning."

The beginning? "Back in the brig, sir?"

"You're shipping out to Baghdad. I have someone for you to speak with at the morgue. I'll leave it to you how to proceed, but keep me informed at all times. That's important."

"Yes, sir."

"And, Lieutenant, I'm pretty sure there is exactly twenty-five million dollars in each of the graves."

"Yes, sir. Oh, one thing. If there is more money in one of the graves, what should I do with the extra?"

"Your plane leaves in two hours, Lieutenant."

I sat in the terminal letting my mind go blank. Families waited for their fathers and mothers to arrive. Some of the kids ran around according to some mysterious game. Other kids sat tight and nervous and, probably, scared. A plane arrived, everyone stood as if they had been told "All rise" in church. The kids who had been running around were ordered to stop and stand with the rest of the family. Every one of them got it immediately. Marines, men and women, strode from the tunnel, most of them looking around expectantly with sharp, cautious eyes that softened and teared when they found who they were looking for. A sergeant fell to his knees and kissed the dirty tile floor, and a specialist wasn't paying attention and tripped over the sergeant. Others helped them both up and everyone laughed and kept moving. Some kids were shy about greeting their parents; some hogged the hugs.

The outbound passengers around me watched it all carefully with their spouses or girlfriends or boyfriends or parents or kids. I don't know how many were jealous of the new arrivals. They all should have been, but it's a difficult thing to admit. Probably quite a few had already been through it before. Except for one blubbering teenage daughter, the tears had not yet started for the outbound group.

My plan was to have no plan, get a slow start in the hope I could see it all with fresh eyes. But Dan had some ideas to plant and would not be denied.

"*Thank me,*" he said. "*I got you the best job you've ever had. SHADE. You could get rich.*"

"*I'm not going to steal the money. None of it.*"

"*I know that, Rollie Boy. You're too smart for that. But you're going to Iraq. There's turmoil. Maybe to Kurdistan. They're hungry. Want their own country. They have oil. You can offer them help. Information. Contacts. You're in a position to have the greatest job of all.*"

I knew the answer, but I asked just to hear him say it. "*What's that?*"

"*Middleman.*"

ACKNOWLEDGMENTS

This is my first novel. I needed plenty of help and I got it.

Howard Blum went above and beyond the call of friendship. I would not have started without his steady encouragement, and would not have finished without the benefit of his shrewd advice and acute insight. I owe him.

P. J. Morrell generously provided Spanish vernacular translation. Peter Keeler, gunsmith, tutored me on weapons. Jack Barthell, Alan Holleb, Neil Steiner, and Clay Frohman, all always gracious, housed and fed me on the West Coast.

Guy Prevost, Mack Reid, and Margy and Norman Bernstein tirelessly listened, critiqued, and proofed without complaint or delay. Paul Bracken let me view the wars in Iraq and Afghanistan through his unique lens. I never came out of a conversation with him the same as when I went in. Geoff Baere spotted the hidden quicksand in the story and posted warning signs.

Avoiding those traps kept me laughing the whole way through.

Kim Witherspoon, refreshingly direct, said what she was going to do and then did it. Rare.

Ben Sevier took the chance, and, along with Jess Horvath, has made it all so easy, smooth, and fun.

I thank them all.

Don't miss the next Lieutenant Rollie
Waters novel by David Rich,

MIDDLE MAN

Now available from Dutton

1.

Snowflakes appeared in Havre, Montana, then disappeared when they hit the ground. The headstone had been pulled out of the ground and laid faceup. It said: ETHAN WILLIAMS 1979–2004. He had been a father, a husband, a son, but none of that was mentioned even though the Army would have paid for the listing. The headstone was probably going to become obsolete as soon as we opened the coffin, but the family might not get a chance at a replacement: My job was to find the money, not the bodies.

A police cruiser pulled up to the curb near the cemetery entrance. The cop did not get out. Our car was parked on the opposite side of the small cemetery, near the exit.

Sergeant Will Panos shrugged. "Had to notify them." He shifted his gaze across the grave. "Who's the smoker?"

The family was clumped together, with one exception. "Must be the father. Met all the others."

"They all keep looking at you."

"It's the uniform." We wore our service uniforms; this wasn't an occasion for dress blues, according to Sergeant Panos.

"Got my eye on the widow. Does that make me a bad guy?"

"That isn't what makes you a bad guy, Will." We had been working together for weeks, traveling around the country and to Iraq, and I had not discovered too much about him that was bad. He was the only one who thought he was a bad guy. I figured he was the expert. Sergeant Will Panos had a fleshy face and saggy eyes. His skin was pockmarked, dark and rough. His nose was crooked from fighting. It was the face of a tough guy, a slob, a bruiser. His face lied: Will Panos was a refined, meticulous, careful man who navigated Marine regulations so precisely that I wondered if he had written them himself.

The widow, Kristen, was a pretty woman, wary, about thirty, short, with her dark roots pushing the blond hair away. Her parents and a sister and the sister's husband huddled together in their winter coats near the foot of the grave. I had met them last night at Kristen's house. She had papers to sign. We had waited thirty minutes for Ethan Williams's father, but he never showed up, and no one found that noteworthy.

The smoker stood alone, smoked his cigarette to the

stub, tossed it down and lit another. I walked over and introduced myself. Up close, he looked ragged. Random patches of his beard had evaded the razor. He was too young to look like that. "Marine Lieutenant Rollie Waters, sir." He didn't reply, so I said, "Are you Specialist Williams's father?"

His eyes narrowed and he seemed to hiss. "You don't fool me," he said.

"I'm sorry we have to do this." I just wanted to get away from him. The smell of liquor cut through the tobacco on his breath. Watery film covered his eyes and he could not hold my gaze.

"You've never been sorry for nothing," he said.

Kristen stepped in close to intervene. "I realize I didn't introduce you two. Lieutenant Waters, this is Ethan's father, Jim." The father pointed at me and said, "That oughta be you in that grave and we both know it." His right hand turned up and I saw something black in it, and a second later the blade popped out the side.

Kristen said, "Jim! I'm over here." He looked at her. "Put the knife away, Jim. There's no danger." She moved closer to him.

"Mrs. Williams . . ."

She was half his size and the blade looked like it would go all the way through her even with the puffy down coat she wore. Jim noticed me again and his eyes narrowed like they were going to take over the hissing, but they wavered. He was afraid. Kristen put up one hand to stop me from making a move, and put the other on Jim's shoulder. I stood still.

"Jim, give me the knife. This'll be over soon." Her voice was soft and understanding, as if they had been partners in some harrowing experience. She put out her hand. He retracted the blade and put the knife back in his pocket. He was back in this world. Kristen checked with me and I nodded that I was okay with that.

Jim spat on the ground next to me, then shuffled a few feet away. Kristen waited for my reaction.

"Usually people wait until they get to know me before they do that."

"He's just . . . it's been hard," she said. She stood silently beside me for a while. "How many of these have you done so far, Lieutenant?"

"I've lost count." I glanced toward Will. He was watching us jealously.

"Lots of tears? Fainting?"

"Some."

"The sergeant is acting as if I'm going to fall to pieces."

"He's seen what happens. . . . He's a good man." I waited too long to give the recommendation and it sounded forced to me, but she ignored it.

"This one will be different," she said in a way that made me believe her.

I wanted to believe her. This job, my first for SHADE, had cloaked me in respectability. The families treated me like a black-swaddled Keeper of Some

Holy Secrets; they feared and resented me. Being mistaken for someone I'm not has always been a private pleasure and I always enjoyed feeding the misconceptions about me. But this identity, Exhumationist, a joke at first, became an open wound. I started thinking that one day I would unzip a body bag and find myself inside.

Kristen rejoined her family. They were not crying either, yet. A preacher had tagged along, ignored by all, stationed on the opposite side of the grave from Jim. I glanced at the man working with a rake about one hundred yards to my right, on a small rise. He was Mack Rios, a Marine sniper I brought along as a precaution: Millions in cash is a temptation for everyone, even the bereaved. The small white tent where we would open the coffin stood between us. Exhumation is a private business. This one, even without tears, felt no different from the others.

I wished it did.

The first time we dug up a grave and unzipped the body bag and found money, I got that thrill that comes from being right. Hard work rewarded. We had to count the money even though the game was still going on and counting brought questions, which deflated the good feeling. We expected to find twenty-five million dollars in each grave: The first had one million; the second had a million and a half. Something was wrong. We did not understand what it was.

The snow stopped. The winch operator signaled to

Will that he was ready. Will nodded. The winch spun. Everyone stared dutifully at the hole in the ground as if they did not know what was going to emerge. But the grave seemed to be two miles deep. The creaky chains rolled up slowly. Maybe the winch man was holding out for overtime. I snuck in behind Jim Williams and grabbed his right arm into a quick hammerlock and slipped my hand into his pocket and extracted the knife. He hissed once more.

At last the casket floated up from the grave and hovered like an alien drone that we had foolishly unearthed and activated. It swung hypnotically and Kristen flinched. It almost hit the preacher, whose eyes were closed, but no one interrupted his reverie. Each exhumation was like a combat patrol. This was my third exhumation, so I felt like a veteran: weary but addicted. I tried to watch the family without staring. I wanted to know what they were hoping for. If I was wrong, if the body was in the grave, then hope was crushed forever. If I was right and the grave contained a body bag filled with money, then hope, which I knew I had revived when I contacted them, would rise up and slam them to the ground and stomp on them, probably as long as they lived. I wanted to watch them to see which choice they thought they preferred. But this was only the third grave and it would take thousands to make a good sample.

The explosion was small, a flash and a pop, but so

was the tent. Dirt pelted us, speeding through the strips and bits of white canvas swirling around us. Beyond the tent, Mack Rios went down with the first shot. The second shot hit Will Panos, who had jumped in front of Kristen to shield her. He yelled, "Damn, damn, damn," and tottered and brought her down when he fell. A hand pushed me in the back and I bent forward to maintain my balance. Jim Williams said something like "You, damn you . . ." The rest was drowned out by the third shot, which went through his neck.

For a moment I thought the silence was complete, but the creaking of the chains holding the coffin kept a steady beat as I ran up the hill to Mack. He was dead, shot in the face, lying on his back with his rifle just inches from his left hand.

I stood up and looked back toward the grave. At first, the area was diorama still, then the figures began to move as if a spell had been cast off. The gently swinging ticktock of the coffin accentuated the stillness of the scene. The shots had come from the big, peaceful field of headstones lined up like seats in an auditorium beyond the grave site. A shooter could have hidden behind any one of them, but no one was out there now.

The sirens were close by the time I got back to the graveside and Will Panos. His wound cut across the front of his right thigh. He was trying to stand. I pulled him down and kneeled next to him. "How is it?"

"Not bad," he said while wincing, because the only bullets that don't hurt are the fatal ones.

Kristen had crawled out from under him and gone over to her parents. The flashing lights from the cop cars coated the scene in glimpses of red, so it took me a moment to realize the back of her jacket was smeared with Will's blood.

"Get the attention of the first cops. Howl if you have to," I said. "I'm going to try to get out of here with the money."

I left Will and went to the winch operator and pulled him up. "Lower the coffin to the ground. Right where it is. Now," I said. He was staring at Will, still on the ground. "Just do it. Do it now. Where's the crank?" He pointed to a tool chest next to the winch. I pushed him toward the controls and he went to work. I meant for him to drop the thing, but he lowered it as if the world's last bottle of bourbon were inside. As soon as the casket was on the ground, I put in the crank to pop the lock, then wedged the crowbar in the middle to lift the top. The winch operator sat there as if waiting for further instructions.

The cops were getting out of their cars. An ambulance was pulling up. I was not sure how I was going to get out of there with the money, but I knew I did not want the local police claiming it. I lifted the top of the casket and reached inside and unzipped the body bag and I flinched. The skin was thin as fancy stationery and the hair was sparse and the remains of a man wore a Marine uniform. From behind me Kristen said, "Who the hell is that?" I stared at her and might have kept staring at her while I tried to comprehend the situation, but I saw cops coming toward us. I zipped up the bag and closed the lid.

2.

My father, Dan, dead now, though not departed, the former and forever Minister of Collateral Damage, had sniffed out the plot by a bunch of officers to ship millions home from Iraq in body bags in the early days of the war. Dan only knew about one shipment. Retrieving it and relocating it came as naturally to him as burying nuts is to a squirrel. He stole it, but he did not want to spend it. The money lay hidden for years until about six months ago, when the plotters dug up the grave Dan had already looted and found nothing but stale air. Dan's last, and only, gift to me was a clue about where he had hidden it.

Colonel McColl and his gang killed Dan and followed me while I followed Dan's clue; I found the money and used it as bait to kill them for what they had done to him. That brought me to the attention of Major Hensel. He had just formed SHADE, which is short for Shared Defense Executive; it's a division of the Defense Intelligence Agency. "Concerned with national security issues involving the military," according to the Major, who is the only one who would know. That is how I came to have the job these past months hunting down the other money-seeded graves McColl had boasted of.

I didn't burn Dan's body with the intent of ridding myself of him forever, though I thought that would be a side benefit. For any decent father, a son avenging his murder would have put the matter to rest, but that sort of decency eluded Dan even in death and he has been stalking me relentlessly, with the same irresponsibility, unpredictability, and irritating selfishness that he perfected in life, dogging me with stories I had heard many times and stories I had never heard before.

Though I studied desert combat, small arms combat, mountain combat, survival techniques, counterinsurgency, tai chi, aikido, yoga, petty thievery, breaking and entering, and other arcane street lessons, Dan studies was my major, my minor, my hobby, my relentless affliction. I hated him while he lived and avoided him as soon as I could, but his death defeated my hatred. Dan fascination, long unacknowledged, often denied, found no new poison after his death and so flourished.

Dan accompanied me out of Havre to the Canadian border, going on about the scene at the grave before the shooting.

"Nice of the old man to save your life like that."

"He was a great guy."

"I'd have done the same."

I laughed.

"Tough having to put your son in the ground and then having to stand there again to find out if you did it right the first time."

That's when I knew the purpose of this chat: Dan had been robbed of the grand stage my graveside would have provided him.

What stories would he have concocted on the spot? My last letter: He would pull a few pieces of paper from his pocket, hold them a moment, then shake his head and put them away. He could recite it by heart: a letter foreshadowing my tragic death and revealing to him the ways he had always inspired me. Funny stories would follow, oozing fatherly wisdom in the face of the stubbornness of impetuous youth. If I left an attractive widow, the show would be directed toward her. Whatever tears and laughs he evoked would be in service of that conquest.

Dan spoke up at that thought: *"I would not."*

"Because you had already succeeded, or because you had already been turned down?"

"Because at some point she would start feeling guilty and ruin all the fun."

But he would not feel guilty.

Canada looked just like Montana. A thin white coating over a flat sheet spreading to the horizon like an exposed bed you could never roll out of. The snow started again, just enough to make a dusting on the road and on the windshield. I pulled onto the shoulder about fifty yards before the border and parked myself on the hood of my car. I took off my jacket and enjoyed the bite of the cold air. I wanted to linger, to clear my mind so I could begin to understand the puzzle of the graves. Dan receded, but just a moment later a border guard emerged from the small station on the left, which looked like a drive-through coffee stand. He wore a parka with an American flag on the sleeve and a Home-land Security patch.

"You waiting for something?"

"Yes."

"What's that?"

"A revelation."

He looked around for a moment, stared as if he could see the North Pole, brushed snow off his coat. "Well, trust me on this; I been working this station fifteen years and unless you're waiting for Santy Claus, you're facing the wrong direction." He tapped on my roof and gestured with his gloved hand. "If this isn't government business then you gotta move along."

When he got about ten yards away I said, "Truth is, I'm waiting for Ethan Williams."

His head slowly tilted and his eyes got squinty as if I had asked him to complete a tough math equation. A car was coming up from behind me. The guard consid-ered hustling back to his post. Instead, he put up his hand to stop the car. It slowed down and stopped next to him and he leaned down. I could only hear his end:

"Hey, Bill. You got anything I need to know about . . . ? When you coming back . . . ? It's fine. No problems . . ." Bill drove across the invisible border and the guard returned to me.

"Who'd you say?"

"Ethan Williams."

"You a relation of his?"

"No."

"Well, if you're waiting for Ethan, you better be patient. That boy died in Iraq years ago."

"You knew him?"

"I know about everybody here. Except you."

It took a day and a half to get to Chicago. Only Dan interrupted my guilty silence.

"This isn't on you. You didn't cause this."

"Man down, a good man. Another man wounded."

"It might have been worse if they hadn't been there."

"How?"

"Did I ever tell you the story about the time I fell in love? Beautiful woman, lived up in San Francisco."

"Before I was born?"

"I think you were staying with someone in Arizona and I didn't want to interrupt your life. It wouldn't have been fair to drag you away." Fair to him, he meant. *"A beauty she was, and rich, too. Her father was a financial wizard on the East Coast. She ran an art gallery. The walls lined with paintings I couldn't look at and the*

floor filled with rich friends I couldn't take my eyes off of. All of them eager to spend their money. For me, it was like being the house at a craps game; I could make a deal every time I blinked my eyes. The biggest problem was keeping track of them all. Sometimes I would hide from people trying to give me checks, which you know made them increase the size of those checks. She was perfect; I don't think she cared what deals I made. And then, suddenly, she broke it off. Not only did the checks stop coming in, everybody wanted their money back. I was devastated. At least I convinced myself of that, at first. Played the part. Of course that helped me with all the investors who suddenly needed their money back. I was too distracted to bother about such small matters. But I must have bought into my show of distress because they seemed to believe me."

"How long did that last?"

"About a week. But I could never believe anyone's tears, not even my own. I felt lousy, but it wasn't about the woman. I felt lousy because I didn't feel lousy about the woman. I was relieved it was over. Love was a burden I did not like to bear. That was not easy to face. But once I admitted that I disliked being in love, I was elated and left town immediately with all the money."

"Who did she catch you with?"

"She didn't catch me with anyone. Her sister confessed. Unsolicited. More of a boast than a confession."

"Your story does not help me. There's no correlation with my situation. A woman caught you cheating; a *sniper killed two men and wounded another on my watch. Not the same thing."*

Even in death, Dan did not argue or explain, though I would have welcomed either. *"Okay,"* he said.

I knew what I had to do and did not want any orders getting in my way, so I ignored Major Hensel's calls, but I left the battery in the phone. When he knew where I was, he would know what I was doing. Dan's story was like a thorn in my shoe: The irritation lingered. I had to let go of the idea of Dan dispensing wisdom. Dan did not dispense, not anything of value. Dan led you toward the truth and stood there watching you find ways to ignore it, twist it, disguise it. That was his thrill in life. As a shadow he was the same, only more so, though I suspected the thrill was gone.

The humiliating possibilities outlined in Dan's story slouched in front of me like criminal candidates in a police lineup: relief, excitement, delight, elation. Whichever I chose incriminated me. But even if I put aside the guilt and ache of losing my man, I could not place any one of those snickering partners with me at the scene. I longed for change, longed to be released from the drudgery of interviews and paperwork. But longing for change does not cause change.

The plane felt like a cage. Behind me, a young boy started to cry in a throbbing rhythm that matched the drone of the engines. The woman in the aisle seat woke herself with a snoring snort. She wiped drool from the side of her mouth and looked past me at the dull black outside the window. She closed her eyes again and her head tilted back sharply, as if she had been hit. Below, a cluster of lights looked like the marking of a drop zone. The exit row was just three in front of me.

All I had to do was admit that I was relieved and I would not mind whatever condemnation came along with it. I would be free. That temptation, posing as my shadowed reflection, winked at me in the window, tempted me to open it up. But I did not want to follow Dan's lead. I never did. Love was a burden he did not want to bear, as was the truth. Dan was a ghost and had been a ghost for many years before he died. I was not ready to become a ghost. I was not ready to open the window and get sucked out.

I was released, not relieved. Released from the routine and administration that my first job with SHADE had devolved into. Released from the lies and paperwork and permits required to retrieve the dead. The bundled emotions were easier to carry than any single one of them would have been.

The list of graves was wrong. I was certain we had followed the right path to obtain it, but the list was wrong, and hoping the next graves would have millions inside them would mark me as an arrogant, ignorant mark. I closed my eyes and rewalked the steps that led to the list, trying to understand where I went wrong.

From #1 *New York Times*
bestselling author
DANIEL SILVA

The Unlikely Spy
The Mark of the Assassin
The Marching Season
The Kill Artist
The English Assassin
The Confessor
A Death in Vienna
Prince of Fire
The Messenger
The Secret Servant
Moscow Rules
The Defector
The Rembrandt Affair

"Silva continues to provide some of the most
exciting spy fiction since Ian Fleming put down
his martini and invented James Bond."
—*Rocky Mountain News*

Learn more at danielsilvabooks.com

Available wherever books are sold or at
penguin.com

From *New York Times* bestselling author

STUART WOODS

The Stone Barrington Novels

L.A. Dead

Cold Paradise

The Short Forever

Dirty Work

Reckless Abandon

Two Dollar Bill

Dark Harbor

Fresh Disasters

Shoot Him If He Runs

Hot Mahogany

Loitering with Intent

Kisser

Lucid Intervals

Strategic Moves

Bel-Air Dead

Son of Stone

D.C. Dead

Unnatural Acts

Severe Clear

Collateral Damage

Unintended Consequences

**Available wherever books are sold or at
penguin.com**